D0496780

Richmond upon Thames Libraries

Renew online at www.richmond.gov.uk/libraries

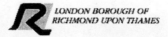

LONDON BOROUGH OF
RICHMOND UPON THAMES

THE KINGDOM OVER THE SEA

THE KINGDOM OVER THE SEA

ZOHRA NABI

Illustrated by Tom Clohosy Cole

SIMON AND SCHUSTER

First published in Great Britain in 2023 by Simon & Schuster UK Ltd

Text copyright © 2023 Zohra Nabi
Illustrations copyright © 2023 Tom Clohosy Cole

The right of Zohra Nabi and Tom Clohosy Cole to be identified as the author
and illustrator of this work respectively has been asserted by
them in accordance with sections 77 and 78 of the
Copyright, Designs and Patents Act, 1988.

1 3 5 7 9 10 8 6 4 2

Simon & Schuster UK Ltd
1st Floor, 222 Gray's Inn Road
London WC1X 8HB

www.simonandschuster.co.uk
www.simonandschuster.com.au
www.simonandschuster.co.in

Simon & Schuster Australia, Sydney
Simon & Schuster India, New Delhi

A CIP catalogue record for this book
is available from the British Library.

PB ISBN 978-1-3985-1770-7
eBook ISBN 978-1-3985-1771-4
eAudio ISBN 978-1-3985-1772-1

This book is a work of fiction.
Name of the author's
in ual people
used fictitiously. Any resemblance to al.

tricity

To my parents

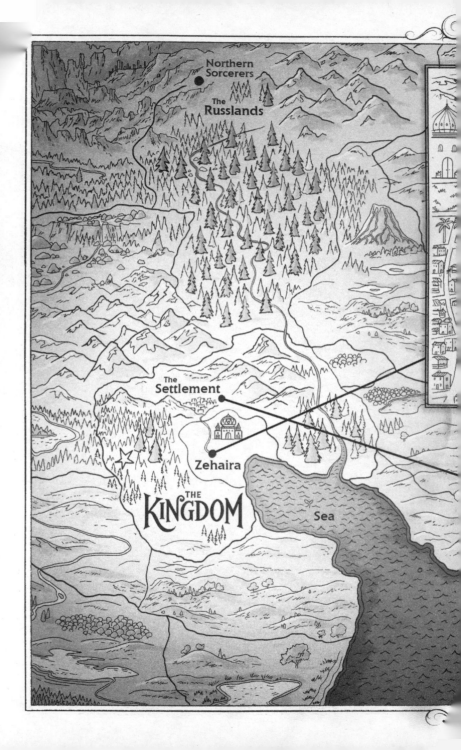

Prologue

A strange dark had fallen over the city of Zehaira that night. A deep, mysterious dark; all thundering skies and pelting rain. A dark that any sorcerer worth their salt would tell you meant there was great magic about.

Of course, magic had always fallen like starlight over the city, but for hundreds of years it had been squashed into its stonework, muffled by the merchant din and swamped beneath the smoke sent up by alchemists at work in the Sultan's palace. In Zehaira the wild jinn were forced to lurk sulkily outside the city walls, snapping at the heels of passers-by from the shadows.

The magic that night was different. It was wild, ungraspable in the way it stole through the city, blotting out the silver sliver of new moon. And since the sorcerers of Zehaira *were* worth their salt, and far more, they had called a council to debate the seriousness of this omen. Putting on cloaks and sombre expressions, they made their way down the underground passages that connected their homes to the Great Library, clustering beneath its amber dome. In the Sorcerers' Quarter the streets ran empty, the only sound the beating of the rain on the roofs.

Empty, apart from a young woman. Clasping a bundle to her chest, she tore through the streets, slipping on the cobbled stones in her haste. Beyond the Quarter there were men's voices, faint but growing louder, getting closer.

They did not sound friendly.

She reached a door, the third to last on the street. As she stopped before it, her face took on a determined look, her eyebrows lowering and her mouth setting stubbornly. Raising her fist, she hammered at the woodwork.

The door opened a crack. A pair of amber eyes peered out from behind it, and the woman let out a sob of relief.

'Sanctuary,' she gasped.

'I'm sorry?'

'Let me in, please. I need your help.'

The person opened the door a little wider. In the light of the house one could make out her overlarge student robes, the young face beneath her turban.

'I'm sorry,' the student said again. 'I can't let strangers in; there's an enchantment on the door.'

She peered past the woman into the night. Suddenly the noise of the approaching men was drowned out by the ringing of bells, each deafening *clang* shaking the city walls. The woman began to tremble with fear.

'They're here for you,' the student said slowly, her eyes running over the woman. 'You're a fugitive.'

'I haven't done anything wrong,' the woman insisted, clutching her bundle even tighter. 'If anything, this is all because I've tried to do the right thing.'

Seeing the student hesitate, she reached forward and gripped at her wrist. 'Please. You have to help. If you turn me away, they will find me and they will kill me, and they will kill *her*.'

'Her?'

At that moment the bundle began to wriggle and snuffle, until finally it let out a great roaring wail of a cry.

The student jumped half out of her skin. 'That is a *baby*.'

'Yes, it is. Although neither of us will be anything much longer if you don't let us in.'

The student bit her lip harder and crossed her arms, warring with herself. Finally she muttered: 'Use the words. Then I have no choice but to give you shelter.'

'What words?'

'I can't tell you what they are!' she said agitatedly. 'Surely you were taught them as a child?'

The woman blinked. Evidently nursery rhymes were far from the forefront of her mind, but she closed her eyes and frowned, hard. The baby, unminding of the woman's effort, only screamed louder.

'Hang on. Morn ... No— Oh, would you be quiet!

'From pitch of night to rose of morn,
I charge you, guard us till the dawn.'

The student sighed in relief, opening the door wider. 'Come on, then, quickly.'

The student led the woman down a long corridor, past walls painted with intricate geometric patterns and mosaics that mapped the constellations, until she came to a small room at the back of the house. It was a cosy space, the walls lined with bookshelves that you could tell at a glance had been loved and tended to. The baby, to her credit, responded well to these surroundings, forgoing screaming for a contented snuffling.

'The servants have all gone home, and Professor Al-Qamar won't be back until morning,' the student explained. 'You'll be safe here.'

'The Professor's out? But I need to speak with him.'

'He'll be back by dawn, I'm sure.'

'That's too late; we have to be gone by tonight. I came because we need a safe passage spell.'

The student blinked, surveying the woman intently.

'That's ancient magic. How in the seven spheres did you come to hear of it?'

The woman didn't answer. Her face was flooding with despair.

'Well ...' The student swallowed, and then steeled herself. 'I suppose ... I know the theory of it. I might be able to help – perhaps. I would need something from you, of course.'

'I can pay you well.' The woman dipped her hand into the baby's shawl and brought out a gem that glittered and gleamed even in the low flicker of the lamplight. 'It's a ruby – surely worth one little spell?'

The student's forehead creased. The woman in front of her was by no means badly turned out, but everything she wore – from her salwar to her shawl – had the slightly shabby appearance that comes when something has been darned at least twice. The gemstone meanwhile was glowing as though a small fire had been lit within it.

Finally she said, 'You stole that.'

'No, I didn't.' The woman narrowed her eyes. 'The lady who owned this, she would have wanted me to have it.'

'But she didn't give it to you?' The woman was silent. 'Then I can't accept it.'

'Why not?' the woman flared. 'One spell or we don't

have a chance. Does it really matter if I can't pay you?'

'It's not about payment,' the student snapped back. 'A spell like that needs power, and that power can't come from something that doesn't mean something to you. You don't have . . . oh, I don't know, a mother's necklace, or a grandmother's ring?'

The woman looked around her. She had so clearly fled with nothing that the student felt sorry for even asking the question. But then the woman looked down at the baby, now asleep in her arms.

'What about her?' she asked.

The student frowned, as if she didn't quite understand, and then her eyes widened almost comically.

'Excuse me?'

'She belongs to me, in a manner of speaking. What if I promise her to you?'

The student tensed. 'You don't know what you're doing,' she said, her voice tight. 'Take it back. Take it back this instant.'

'I know exactly what I'm doing,' the woman insisted. 'I promise you the baby in exchange for your help.'

The student closed her eyes in horror, burying her face in her hands.

'Oh, by the nine stars,' she mumbled. 'This cannot be happening.' She turned to the woman. 'What am I supposed to do with a baby? What about my life, my plans? I am eighteen, I am top of my class – I might become the Grand High Sorceress one day. You want me to give all that up to raise a child?'

'Well, let's not get ahead of ourselves,' said the woman. 'Who said anything about raising her?'

The student peeked from between her fingers. 'What do you mean?'

'The spell needs me to promise her to you. There's no reason you have to bring her up, is there? So long as it's clear that she's yours. You perform the spell and I give you the baby, sure, but then I'll borrow her from you.'

The woman set the ruby down with the triumphant air of someone who has just solved a difficult riddle. 'You can keep that till I bring her back.'

The student lifted her head from her hands, her forehead still pinched.

'I suppose … I suppose that could work,' she said slowly. 'Only this sort of magic doesn't like being tricked. Fate might work in terrible ways to bring her back to me – you could be putting yourself in danger.'

The woman hesitated and looked down at the baby for a long moment, as though truly seeing her for the first time. Then her eyes softened, and she shifted the infant to her shoulder, placing a quick defiant kiss on her head.

'Well, love, no way of knowing until we try.' She

held out her spare hand to the student, who, with a last reluctant twist of her mouth, accepted it. 'I hereby give up this child in return for safe passage from Zehaira, on condition that I am permitted to bring her up for as long as I am alive. I thus promise her to . . . ?'

'Leyla,' said the student grudgingly. 'Leyla Khatoun.'

Twelve Years Later

Chapter One

My own Yara,

I hope that you will never need this letter. I want to tell you everything myself — but if you are reading this, then something terrible has happened, and you are on your own. There is a lot I haven't told you, so much that I don't know where to begin. But I can tell you how to return to the city you were born in, and whom you can go to for help. I wish I could tell you to get on a plane and that there will be someone to meet you at the airport — but it will be far more difficult than that, and far more frightening. Yet it is a journey you must make.

To return to the city of Zehaira, take the number 63 bus to Poole Harbour, walk right to the end of Ferry Way and read out the words on the back of this letter with all the command

and confidence that I know you have. Persuade whoever arrives to take you with them — you must make them know that you will not take no for an answer. Pack food and warm clothes and a waterproof coat. When you arrive at your destination, ask for the sorceress Leyla Khatoun, at the third-to-last house on Istehar Way, in the Sorcerers' Quarter. I know that she will give you the help that I cannot.

I love you so, so much — more than the moon, more than the stars, more than my own heart.

Good luck, my brave girl.

Mama

Yara Sulimayah's eyes moved over the swooping curves of her mother's handwriting for a second time, the letter clutched so tightly in her hands that the paper was taut, her knuckles pale. Her dark fringe fell over her eyes, and she brushed it away as though it had caused her personal offence. She was reading the letter fifty metres above the ground, although this was by no great feat of magic or acrobatics. Rather, she had lived on the sixth floor of a tower block since she had come to England as a baby and had not strayed far from it in the twelve years that had followed.

Yara began her mum's letter for a third time, each word

more confusing to her than the last. She lingered on one: 'sorceress', and her heart began to pick up pace in her chest.

'Yara?'

She turned, stashing the letter in her pocket. Stephanie, her social worker, was standing at the door; her palm pressed against the wallpaper in a way that would have made Mama seethe, her eyes warm with concern behind her glasses. 'Find anything?'

Yara steadied herself. 'Nothing, really. Just her passport and stuff.'

'Ah, well. Is there anything else of your mum's that you want? Maybe a shawl?'

As she spoke, Stephanie's gaze fell to the open drawer where her mother had kept her headscarves, each neatly folded into squares. Yara got to her feet and ran her hand over smooth silk, chiffon and crepe.

'That one's pretty.' Stephanie came further into the room, her hand hovering above Yara's back. She pointed to a metre of deep green material, with pink and red flowers embroidered in a close print.

Yara shook her head. 'She never wore that one. She was saving it for a special occasion.'

Her hand settled on a shawl of faded blue, the gold embroidery like tiny, fraying stars. When she was little, her mother used to take it off and spread it on the table, pretending that Yara's dolls were travelling through the night sky. Picking it up from the drawer, Yara brought the headscarf to her face, inhaling the scent of castor oil and rose water that clung to the fabric.

It had been almost a fortnight since her mother had not returned from her shift. Since Stephanie had met her at the school gates and explained that there had been an accident on the main road. Since she had taken Yara to a foster family, and then to a funeral. Now she had brought her here, home; to pack up her things properly. To say goodbye.

Almost a fortnight. The days seemed to have blended into one terrible moment, as though she had missed a step and was still falling, her stomach still plummeting. She had never spent this long without her mother. Fresh tears welled in her eyes.

'Oh, sweetheart.' Stephanie squeezed her shoulder. 'I know.'

Yara stiffened beneath her touch, dropping the headscarf back in the drawer and blinking furiously. She was small for twelve, but she made up for it with eyes that were dark and fierce, and thick eyebrows that would knit together stormily. The full force of her glower would normally stop adults in their tracks – but Stephanie, looking around the flat, did not seem fazed.

'You're sure there isn't anywhere else your mum kept things?'

'No. The top drawer was her last hiding place.'

'And nothing about any family at all – no postcards, no photographs?'

Mama's letter burned hot in her pocket. Her words: *It is a journey you must make.*

'Mama always said there was no one else. That it was just the two of us.' She picked up her school bag, interjecting before her social worker could say anything else. 'So everything's packed?'

'All your things are, yes. The removal crew are coming for the furniture this evening.' Stephanie checked her phone. 'Right, it's eight o'clock; we'd best be off. Are you sure you want to go to school? I'm sure if we called the office and explained—'

'Actually,' Yara said slowly, 'could I have a bit of time by myself?' Seeing her social worker's hesitation, she attempted a desolate look. 'I . . . I need to say goodbye.'

Stephanie's expression softened. She gave Yara's shoulder another squeeze. 'Of course. I know it's difficult – but the Browns will look after you, I promise.'

Yara nodded, and now there really was a lump in her throat. She blinked and swallowed around it furiously.

Stephanie checked her phone again. 'All right, then. I'll be outside.'

Yara turned to the windowsill, looking out at the estate below to hide her face from her social worker.

She waited, pretending to be lost in thought as she heard Stephanie gather her handbag and coat, stop to look at Yara in the empty flat one more time, and then step out into the hallway, closing the door behind her.

Yara moved immediately. She pulled the letter from her pocket, reading her mother's words to herself again. Sorceresses, mysterious summons that had to be read right by the sea – if it hadn't sounded so unmistakably like her mum, right down to the instruction not to take no for an answer, she might have thought the letter had been written by a stranger. Perhaps it was some kind of game, like the treasure maps Mama had made for their adventures when Yara was much smaller. Perhaps she had forgotten about it, and put it away with their documents by mistake.

Only she couldn't think of anything *less* like her mum, with her eagle eyes and knack for precision, who knew instantly when Yara had forgotten to put her homework on the dresser or hadn't folded her laundry properly.

Looking up, Yara scanned their living room, hoping for something that might provide a window into her mum's mind. But each thing she saw – the biscuit tin where Mama kept her sewing kit, the tea caddy where she kept her secret stash of custard creams, the hospital scrubs carefully hung up on a peg – only seemed to emphasise how ordinary Mama had been.

Anyway, what was the alternative? That Mama was serious, and genuinely expected her to get the bus to Poole Harbour and voyage to a country using only words and determination? That there were such people as *sorceresses*, and that she needed one's help? It obviously wasn't true. It *couldn't* be true.

Except.

Except that Mama had always been vague about where they were from. It said Iraq on their documents, but her mum had explained that she hadn't known exactly where they had lived before, and had to hazard a guess as to which country it was. Yara had been desperate to know, had pleaded and argued and sulked for the story of their journey to the UK; but every time she asked, Mama's voice would get tighter, and pain would furrow her face.

I'll tell you when you're older. At first it had been a promise. More recently it had sounded like a plea for more time. But that was time they would never have now.

Yara looked down at where Mama had underlined her instructions so vigorously that the pen had almost gone through the paper, and the dull ache of her mother's absence flared into sharp pain once more. She bit her lip, hard. Whatever reason Mama had for talking about magic and sorceresses, this had been her attempt to give Yara some answers to the questions that had been burning inside her for years. She couldn't throw that away, not if there was the slimmest, smallest chance she might find something out.

'Right,' she said aloud, steeling herself for the absurdity of what she was about to do next. 'I suppose I had better get packing.'

She didn't have long. If she really was going to follow Mama's instructions, she needed to pack and be well away from the flat by the time Stephanie realised she was missing. Another twelve-year-old might have been daunted by the task, but Yara, who had been helping organise protest campaigns since she was old enough to understand that there were people in the world who wanted to *shut down libraries*, got to work.

She checked the letter again: *Pack food and warm clothes and a waterproof coat*. She was in her school jumper and trousers, and most of her regular clothes were in a suitcase at her temporary foster home. Only her salwar qamis were left in the flat – and not even the two pretty ones she had chosen to take with her, but the plain ones her mum had insisted on buying the fabric for, ignoring Yara's complaints. She stuffed them into her school bag and pulled on her blue waterproof. There wasn't much food about, but Yara knew she wouldn't have time for a supermarket trip. She opened the freezer, rummaging until she found the sambusak she had made with Mama before the accident. There was only one of the little pastries left, but it would have to do.

What else? Wash things, a book called *The History of the World* that Mama had given her for her birthday and which she had still not read. A photo of her mum, and of her and a friend holding a poster together outside the library. As she looked at their twin smiles, Yara's breath hitched in her throat. Rehema had tried to reach out to her over a week ago, but, lost in a haze of grief, Yara had found herself unable to reply to her messages. She wondered how she would explain what she was doing to her friend if she were here.

There didn't seem much point in packing anything else apart from a pocket atlas, which she took largely as a reminder to herself that places reachable only by magical summons did not exist. Then, as she was poised to leave, she had a change of heart. Running back, she picked up her mother's blue headscarf and wound it round her neck.

Then there was nothing left to do, nothing except say goodbye to the flat she had lived in since she was barely a month old.

'Yara?' Stephanie's voice sounded through the letterbox. She was out of time.

'Just two more minutes,' she called back, and looked around. With sudden clarity she realised that she was standing in an empty place, with walls where Mama had measured her height and pinned up her essays, and a kitchen where Yara had sat on the counter, peeling vegetables and talking to Mama about the latest injustice she had discovered in the world. It was already a place where they had once been.

'Goodbye,' Yara said softly, as though louder tones would disturb what little trace of them was left. As quietly as she could, she slipped into the kitchen, out through the back door and down the iron steps of the fire escape.

Chapter Two

The number 63 bus was already screeching round the corner when Yara came out, and she had to run, barely flagging it down in time. She hopped on, finding a seat by the window and trying to ignore the roiling in her stomach. She had taken the bus by herself countless times, but never all the way to Poole Harbour. After a few stops, her phone began to buzz, and as Yara took it out of her pocket to silence it, she saw frantic messages flashing on her screen. Her panic rose. Each passing car made her jump; each siren in the distance signalled that the police were on her tail.

They stopped outside the library, and through the window Yara could see Rehema helping her mum shelve books. Rehema's mum was a librarian, and on a usual Wednesday morning before school Yara would go in to help, and perhaps talk about a new project for the library to champion, or what might come up at their

Local Action meeting on Friday. This time she ducked in her seat, pulling the hood of her raincoat further over her eyes. She felt hot and ashamed as she did so, and wondered whether she should simply turn round and forget the whole thing.

Desperate for a distraction, Yara got out the letter and looked it over once more. *Read out the words on the back of this letter with all the command and confidence you have*, her mum had said. But when she flipped over the page, what she read seemed so bewildering that she put it down quickly and looked around her instead, surveying the small assortment of passengers.

There was a family sitting together in the pushchair area: the youngest asleep in her pram; a toddler sat on a large suitcase; a little girl holding her father's hand with a serious tired expression on her face, either too well behaved or too exhausted to shriek and run around the bus. Their mother was gripping the pole tight, her niqab spotlighting the apprehension in her eyes.

Catching her eye, Yara offered the woman a tentative smile. The woman smiled back, and she spoke in quick syllables to Yara, who shook her head.

'I'm sorry, I don't understand.'

The father turned his head to their exchange, his brow furrowed.

'Where are you from?' he asked her in English.

'Iraq, I think.'

The couple smiled, the man's forehead uncreasing and the woman's eyes crinkling.

'Us as well. What language do you speak?'

Yara hesitated. Then she changed her speech, trialling the lilting notes of the language she had spoken only with her mother. 'My mama wasn't sure exactly where we were from. She said we used to live near a harbour.'

But the man and the woman only looked at each other in bafflement.

'We have lived in Iraq all our lives,' the woman said finally, 'but I have never heard anyone speak as you do.'

Yara nodded, averting her gaze. This wasn't the first time this had happened – someone trying to work out where she was from, only to stare in confusion once she had spoken. After giving up on getting the truth from Mama, she had spent hours online, scrolling through dictionaries and trying to understand long articles about dialects, but it was as though their language didn't exist. With Mama gone she had thought she might never speak it again.

'Ah, well.' She was interrupted from her thoughts by the renewed cheerfulness of the man. 'It's nice to meet you anyway.'

Yara smiled back, but a snort came from behind her, a low mumble in a woman's voice, loud enough for Yara alone to hear.

'Flipping migrants. Go back to your own country if you don't want to speak English.'

Yara felt herself go white and then red. She tried to force herself to count to ten, but her temper rose within her. She whipped her head round.

'Well, in this country it's considered rude to interrupt other people's conversations,' she hissed. 'And if all you can say is something as nasty and stupid as that, then just *don't speak at all.*'

The woman opened her mouth wordlessly and clutched at her throat, her eyes popping out of her head. Quickly Yara hopped out of the seat and pressed the bell, three stops before she had meant to get off.

'Good luck,' she said hurriedly to the man and woman, who fortunately appeared not to have heard the exchange.

'*Ma'a salama,*' replied the woman. 'Good luck to you too.'

The bus came to a stop, and Yara leaped off, breaking into a run down the long road to the harbour.

For a while all thoughts of her mum's strange instructions were pushed out of her mind by rage.

Yara had a tendency to charge head first at bullies, and not stop to think until she was sitting outside the headteacher's office. If Mama had been there, she would have told her to stay quiet, to keep her head down and not put herself at risk – only it seemed to her that far too many people got away with far too much in the world, and the thought of sitting silently while someone said *that* made her blood boil.

Anyway, she reminded herself, *Mama isn't here any more.* The thought filled her with a horrible blind misery, and she didn't notice where she was walking until her path was blocked by the red barrier to the ferry port. With no operator in sight, she ducked underneath.

It wasn't a particularly magical outlook: a grey car park littered with empty crisp packets and crumpled beer cans, the waves lapping listlessly against the coastal path. A fox was curled up on the bonnet of an abandoned car, and Yara thought she felt its eyes on her back as she walked to the end of the car park and on to the dock, her footsteps creaking on the damp rotting wood. She was half afraid that the cracked planks would give out altogether and deposit her into the waiting sea.

Yara brought out Mama's letter with shaking hands. The reality of her situation was fast catching up with her, her stomach churning at the thought of how much trouble she would be in if – no, *when* – nothing happened. Nevertheless, she turned the letter over again, and found the part her mum wanted her to read aloud. For the first time she noticed that it was arranged in verses, like a poem. The lines seemed to rhyme too; she glanced at the first couplet.

Beneath these stars and on this sea,
An ancient spell once carried me . . .

Even in her head the rhythm of the words seemed to lift them up off the page and into the air, hovering around her head like a strange breeze. It was as if she had played a note on a musical instrument, and although the sound had gone, it was still vibrating through her. Then the wind changed, and she could feel something shifting, swirling, prickling at the hairs on the back of her neck. She looked up, and gasped.

Where before the end of the dock had seemed the furthest point out to sea, now she could see three steps going down, carved out of stone. Yara blinked and rubbed at her eyes, trying to make sense of what she was seeing. *It was high tide*, she thought frantically. *It was high tide, and the steps must have been hidden. That must be it.* She moved closer to the edge, her heart beating somewhere in her throat, and saw that the steps led to *a road* of raised stone, which carved through the waves until it vanished into the October mist. Behind her people continued to walk past the car park, seemingly unaware of the strange new pier that had emerged from the sea.

Excitement began to bubble low in Yara's stomach, spreading until her whole body seemed to be fizzing with it. Mama must have meant for her to take this path, and if that was what she meant, then the rest of her letter – the journey, the city she was born in, the *sorceress* – maybe that was all true too.

One step at a time, Yara told herself, digging her nails into the palm of her hand. There was further to go yet.

Holding her breath, she lowered one foot. She half expected to fall through thin air, and was almost startled when she found solid ground beneath her. She exhaled unevenly and brought the other foot down, descending the last two steps until she was on the stone pier itself. She looked beneath her, trying to work out how it could possibly support itself all the way out to sea, but the waves were dark and opaque, and there was nothing beneath the stone that she could make out.

Yara took a step forward, and then another, until she was walking along the pier, the echo of her footsteps the only sound other than the insistent murmur of the sea. She dared not look behind her. She had a feeling that if she did, she would no longer be able to see the car park. In fact, the further she walked, the more she was convinced that she was no longer in Poole Harbour – or, at least, no longer in the Poole Harbour that tourists came to visit on coaches and which archaeologists from the university poked at with trowels. She was somewhere different.

She checked her watch. The second hand was stuttering, trembling halfway between numbers, and when Yara reached into her coat pocket to check the time on her phone, her chilled fingers pressing frantically at the buttons, the screen stayed black.

She stopped in her tracks. The fear that had been swirling inside her rose suddenly to her chest until she couldn't breathe, until she was conscious only of how alone she was, out in the wide open sea. She wished, suddenly and desperately, that Mama was here with her.

Yara looked down. Without noticing she had clenched her fists, crumpling the letter. At the sight of it breathing came a little easier. She had to trust her mum – she would never put Yara in danger. Tossing her head back, she forced herself forward, faster than before.

Finally, she made out another dock at the end of the pier. This one had no signs of rot, no smell of mildew and decay. The stone platform was as smooth and burnished as if it had been hewn that same hour. This must be the place.

Fear rose up in her again, and she was shaking so

badly that she thought it impossible that she could speak as confidently as Mama had told her to. But looking down at her mum's writing, at the firm curves of her consonants, she mustered her courage.

'Beneath these stars and on this sea . . .'

Her voice faltered and caught on the words, her face growing hotter as she thought how ridiculous she must sound. She cleared her throat, willing herself on.

'Beneath these stars and on this sea,

An ancient spell once carried me.

Borne by wood and left on stone,

I bid your ship come take me home.

Unravel now these threads of time

Spent in foreign land and clime.

My time beneath this sky has passed.

I bid you, take me home at last!'

At first it was as though she had not spoken. The horizon remained clear, the sea unchanged, and were it not for the profound sense that something astonishing was about to happen, Yara might have felt embarrassed at having ever taken her mother seriously.

And then ... she could see something. A black dot on the horizon, getting closer. Something with a mast reaching up and a blue sail billowing behind it like a taut bow, its movement as seamless as if it were cutting through silk. There was a strange urgency in the air now, as though the entire harbour were holding its breath for the vessel's arrival.

Yara thought that if her heart were to beat any faster, it might burst out of her chest and take flight back home to Bournemouth.

The boat – it was no bigger than a small fishing vessel – drew nearer, and then it was near enough that she could make out a figure at the helm, wrapped in blue cloth. It came to a halt at the dock, and the figure began to move towards her with slow steps. Yara could see his eyes now, which seemed to flicker darkly without settling on a colour, his pupils tall and narrow – like a snake, she realised with a jolt. Even standing in the boat, he towered over Yara, and she held her breath as he began to speak.

'The daughter of Nahzin Sulimayah?'

He spoke in a deep rumble that seemed to rise up from the bottom of the sea; every syllable rang with the authority of one who has lived a great many years and knows all there is to understand about people.

Yara had to crane her neck to answer him. 'Um, that's my mum?'

'Yes. This is the safe passage spell belonging to Nahzin Sulimayah and her daughter, who has no recorded name.'

'You mean ... you mean, I've done this before?' The man was silent, and Yara tried again. 'Who are you?'

'I am the Ferryman. I voyage between the seas of the seven spheres.'

'You mean the seven seas?'

Once again the Ferryman did not answer, and Yara gave up. 'My name is Yara Sulimayah.'

'Well, Yara Sulimayah, why have you summoned me?'

For a moment Yara simply stood there, stunned. She *had* summoned him. He was here because Yara had recited that verse. Then she remembered her mother's instructions: *Persuade whoever arrives to take you with them – you must make them know you will not take no for an answer.*

'I demand to be taken aboard your ship.' Her voice sounded small even to her own ears, and she tried to look commanding. 'You will take me to my mother's country. To –' she racked her brains – 'to the city of Zehaira.'

'Zehaira.' The Ferryman rolled the word on his tongue. 'A long way to travel. Why should I take you?'

Yara faltered. She knew how to be persuasive – she had a particular knack for getting people to sign petitions – but there was something so mysterious about this person that her confidence deserted her. As she stumbled over her sentences, she felt a sudden terror that she might get this wrong, and that she would be left on this dock with no means of return.

'I, um . . .'

At her hesitation the Ferryman shook his head, moving back towards the helm. Yara's nerves gave way to a keen outrage.

'You're not actually going to leave me here on my own in the middle of the sea? I have no one and nothing left in the world but a letter telling me to return to Zehaira, and I am not going to let you turn me away. You will invite me aboard your boat and take me home because it is the right thing to do. I won't let you say no. I won't *let* you.'

She flushed, feeling certain that she had lost any chance of getting on to the boat – but to her surprise the Ferryman nodded.

'To hear is to obey. Yara Sulimayah, I invite you aboard my vessel. I will make it my solemn duty to take you home.'

He extended a hand but Yara recoiled, the brief pleasure she felt at her success washed away by fresh fear.

'Wait. I haven't told anyone where I'm going. There are people who won't stop searching for me – I should tell them . . .'

'Once you step on this ship, your life on this land will melt away as though you never lived it,' said the Ferryman, and it was as though he were speaking his words into existence. 'Your possessions will remain, but no one will know who owned them. Your actions here will remain, but no one will remember who it was who did them. Your outline will remain in the minds of the people in this country, but your presence will fade from their memories until you are no more real to them than a breeze on the back of their necks.'

Yara bit her lip. She thought of Stephanie pacing the flat frantically, only to stop and go about her day as though nothing had happened. Of Rehema, coming across the climate-change posters they had made together for the library and puzzling over who could have painted them. She didn't exactly have many other friends – but secondary school was supposed to have been a fresh start, and now no one there would ever think about her again. Surely Mama would have understood that this was too much to ask? To give up everything she had ever known.

And yet . . . Mama was gone, and across the sea there was a land of spells and *sorceresses*, where all the secrets and mysteries of her past lay waiting for her.

'So I invite you once again.' The Ferryman's voice cut through her thoughts. 'There will not be a third invitation.'

She glanced over her shoulder and something loosened in her chest. This was a place where she had lived with her mother once. Now the only way was forward.

She took his offered hand.

'I accept.'

Chapter Three

Yara had lived by the sea all her life, had watched waves smash themselves to pieces against rocks from her bedroom window since she was a little girl. Yet the sea she made her voyage across was like nothing she had ever encountered before.

The wind was a constant shriek in her ear, tossing their boat violently from one wave to another as though determined to tear them to shreds. Lightning split the sky, and the thunder bellowed in answer. Beneath the boat, the swell and rush of the sea as it rose to ten times Yara's height seemed like a great mouth opening to swallow her whole; time and time again she thought she would be flung from the boat and drowned.

'Stop!' she cried, until she had no voice left to shout with. 'Stop, I've changed my mind, let me off!'

But each time the Ferryman ploughed forward, guiding the rudder as though wrestling with a wild horse.

Yara clung to the mast, hair plastered back with rain and sea water. The dark had descended without warning, and now it was pitch black, the air so cold that her chattering teeth drew blood on the inside of her cheek.

Above her the storm clouds parted, and Yara tilted her face towards the sky, desperate for a glimpse of light, but she could scarcely register what she was seeing. The moon was careening across the horizon, waxing and waning by the second – and the stars, the stars were tangling themselves in labyrinth-like movements, shifting in front of her eyes.

Too frightened to scream, Yara fled to the furthest corner of the boat, hoping that if she pulled her hood over her eyes and put her hands over her ears she might wake up, and the whole thing would prove to be a nightmare.

She must have managed some sleep, because when she opened her eyes again, the waters were calmer; and when she risked a glance up at the sky, the stars seemed set in their place, the moon a scimitar crescent cutting through the darkness and casting a pale light on the sea. As the rain ceased to fall and the clouds melted away, Yara could make out a dim outline in the distance.

Land.

They came to a dock, not unlike the one she had found at the end of Poole Harbour, her way forward illuminated by the moonlight. The wind dropped, and the boat came to a slow halt.

'This is where we part ways, Yara Sulimayah,' said the Ferryman. It was the first time he had spoken since she had climbed aboard his boat.

'But I . . . I don't know where to go.'

'Affairs on land are not my concern. You must make your own way from here.'

His tone did not change, and yet Yara found herself compelled; she climbed to the edge of the boat and jumped down on to the dock, clutching her bag tight. She had to steady herself to stop her knees from buckling and launching her into the sea.

'Thank you.' Her voice cracked, hoarse from her earlier screams. 'How will I find you again if I want to go home?'

'I believe the two of us will not meet again for some time. Until then, Yara Sulimayah.'

The wind rose and the boat moved away, the Ferryman at the helm. As it disappeared into the night and the rising mist, there was a change; as though a great veil of mystery had lifted, and even on this strange dock far out at sea, things felt more ordinary again.

Yara shivered in the dark. The road was long, the land

itself still hazy in the distance. For a moment she stood, overwhelmed by the vast, lonely scene. Moving forward seemed like an impossible task, and yet somehow, still not entirely steady, she found herself walking.

The sky began to pale at the edges. She saw the mountains first, snow-capped and blushing in the twilight. Then, as the dark faded and the mist rose, she could make out golden domes in the distance, like small lanterns lighting the way.

The dawn came, and the city stirred. As she drew closer, great dhows streamed past, the ships throwing their anchors down at the harbour, where people were pitching stalls. Closer still, and she could hear the shouting of the merchants as they docked and the bustle of the market traders, the air alive with the smell of fresh herbs and spices.

Yara reached the end of the path and looked around in open-mouthed wonder.

Back in Bournemouth, a market had either meant seaside souvenirs and sticks of rock, or cheerful crates of coriander and green chillies. Here there were tents and displays as far as the eye could see, and more colours than Yara had ever seen in her life. Fruit that glowed like precious stones, silks and chiffons cascading into each other like bright waterfalls. The largest tent displayed tapestries with intricate patterns and rich embroidery, and she could even see a stickily studded sweet stall encircled by a cluster of children, each begging for a taste.

Perhaps most bizarrely of all, Yara could understand their pleas, just as she could understand the merchants and the market traders. Her mother's language. Spoken for the first time not as some intimate form of communication between the two of them but as something yelled around her by strangers on the street.

This was her mother's city. No, this was *her* city. She had been born here. This country wasn't on any map; forces other than the movement of currents and a surprisingly resilient boat had brought her here. There were no cars or lorries in this port. There wasn't a speck of concrete in sight, and not one person was looking at a mobile phone – meanwhile, her own screen remained resolutely black. Wherever she was, it was very far from home.

Yara felt dizzy with the force of her discovery, with the new sights and smells and sounds that pressed on her from all sides until they overwhelmed her senses. It was as though something was stirring within her, desperate to get out under this new sun; she wanted to explore and taste and ask a thousand questions. Even with the cool salt spray on the back of her neck, it seemed warmer than any summer day she had known before.

The sky was bluer too, a deeper blue than she had ever realised it could be.

Yara jumped down from the dock, her palms skimming the heated stone of the ground as she landed. As she got to her feet, people's heads turned to look as though they were seeing her for the first time, a hundred eyes sizing her up. It wasn't as though she was the only one dressed differently – the people disembarking from the dhows seemed to be arriving from all corners of the world – but no one looked quite like her, with her bobbed hair and waterproof jacket. Yara felt colour flood her cheeks. Ducking her head, she retrieved her mother's letter from her bag, now dog-eared and smelling of the sea.

'*The third-to-last house on Istehar Way, in the Sorcerers' Quarter,*' she muttered to herself. It felt strange saying the words aloud – even after the voyage, she wasn't entirely convinced that such people as *sorcerers* existed.

'Excuse me?' She tried to stop a passer-by, but he threw up his hands and hurried on. After her third attempt was met with the same result, Yara felt panic flutter inside her. She was in a strange country with nowhere to stay and no one she could ask for help.

No, she told herself. There was someone she could ask for help, she was sure – she just needed to find her. In the meantime, she had a few pound coins in her pocket. Perhaps if she bought some food, one of the stallholders could point her in the right direction.

Yara scanned the signs above the nearest market stalls, wondering how difficult it would be to be a pescatarian in this country. While speaking her mother's language came naturally, reading required more concentration; the only practice she got at home was deciphering shopping lists. A few stalls down, she recognised the words 'fish stew' scrawled in hasty letters, and jangling the change in her pocket, she walked over to where an old woman stood hunched over her pot, handing out bowlfuls of the stuff to sailors.

'Two silver pieces, lovely.' She grinned at Yara toothlessly, palm outstretched.

Yara parted with two fifty-pence coins, shrinking before the woman's suspicious gaze.

'This foreign?'

Yara gave a nervous nod, and the old woman relented. 'Well, it all melts down the same, I suppose.'

She gave Yara a full bowl of stew with huge chunks of potato and pungent white fish, red and gold spices swimming at the surface. It smelled wonderfully familiar, and, realising that she was starving, Yara fell upon the bowl.

The old woman watched her appetite with an

approving gaze. 'Didn't they feed you, where you come from?' Yara shrugged, her mouth full. 'Where would that be anyway?'

She swallowed and answered. 'Somewhere far away.'

There was a murmur of acknowledgement from those around her. Apparently this was not an uncommon answer in the Zehairan port.

'And all on your own?'

'I'm looking for someone.' Yara raised her eyes from her bowl. 'In the Sorcerers' Quarter?'

It was incredible how swiftly the atmosphere changed. The sailors, who had been eavesdropping with expressions of good-natured curiosity, narrowed their eyes and began to mutter among themselves. Yara could feel glares directed at her back, and her stomach clenched with anxiety.

'I don't think you are, darling. Sorcerers are a wicked, treasonous lot – there's no quarter for them here.'

'Foreign witch,' came a hiss from behind Yara.

'None of that.' The old woman's voice was sharp. 'She didn't mean it.'

'But I think I did.' Yara clutched her bag to herself. 'I want to find the third-to-last house on Istehar Way?'

She could feel the antagonism of the sailors and traders swell – even the old woman with her soup spoon was now regarding her with frosty hostility.

'Well, you won't find any sorcerers there. Only the Sultan's alchemists, and they won't take kindly to a foreign brat poking around their business.'

She reached across her pot and snatched the half-emptied bowl from Yara's hands. 'Now go on. Get out of here.'

Unsure of what she had done wrong, but recognising menace in the faces of those gathered around her, Yara made a hasty departure, snaking her way back through the crowd.

Shaken, and beginning to feel hopeless, Yara wandered through the market, a lump forming in her throat. This had been a mistake, a horrible mistake. She should summon the Ferryman and beg him to take her back to England – but would he answer her summons? She only had the spell to take them one way. She was stranded. Her chest squeezed until she couldn't breathe, a tear escaping and spilling down her cheek.

'Can I help?'

Yara turned round, sniffing and wiping her eyes. Quite by accident, she had found herself in the middle of the bazaar and directly in front of a wizened man with a beard down to his knees.

'I'm new to the city,' she explained, once she had managed to work her voice around the tightness in her throat. 'And I think I'm lost.'

'Understandable,' the man said kindly. 'I see at least three travellers a day who come to me, telling me that they are lost. But you are in luck!' He moved back, and Yara saw that behind him were large sheets of parchment with mysterious lines and symbols drawn in ink. 'Your voyage has taken you to the stall of Umr Ibn Munir, the greatest cartographer beneath these skies! Is it a map of the city you require? Or do you wish to venture beyond the walls of Zehaira and into the mountain provinces of the kingdom? Or perhaps you are going even further . . . ? I can provide coordinates for the most barbarous corners of the earth.'

Yara followed his gesturing and was startled to find herself looking at a map of Europe. At least, she thought that it must be Europe, because she could see the UK at the far west, and the boot of Italy – but the majority of the continent had labels she had never heard before in her life. Most of it seemed to be taken up by *The Holy Frankian Empire*, but she could see *The Dane-Mirks* in the top-left corner, and *The Russlands* in the top right. As for her own country, Ibn Munir had written in careless handwriting: *Small wet island. No culture of note.*

'Well?' Ibn Munir asked. 'Where is it you need to go?'

Yara tore herself away from the maps.

'I . . . I only have a pound coin.' She brought it out to

show him. She secretly had a bit more than that at the bottom of her school bag – though who knew if anyone else would take her money? But Ibn Munir *tsked* at her extended palm.

'Do you think that the noble explorer Abdul Tariq would have begged a small coin for guiding a child in the right direction? Or the astronomer and renowned gourmand Malik Hussein demanded recompense for pointing out the Eastern Star to a frostbitten scientist?'

He seemed to be awaiting her answer.

'Um, no?'

'No! And yet you presume this mercenariness of the greatest cartographer in the kingdom, merely because he has the misfortune to be keeping a stall in the Grand Harbourian Bazaar instead of charting new territories beyond the mountains.' His face took on a tragic demeanour. 'Is it the fault of the noble map-maker that his daughter's husband is an oaf, and the Sultan a blind fool who wouldn't understand an expedition of scientific import if it bit him on the—'

'I'm sorry,' she interrupted, recognising that the cartographer would descend further into gloominess unless she stopped him. 'I just didn't want to be ungrateful, that's all.'

'Well, then, we shall say no more about it.' Ibn Munir tilted his head, mollified. 'After all, there are many in this wretched city who would have snatched the coin from your hand without a second thought. Now, where is it that you wish to go?'

Yara hesitated. The cartographer seemed less threatening than the woman serving stew, but it was hard to forget the hardening eyes and clenched fists at the mention of the Sorcerers' Quarter. She should be careful.

'I ... I was told by someone that I should go to the third-to-last house on Istehar Way,' she said, ready to retract her words at the slightest sign of alarm. 'It's important.'

To her relief there was no hostility in the old man's querying look.

'Are you a messenger?' he asked finally.

Yara seized on the excuse. 'Yes. I have a message. For the Sultan's alchemists,' she added, remembering what the woman at the stall had said.

Ibn Munir sighed.

'Very well – I suppose there's no harm in giving you directions, although I must say, I would not want a daughter of mine venturing there. Do you see that street to your right? Head down there until you reach a square with a eucalyptus tree in the middle, and then take the second street on the left. That's Istehar Way. The third-to-last house should be obvious enough.'

Yara let out a breath.

'Thank you. Are you sure there isn't anything—'

'Get on with you.' Ibn Munir waved her away. 'If you truly have a message for the alchemists, it is wisest not to keep them waiting.'

Chapter Four

Taking the cartographer's advice, Yara wandered eastwards, leaving the bright stalls of the bazaar behind. The street was narrow, terraced sandstone buildings rising on either side of her until she felt as though she might be travelling in a valley of dunes. It grew quieter too, away from the stalls. Every now and then Yara would glance up at an open window – but for the most part she saw closed shutters, and only the occasional pair of eyes peering out furtively from behind them.

Yara didn't linger long. The further into the city she went, the more unmoored she felt, each curious glance a sharp reminder of how little she belonged here. She wound the headscarf tighter round her neck, repeating her mother's words in her head like a mantra. *Ask for the sorceress Leyla Khatoun ... she will give you the help that I cannot.* Perhaps this woman was a relative. Perhaps she was a friend of her mother's. Perhaps she could answer all the questions Yara had had since she was a little girl about why they had moved to the UK.

She was so lost in her daydreaming that she didn't notice the eucalyptus until she was walking directly beneath it, the air heavy with its perfume and the pale branches forming a canopy that made shadows play across the square. Yara stopped, fascinated. The air around the trunk was shimmering with a strange quality, the leaves rustling together as though they were whispering among themselves. Almost unthinkingly Yara reached out with her free hand and spread her palm against the trunk.

She gasped.

It was as though the bark was vibrating beneath her hand – not in a juddering, mechanical way, but with a warmth that shot up her wrist and spread right to the tips of her toes. Something strange and electric began to prickle inside her, needling beneath her skin. As the feeling grew, the branches seemed to bend towards her, the whispering of the leaves growing more urgent until she thought she could hear their murmur. '*Yara, Yara, Yara.*'

She sprang back, looking up at the tree in disbelief. Its leaves fluttered in the breeze innocuously, until Yara convinced herself that they had merely been rustling in the wind.

The second street on the left, Ibn Munir had said. As Yara rounded on her destination, her jaw dropped. Gone was the sandstone brick, the uneven bubbling of the cobblestones. The ground was paved a smooth obsidian, the marble stone rippling as though the rock were still molten and moving beneath the surface. And covering the houses on either side of the street, *gold*. More gold than she had ever seen in her life, creeping up the walls like ivy, flashing coldly in the sunlight until Yara had to shield her eyes from the glare. Clearly whoever lived here was rich beyond all reason, but the street was empty; there were no children playing, no one working at the windows.

With the first staccato *tap* of her shoes on the ground, Yara knew instantly that this place didn't want her here – a thought that would never have crossed her mind about a street at home. It was as though some new instinct had awoken inside her, something that was telling her in no uncertain terms that she should *get out*.

Her footsteps echoed as she walked, and her feeling of unbelonging grew, the warmth she had gleaned from the eucalyptus tree long gone in the cool air of the street. The blue of the sky was no longer visible, obscured by pale, wisping smoke.

A few steps more, and then there it was. The third-to-last house.

Yara stood outside the front door for quite some time, her breathing unsteady and her heart thumping. The house was cloaked in the same gold-leaf patterns as the rest of the street – but, as she got closer, she could see that they were not patterns but calligraphy, sentences running into each other until Yara could not tell where one ended and another began. Rather, she could only slowly spell out a few words. '*Greatness . . . vanquish . . . triumph.*' Then one she recognised on sight, a word that had been burned on to the back of her mind since discovering her mother's letter. *Sorcerers.*

The sight of the word ought to have comforted Yara, but if anything it only increased her dread. Reminding herself that Mama would not put her in danger, she lifted her hand to knock.

Mrrow?

Yara looked down. A black tomcat had appeared by her feet. He was a scrawny underfed thing, with jutting ribs and thinning fur; the mere sight of him tugged at Yara's heartstrings.

'Hello. Are you lost?'

The cat sniffed at her fingertips, then gave a lonely, plaintive whine.

'Oh, you poor thing.' Yara hunted around in her bag, and her fingers closed round the half-forgotten sambusak. As she held it in her palm, the thought of making the pastry while Mama quizzed her on her schoolwork brought with it a wave of sorrow that felt powerful enough to knock her off her feet.

Stop it, she told herself, sternly. *It's only pastry. It was never going to last for ever.*

She offered it to the cat, who, after regarding it with some suspicion, began to gnaw at it, his purr like a rumbling motor. Seeing his enjoyment made the tightness in her chest recede a little, and she crouched next to the cat, stroking his head and determinedly blinking back tears.

'I wish I could stay out here with you. This isn't your house, is it?'

The cat cleaned his whiskers of crumbs. Then, brushing past her legs, he walked to the side of the building, looking back at her expectantly until Yara got the impression that she was being asked to follow. Feeling foolish, she nonetheless found herself walking behind him until they reached a narrow staircase spiralling down to below the house.

'You want me to go down there?' she asked doubtfully. Skulking around in the basement would hardly endear her to Leyla Khatoun, but the cat was circling her legs with impatience, nudging her calf with his nose. 'All right, all right. I'm coming.'

She took the steps quickly, the cat at her side. At the bottom was a passageway, the floor tiled with mosaic and stone arches holding up the ceiling. The cat sprinted across, not stopping until he reached a wooden door, where he began to miaow insistently, scratching at it with his claws.

Yara huffed. After all that, the cat had only wanted her to let him into the cellars for more food. All this talk of sorcery must have turned her head.

As she made up her mind to go back and try the front door, Yara heard a sound that made her stop dead in her tracks. It was a low wailing noise; she might have dismissed it as the rushing of the wind were it not for a note of sorrow that made it unmistakably human. Someone was in trouble. No, more than that – someone down here was filled with an unhappiness so unbearable that it could only take form in a wordless cry. Yara felt something surge within her in answer, and she moved closer to the door.

'Hello?' she whispered. 'Are you all right?'

Just then, there was the sound of footsteps, and instinctively Yara pressed herself against the wall. The door opened and a man carrying a crate of linens breezed past without seeing her – but before it could close behind him, the cat darted forward and stopped it with his body, looking up at Yara expectantly.

The wail started up again and, half hypnotised, Yara followed him through. A winding corridor lay in front of her, dark enough that torches had already been lit. Feeling for the wall on her right, Yara stole through the passage, the cat just ahead and glancing periodically over his shoulder, as though to check she was keeping up.

The way grew narrower, the flickering torches fewer, until she could hardly see her own hand in front of her. A cold shivering feeling made its way down Yara's spine. Not that long ago she had been fretting about skipping school, and now she was creeping through the cellars of the grandest house she had seen in her life. She should turn back.

Before she could act on the thought, the cat stopped sharply, his tail upright and his back arched. Yara could hear a growl beginning in his throat, and she picked him up quickly, stroking the back of his head. As she did, she saw what had perturbed him. A door next to them had been left open, and moving in front of them were two men. One was tall and dressed in black-and-gold robes, staring in deep concentration at a row of copper beakers and bubbling solutions; the other was stooped and strutting, twisting rings on his fingers.

'Will this take much longer, Firaaz?' he blustered.

'Patience, wisest of viziers.' The taller man had a voice that was as smooth as oil, but there was an undercurrent of amusement there too, as though its owner were privy to a joke that no one else was part of. He stepped forward, and Yara could make out a pair of pale eyes, bright as cut green glass. 'The purification of metals is a delicate art, and the greatest experiments take time.'

Rafts of smoke began to rise from the worktable, and no matter how hard Yara squinted, she couldn't see through the fog.

'Now you see,' Firaaz continued, 'one drop of the tincture on the sorceress's hair, and ...'

Yara, drawn in by the mention of a sorceress, opened the door a little further, straining to catch their conversation. The cat began to hiss, struggling in her arms – but the men were too absorbed in the success of the experiment to notice.

'Remarkable.' The Vizier's voice had lost its pompousness; he spoke in hushed tones. 'When will it take effect?'

'Almost immediately in Zehaira. It may take longer outside the city walls – but I will send my men to make sure it spreads.'

'And it won't harm the citizens? The ordinary ones, I mean.'

'Not a soul,' Firaaz promised. Yara could see his eyes glinting in the torchlight before he moved to stand next to the shorter man. 'You see—'

At that moment the cat, no longer able to contain himself, gave an ear-splitting yowl and sprang from Yara's arms.

'What the—'

Firaaz looked up, and his eyes met Yara's across the room. His face slackened in shock, then contorted in a fit of rage.

Yara froze, seized with fear. Firaaz moved, and might have grabbed her, but just then several of the flasks shattered in the heat, and Yara turned on her heel and pelted back the way she came.

'A spy! A saboteur! Stop that child!' came the howl behind her, and she ran faster. She sprinted down the corridor, out of the basement door and back up to Istehar Way.

Yara slipped back through the streets, knowing her pursuers would not be far behind. Sure enough, as she turned her head, she saw three men in black uniforms running towards her, their swords drawn. She let out a breathless sob. Her legs were jelly-like after the voyage, her heart banging sickeningly against her chest as she hurtled down an alleyway. A network of warehouses towered labyrinth-like above the narrow streets, and

Yara only hoped that she would be fast enough to lose them in the maze.

A glance behind her told her that was not the case. They were close enough now that she could hear their snarls:

'Little demon.'

'You'll see what we do with your kind here.'

The threat spurred Yara on, her hair flying behind her as she struggled to keep going – but her trainers, second-hand and too big for her, caught on the uneven ground. She went flying, hitting the ground with a hard *thwack*.

Too stunned to pick herself up, Yara could only scramble backwards.

'Please. I'm sorry, I'm sorry! I didn't see anything.'

The men slowed, their faces broadening with identical grins as they walked towards her, backing her against a wall.

'Let her go.'

It was a woman's voice, clear and ringing, but Yara couldn't see past her assailants.

'Stay out of this,' one of them growled, not turning round.

'It wasn't a request.'

And then time seemed to choke and sputter like an overheated engine. One moment the men were leering over her, their teeth bared in triumph. The next, the air rippled, and they swayed and crumpled to the floor, their eyes rolling back in their heads. As they fell, they parted to reveal the woman behind them, who was standing with her hand outstretched, panting.

'Goodness me. I haven't done that in a while.'

Chapter Five

Yara gaped, her thoughts tripping over each other in their haste to catch up.

'Was that ... was that you? Was that magic?'

The woman grinned ruefully, pulling up her headscarf from where it had slipped to her shoulders, her bracelets tinkling on her wrists.

'Sort of. I'm a little rusty, but I suggested that the blood might like to rush from their heads, and then physics did the rest. It won't knock them out for long, though.'

She was right. Even as she spoke, one of the men began to twitch and stir. 'Oh, crumbs.'

Stepping over the limp forms of the men, she grabbed Yara's hand and hauled her to her feet. Yara reeled, still not quite able to believe what she had seen.

'I don't ... Who are you?'

'Someone who doesn't wish you any harm,' said the

woman firmly. 'Which is more than can be said for these men, who will be staggering to their feet within seconds. Now come on – we have to move.'

Realising the truth of her words, Yara took the strange woman's hand and began to run.

She sneaked a glance at her companion as she did so. The golden brown of her skin had turned bright pink in her exertion, and clouds of dark auburn hair frizzed round her face in the heat. Yara thought this person must be quite a bit younger than her mum, but she was sure that Mama had never been quite so beautiful.

Just then, the woman made a sharp left, pulling them into a gap between two warehouses and down a narrow passage. She stopped then, leaning against a wall and closing her eyes. 'They won't look for us here,' she panted. 'Just need a moment ... haven't ... cast a spell in a long time.'

Yara nodded, struggling to regain her own breath. 'You did magic,' she blurted in between gasps. 'Does that mean ... ? Are you ... ?'

'A sorceress, yes, and one who just saved your life.' The woman gave her a sharp glance, and Yara felt her face go red.

'Yeah, thank you so much.'

The woman relaxed. 'That's all right. You're not hurt, are you?'

Yara had a 'no' on the tip of her tongue, but then she looked down. Both of her knees were grazed badly and wet with blood. The woman followed her gaze.

'That looks sore. Shall I take you home?' She looked at Yara, taking her appearance in for the first time. 'Oh, I'm sorry, I thought you were from around here. Where are you from? Do your parents know where you are?'

'I don't have any parents.' Yara lowered her eyes. 'And I am from here, sort of. It's complicated.'

She risked looking up, daring the other woman to feel sorry for her. But while her eyes had softened, there was genuine friendliness in her voice when she replied.

'Well, how about you come back to my shop and explain there? I can patch you up.'

Yara nodded, trying not to look as nervous as she felt. 'Don't go home with a stranger' had been drummed into her since she was a small child, and going home with a strange witch – or sorceress – seemed like even less of a good idea.

The woman seemed to read her thoughts and gave her a warm smile.

'Don't worry. I'm not the sort to bake children into pastries. Lifelong vegetarian for one thing.'

Yara smiled back shyly. 'Okay, thank you. I'm Yara by the way. Yara Sulimayah.'

'Meriyem Shereen.' The woman brought the palm of her hand to her heart. 'Call me Meri.'

They came out of the alleyway, Yara shielded from view by Meri's shawl. There were people about again, and there was a warm undercurrent of noise as they leaned out of windows and stopped on street corners to chat. Hearing excitable chirrups from sparrows, she realised that the birds had not sung on Istehar Way. Perhaps they found it as frightening a place as she had.

Even so, Meri swept them along, keeping to the shadows of the warehouses. It might have been Yara's imagination, but it seemed that people kept their distance from Meri, and more than once she saw a hostile glance thrown in their direction. The few times someone did call out to her, she would offer a brief smile and press on, citing burning bread.

'I really do have quite a few batches in the oven,' she explained to Yara, 'but even if I didn't, I wouldn't want to linger. If those men are who I think they are, then you're in terrible danger.'

'Who do you think they—'

'Shhh,' Meri hushed her. 'Walls have ears. Any one of these people could overhear something and turn you in.'

'But I haven't *done*—'

'*Shhh*. We can speak when we get back to the bakery.'

They came out at another square, this one bordered by bay trees and vaulted shopfronts. Meri led them to one with rows of flaky pastries stacked enticingly before the window, twisted bread hanging from pegs like looped scarves, embroidered with olives and chillies. As they approached, the most fantastic aromas began to fill the air – of toasted spices and nuts, of bread rising and buns baking and fruit growing fat and sticky with sugar.

Yara, who had always had a sweet tooth, sniffed the air. 'Oh my *goodness*.'

Meri laughed, lifting the latch and inviting Yara in.

'I'm glad you like it. It's the second great love of my life, this place.' Venturing inside, Yara could see that she meant it. The walls were stained a cheerful pink, the floor swept and the counters scrubbed within an inch of their lives. 'My apartment is upstairs. Let's get you cleaned up.'

Meri led her into a small, pleasant room, with arched windows that let the light stream in and a low round table surrounded by cushions. Sat on one of these was a girl who looked roughly Yara's age, her hair curling wildly around her shoulders and her eyes fixed on a scroll of parchment. She looked up, and Yara recognised Meri's bright eyes in her face.

'Here, Mehnoor, I found her.'

Yara blinked. 'Found me?'

'Oh.' The girl – Mehnoor – got to her feet and looked intently at Yara. 'You've come a long way, haven't you? I can feel loud noises and tall buildings and the *sea*, and you've come here to find someone—'

'Mehnoor,' Meri chided, and the girl's mouth snapped shut. 'I'll be right back – I'm sure I keep some medicinal wine somewhere.'

As she left the room, Yara turned to look at Mehnoor in amazement.

'How did you know all that?'

'I'm a soothsayer,' Mehnoor said simply. 'I keep watch for anyone who might need Auntie's help, and I sensed you in the old Sorcerers' Quarter today. You have a very insistent aura – it was determined to get itself heard. You're like a character from a poem.'

'I'm really not.' Yara felt herself blushing again. 'So you can ... *sense* people? Is that what being a soothsayer is?'

'Sort of. It's all kinds of things – feelings, dreams, things that might not even happen ... they all jumble together in my head. It's very confusing. I have to take a sleeping tea to stop the dreams, and I'm barely allowed outside, because I'm bound to blurt something out that'll get us both in terrible trouble.' She looked enviously at

Yara. 'You're so lucky being on an adventure. You have to tell me *everything*.'

Yara didn't feel lucky at all, and was about to tell Mehnoor this when Meri re-entered the room.

'Found it. I always keep some on hand.' She held up the medicinal bottle, which was giving off a pungent vinegary smell. 'Do you want to apply it, or shall I?'

'I can do it.'

But as Yara took the bottle she winced in pain. Her palms had been badly roughed up by her fall, and small specks of stone were lodged in her cuts.

'Let me,' said Meri, guiding her to a cushion. 'That was quite a tumble you took.'

'Thank you. And thank you so much for saving me. That spell was really … cool,' Yara finished, blushing. 'Cool' didn't seem quite the right word for someone who had toppled two grown men with a flick of her wrist – but her reward was one of Meri's warm smiles.

'It was, wasn't it? It's been so long since I've allowed myself even the smallest of spells.'

'Why?'

Meri didn't reply at first, lowering her head and applying the alcohol, careful even as Yara squirmed at the sharp sting of it. When she finally spoke, it was with a heavy, resigned sadness.

'Sorcery has been outlawed for almost twelve years

in our kingdom. If anyone were to find out that I cast that spell, I would be arrested and imprisoned – or killed, even.'

'Killed?' Yara felt a jolt of horror run through her, and Meri looked up in surprise.

'Do you really not know? I thought news of the Inquisition had travelled the world.' She leaned back, her face suddenly drawn with worry. 'You said you were from Zehaira?'

'It's all right, Auntie,' said Mehnoor. 'She's on our side, trust me.'

Meri nodded, taking a deep breath. 'You see, things were not always this way. There was once a great community of sorcerers here in Zehaira, renowned for their wisdom and learning throughout the world. There was a Great Council of sorcerers who oversaw the practice of magic in the city, led by the Grand High Sorceress – one of the most powerful women in Zehaira. Then, nearly thirteen years ago, things changed, almost overnight. The Sultan declared that we were plotting against him, and the guards ambushed and slaughtered the Great Council at their meeting. By the time word got out, everything had been thrown into chaos. People being turned out of the Quarter and executed in the streets, others trying to escape only to be handed over to the guards by those who promised to smuggle them out.' A shadow passed over Meri's face. 'It was a terrible time. There was no one who would speak up for us – even the ordinary people either believed the Sultan's lies or were too afraid to help.'

'But ... but you have magic; you can do spells!'

'We were scholars; we knew nothing of stopping swords. Now we're scattered, too afraid to reach out to one another. Worse still, we lost the Grand High Sorceress. She wasn't just our leader, she was the keeper of a vast resource of magic, contributed to by generations of sorcerers in Zehaira – we needed it if we were to defend ourselves. Then they destroyed our library and our university, and if ever there was other magic capable of defeating the Sultan and his guards, knowledge of it vanished into the flames.'

Meri looked out of her window as she spoke, and Yara followed her gaze. Looking towards the gold and marble of Istehar Way, she thought she saw the ruined walls of something that might have once been tall and domed, and her stomach tightened in horror at the thought of a library disappearing in ash and smoke.

'I'm really sorry.'

'Oh, don't be,' said Meri, with a slight shake of her head. 'Look at me, talking about the past when you've been through such an ordeal. How did you find yourself on Istehar Way?

'It's a long story,' Yara began. 'I was trying to find someone – a sorceress – but now I don't know where to start looking.'

'Do you know her name? I might know what became of her.'

'Yes, Leyla Khatoun,' Yara said, remembering her mother's letter. 'My mama said she would be able to help me, and—'

'Auntie, what's wrong?' Mehnoor interrupted.

Yara looked up at Meri. She had gone pale, her mouth falling open and emotions passing across her face too quickly for Yara to recognise them. She sat down heavily, looking her directly in the eye.

'Yara, I think perhaps you had better tell us everything – right from the beginning.'

So Yara told them about the letter, and the mysterious pier, and the spell. For the most part the pair listened to her, lips parted and eyes wide in amazement, but when she mentioned the strange Ferryman who had brought her to Zehaira, Meri interrupted.

'You're sure it was a safe passage spell? And your mama really told you to find Leyla Khatoun?'

'Yes, she said: "She will give you the help that I cannot." What does that mean?'

Meri gnawed at her lip. 'What was your mother's name?'

'Nahzin,' Yara said hopefully. 'Nahzin Sulimayah.'

Meri's forehead creased. 'I'm sorry; I don't think I ever met her. Your mother never mentioned the Inquisition? Or how she came to travel so far from the city?'

'No, never.'

'What about Leyla? She must have said something about how she knew her.'

Yara frowned. 'I don't think so. She knew where Leyla lived, though; she told me to go to the third-to-last house on Istehar Way.'

'Yes, that's where she used to lodge with Professor Al-Qamar—' Meri's eyebrows rose in horror. 'Oh, Yara, you didn't try to find her there?'

'It was all I had to go on,' said Yara defensively. 'People kept saying that's where the alchemists were, but I thought maybe she was with them. What are alchemists anyway?'

Meri sighed. 'Once upon a time they were scholars too, committed to pursuing science and philosophy. But they were taken over by a faction obsessed with turning base metal into gold. When they succeeded, the city changed; the people grew hungry for wealth, and the alchemists used their greed to make themselves the most powerful men in the city.'

'Did they send the guards after you?' asked Mehnoor.

'Yes, or one alchemist, at least. The other man called him "Firaaz".'

Meri made a small disbelieving sound. 'Omair Firaaz? The Sultan's Chief Alchemist, the richest and most ruthless man in Zehaira? Oh, Yara, what have you done?'

'Nothing, I promise! I just overheard something I shouldn't have, I think.' Yara tried to remember, but with everything that had happened that day, her thoughts seemed to have tangled together in her head. 'He – the alchemist – was showing off an experiment to someone who called himself a vizier. He said that whatever it was wouldn't harm the ordinary citizens.'

'The ordinary citizens. But what of those of us who are not ordinary?' Meri looked out of the window again. 'The workings of the laboratories of Istehar Way are shrouded in secrecy – but there are rumours that the alchemists were not satisfied with the Inquisition, that they won't rest until they have wiped out sorcery for good. And there is no one who hates and fears sorcery more than Omair Firaaz. If a vizier was there too . . .' She trailed off. 'You must leave Zehaira, lie low. I might not be able to reach other sorcerers, but I know people on the outskirts of the city who can keep you safe.'

'But I *have* to find Leyla Khatoun. I don't know

anything about this place, apart from the fact that my mum wanted me to find her. I can't just give up.'

Meri fell silent, her mouth pressed tightly, unhappily shut.

Yara watched her. 'Do you know Leyla?'

'I did,' Meri said shortly. 'Or I thought I did. The last time I saw her, she was heading into the mountains with other refugees – that was over a decade ago, and I haven't heard from her since.' But the sorceress ducked her head as she spoke, not meeting Yara's eye.

Yara leaned forward. 'Please. You must know some way I could find her.'

Meri hesitated, gnawing at her lip again – but then seemed to come to a decision.

'I suppose . . . I suppose there might be a way. I would need to use a spell, so you'll have to wait until after dark if we are to remain undetected, but if you truly are intent on seeking her out, I would rather you do so with my help than without.'

'I am,' said Yara, looking up at her gratefully. 'Thank you.'

'Well, then.' Meri's eyes were still clouded with worry, but warmth came flooding back into her face. 'I'll reopen the bakery in five minutes – that should offset any suspicion. You're welcome to get washed and rested . . . and perhaps you should borrow some less . . .

conspicuous clothes from Mehnoor.'

'It's all right.' Yara clutched her bag to herself. 'I have my own.'

'Then come downstairs and get me if there's anything you need, but otherwise stay out of sight. There's every chance they've already put out a warrant for your arrest.'

Chapter Six

Fairly certain that electricity was a foreign concept in Zehaira, Yara was ready for the torment of a cold bath. To her surprise Meri had a round stone bath with a lit furnace beneath, and a slab of hard soap on the side. By the time she had washed, combed through her hair and put on a salwar qamis she had packed, Yara felt more like her old self than she had done since she had been taken to the foster family weeks ago.

Yara studied herself in Meri's mirror. She had worn the outfit so little that the dark green fabric was almost like new, and she felt a hot prickle of guilt at having been so ungrateful for it. Her old clothes lay in a heap by the side of the bath, scrunched and stained and smelling strongly of the sea. She put them in her bag, extracting Mama's headscarf from the pile and wrapping it back round her neck.

When she went downstairs to the kitchen, Mehnoor

was kneading dough, and Meri was looking more than a little flustered, her sleeves rolled up and her cheeks dusted with flour. She did a double-take at the sight of Yara.

'I almost didn't recognise you. You look like a local girl.'

'Well, I suppose I am one technically.' Yara fiddled with the end of her headscarf. 'Seeing as I can't leave until dark, I was wondering if I could help out? You've been so kind.'

Meri tilted her head to one side, considering her. 'All right, thank you very much.' She looked behind her into the shop, where there was already a queue forming in her absence. 'There's a list of things that need doing on the counter – Mehnoor will show you the ropes.'

Yara set to work. She ground cardamom and cassia with Meri's pestle and mortar, washed up pans in a stone basin in the corner, and rolled out pastry so thin that she could hold it up and see Mehnoor through it. She had always loved helping out in the kitchen – Mama had been so busy with work and night classes that the time they spent there together had felt sacred to the two of them. Even as the memory made her chest feel tight and tears smart at the corners of her eyes, it was a relief to think that she could do something as normal as baking in this new world.

Occasionally Yara would peek through the door to

the front of the shop and watch Meri. Even as the baker joked with her customers and pressed baklava into the hands of hopeful children, she looked increasingly anxious as the day went on. Frazzled, too – there was far too much work for one person. Mehnoor was clearly doing her best to help – but she had an unfortunate habit of daydreaming at crucial moments, and twice Yara had to run to catch flatbreads that the other girl had left to char.

By the time Meri had seen off the last customer, it was already growing dark. She came through to the back of the shop and looked around her appreciatively.

'You know, if it weren't quite so urgent that you leave the city by nightfall, I might offer you a job. It would be wonderful to have another pair of hands around the bakery – and Mehnoor could burn bread just by looking at it the wrong way.'

'Hey!' Mehnoor said indignantly, and Meri laughed, pressing a kiss on her niece's forehead.

'It'll be safe to do the spell soon. Clean up as best you can, and I'll come and help you when I'm done in the front.'

She returned to the shop floor, and Mehnoor looked longingly at Yara.

'Couldn't you stay?' she asked. 'I'm sure we could keep you hidden.'

Briefly, Yara allowed herself to imagine working at the bakery, making delicious food and living with Meri and Mehnoor – and then she shook her head.

'I would love to, honestly. But Mama really wanted me to find Leyla Khatoun. I think I have to try.'

Mehnoor sighed. 'I know. You're on an adventure and this is just a stop on the way. It's just so *lonely* here. All I have for company is poetry, and I've read every scroll we own three times already.'

Yara felt a pang of sympathy. Struck by an idea, she rummaged in her bag and drew out her history book. Parting with Mama's last gift to her felt almost unbearable – but at the thought of Mehnoor cooped up at the back of the bakery, she handed it over.

'Here. You won't be able to understand the words – but there are lots of pictures, and at least you haven't read it three times before.'

Mehnoor flicked through the pages with a look of awe, tracing her finger across an illustration of the Colosseum.

'This is *amazing* – and usually if I concentrate hard enough, I can sense what a manuscript is about.' She looked up. 'I need to give you something in return.'

'Honestly, you don't. You and Meri have been so kind to me.'

Mehnoor shook her head. 'Just wait here.' She disappeared briefly upstairs and came back down with a vial of dark green liquid, which she pressed into Yara's hands.

'What is it?'

'My sleeping tea. It's not much of a present.' Mehnoor frowned, shaking her head as though to clear it. 'Sorry, nothing seems very clear at the moment, but I *think* that it's the best way to repay you. Just make sure you don't let it fall out – and maybe don't mention this to my auntie.'

Yara wasn't quite sure that she followed, but she smiled, putting it in her pocket. 'Thanks. Won't you need it?'

Mehnoor blinked at the question. 'No,' she said, shaking her head again. 'I think ... I think it might be good for me to have the dreams for a while.' She looked at Yara apologetically. 'I'm not very good at explaining – especially when I'm not sure about things myself – but I think this might all turn out for the best.'

'How are we doing?'

Yara jumped. Meri had re-entered the kitchen, a sweeping broom in hand.

'Just finishing up,' said Mehnoor, looking sidelong at Yara.

'Right. It's almost sunset; I think we can try the spell. Mehnoor, I want you upstairs – and don't try to argue!' she said, as her niece opened her mouth in protest.

'Fine.' Mehnoor turned to Yara, her eyes shining as she reached for her hand and squeezed it with her own. 'Goodbye. And good luck – I think you're the bravest person I've ever met.'

Yara's heart contracted, but before she could form a reply, the other girl dropped her hand and flitted back up the stairs.

Meanwhile, Meri closed the doors and shutters, setting her oven and two great stone mixers to work, until they were surrounded by deafening noise.

'The more non-magical energy around, the harder it is for magic to be detected,' she explained, looking around them with trepidation. 'I don't believe that my neighbours would inform on me, but you can't be too careful. Still, we should be able to get away with one quick spell.'

'Should?'

'Don't worry.' Meri retrieved a cooking pot and placed it in the centre of the room. 'If we never took any risks, we'd never do anything at all.'

She kneeled in front of the pot, and Yara came to sit beside her, worrying at her lip with her teeth.

'But, Meri,' she began uneasily, looking at her knees, 'you're not taking a risk for yourself; you're taking one for me. You don't have to do this.'

Yara felt Meri hesitate next to her. And then she felt

the pressure of her hand, warm and still a little damp, against her own.

'Yes, I do,' she said, quietly. 'Because the only true test of your character is how you respond to someone who needs your help.' Yara looked up, and Meri's face was alight with fierce, certain kindness. 'Besides, you helped me too. I never would have sold so much today if you hadn't worked so hard in the kitchen.'

'That wasn't the same at all.'

'Yes it was. You helped me to the best of your ability because I helped you, and now I am helping you again in return. And that, Yara Sulimayah, is the only way any of us can survive in a world that is doing its best to destroy us.' She released Yara's hand. 'Now I need to concentrate. I haven't attempted this spell in years, and it would do neither of us any good if I were to get it wrong.'

Yara watched in silence as Meri drizzled honey into her pot, measuring two, then three teaspoons, before scattering cinnamon bark and cloves into the mixture.

'That's magic?' Yara asked doubtfully. 'It looks like you're making syrup.'

'On another day I might be,' said Meri, stirring anticlockwise. 'Anything that lives and grows beneath the stars has some magic in it. It's only a matter of drawing it out.'

Meri held out her palm, and spoke in slow, solemn tones.

'As green goes to gold,
And gold turns to dust,
So loved ones are lost,
As their memories rust.

As she spoke, she lifted her sleeve and grasped a thread tied round her wrist, picking at the knot until it came loose. As Yara looked closer, she saw that it was not a thread at all, but two locks of hair braided tightly together, one auburn and one jet black. Carefully Meri untangled the two strands. She looked down at the black one for a long moment, her throat working, before she dropped it into the pot.

'But fragments remain,
To ourselves they are bound.
As light follows rain,
So our loved ones are found.'

The thread of hair began to glow and Meri watched it carefully, counting slowly under her breath. Yara, remembering how Firaaz's eyes had gleamed as he had prepared his solution, shivered with unease.

The glow faded, the strand of hair began to darken, and then, just as it looked as though it was about to smoulder, Meri's hand darted into the concoction and pulled it out.

The sorceress exhaled in relief. 'Perfect. Now, if you'll lend me your hand . . .' Meri fastened the black thread round her wrist.

Yara wrinkled her nose, expecting the hair to be sticky with honey – but it was smooth and warm against her skin.

'Can you feel it?' Meri asked.

Yara frowned, unsure what Meri could be referring to – and then she gasped. It was as though there was someone tugging gently at her wrist, telling her to move to the right – but when she looked up, Meri's hands were folded neatly on her lap.

'Is that you?'

'It's a locating spell. It will lead you to Leyla – wherever she is now.' She drew herself upright. 'Now all that's left to do is smuggle you out of the city.'

Which was how Yara found herself curled up in an enormous bread basket on the bakery floor, her bag at her side and Meri peering in anxiously.

'I've packed you some food. From the outside it should look as though I've sealed the basket, but you'll be able to lift up the lid and let yourself out when the spell tells you to.'

'Thank you.' Yara got on to her knees until her face was level with Meri's. 'I know I can't possibly thank you enough, but . . . thank you.'

Meri smiled. 'Here. One last bit of protection.' She reached across and kissed Yara's forehead. 'A witch's kiss. They're said to protect you from ill fortune and the evil eye. Not a guarantee, but the best I can give you.' She drew back, looking directly at Yara. 'Before I close the lid, did you overhear anything else on Istehar Way? Anything at all that might help me understand what the alchemists are planning?'

Just as Yara racked her brains, they were interrupted by a loud thumping at the door.

Meri's eyes widened. 'That's the delivery man. Quietly now.' She lowered the lid, and Yara was left in darkness. Through the gaps in the weave, she could see Meri's sandals crossing the tiles as she went to let the man in, and then large boots treading dust on to the recently scrubbed floors.

'This is it, then?'

'Yes, please. For the House of Youssef, three leagues east.'

Yara shifted. Meri had packed the goods for the

Youssef family around her, and she was uncomfortably conscious of delicate pastry and flaking crumbs. There was a grunt and an almighty heave, and then she felt herself being lifted into the air.

'Weighs a ton.' The man jolted Yara as he adjusted the basket in his arms. 'What's in here?'

'Oh, just the usual,' Meri said lightly. 'The last time I trusted my goods to a driver, they arrived in a terrible state. I thought I would pack them in this time.'

Yara could hear low grumbling above her, but the man began to move, and she held her breath as she was transported through the air.

'Did you hear?' The man's voice came again. 'There's a sorcerer loose in the city tonight.'

'Really?'

'Oh yeah. Well, a young one anyway, speaking in strange tongues and spying on the Sultan's alchemists. That's sorcerers for you – each one more wicked than the last.'

'You shouldn't listen to gossip.' Meri's voice grew sharper. 'And you certainly shouldn't repeat it in here.'

The man stopped in his tracks, setting the basket down on the ground.

'Not gossip,' he said pointedly. 'Got it from the cousin of the wife of one of the Sultan's guards, no less. They're searching the city for it.'

Yara watched as he took slow, menacing steps towards Meri, not stopping until she was backed up against her counter. 'And I heard they're starting with people of a particular ... disposition, Madam Shereen. So I'd watch out if I were you.'

Meri was radiating anger, and yet for the first time that day, her eyes betrayed her terror, her chest rising and falling unsteadily. With visible effort, the sorceress maintained her composure, and the man stepped back, grinning.

'Goodnight.'

The smugness in his voice was unbearable, and Yara half wanted Meri to run after him and wipe the smirk off his face. But when the man picked the basket up again, she heard only one set of footsteps as she was carried out through the open door of the bakery.

Yara was deposited on what she assumed must be the cart with a *thump*, and heard the man climb up to his seat and click his tongue twice. With that she was away, bumping down the cobbled stones of the streets and into the chill of the night. She could feel herself getting further away from the city – further from the men who had wanted to hurt her, but further from Meri and Mehnoor too.

Thinking of everything that had happened that day, she could feel exhaustion creeping up on her. Her eyelids were growing heavy and her thoughts mixing together, until the rattle of the wheels of the cart could be the noises of the street outside their flat, and the basket her own bed. Only Mama wasn't there – she never would be.

Shutting out all other thoughts, Yara closed her eyes, nestled into her mother's headscarf, and wished herself home.

Chapter Seven

'*I*'*m sorry; all I have to give you is a terrible burden. But I love you. Oh, Mama loves you so much.*'

Someone was carrying her in their arms, and she could hear the sound of rain on the street, and low voices, and heavy breathing. Yara felt herself being jostled and bumped, felt herself lurch as the person slipped and almost fell ...

A sharp tug at her wrist jolted Yara out of sleep. For a wild moment she thought that she was still being carried, and she sat bolt upright in alarm. Her head hit the top of the basket, and she was brought back to reality with a *bump*.

She must have been asleep for quite some time; there was light streaming through the wicker, and birds jabbering around her. Closing her eyes, Yara tried desperately to cling on to the dream – but it slipped away like smoke into the morning. She swallowed heavily, wiping away tears that pricked insistently at the corners of her eyes.

Then she felt her wrist being pulled again, harder – the spell seemed determined that she should turn left *at once*. Realising that the cart must now be taking her in the wrong direction, she got to her knees, pushing open the lid of the basket and peering through the gap.

They were travelling through a mountain valley, a wall of cedar trees on either side and the ground rocky and uneven beneath the wheels. Having made certain that the driver had his eyes on the road, Yara began to manoeuvre herself out, hooking her right leg over the basket and balancing one-footed on the edge of the cart, wobbling precariously. If this went wrong ... but her left leg came down safely too, and she let the lid of the basket close, letting out a sigh of relief.

At which point the cart hit a stone, jolted and sent Yara flying through the air. She landed in a patch of tall grass by the side of the road, then tumbled in the dirt until she came to a stop. Lying on her back, unable to do much but gasp for breath, Yara only dimly registered the sound of the cart moving away in the distance, the delivery man oblivious to anything happening behind him.

When she could no longer hear the wheels on the

mountain path, Yara got to her feet. She didn't appear to have injured herself; her qamis, on the other hand, was covered in dirt and badly torn at the shoulder. Still, the most important thing was that she was out of the city, and free to find Leyla Khatoun.

The spell seemed intent on taking her away from the mountain path, and she obeyed the pull on her wrist, walking further into the grass until she was surrounded by rolling hills that were sun-baked and flecked with small flowers. Cypress and crab-apple trees bent and swayed in the breeze, each flutter of their leaves releasing bursts of cool scented air. She was completely alone. The sun rose higher in the sky, and she pulled her headscarf over her head, rolling up her sleeves in the heat and shifting her bag to her other shoulder.

She had never walked this far before – she had barely left Bournemouth. She and Rehema used to talk about the places they would travel to when they were old enough, but in all her imaginings she had never quite realised how quiet the world could be without cars, how vast it could seem with no buildings or people in sight. Yara swallowed heavily at the thought. Rehema wouldn't remember their plans now.

After a few hours, when the protest of her aching limbs and blistering feet grew too much, Yara finally came to a lone tree with fanlike leaves. Tempted by a view of her surroundings, she climbed up, deciding to rest there for a time. Her face was flushed with the heat of the sun; she was dirty and sweaty and stiff from a night spent hunched over in a basket – but, looking out over the mountains, she felt as though she might be content to sit here for ever.

Suddenly starving, Yara opened her bag. Meri had packed her a flask of mint tea, some flatbreads and a bag of brown flaky pastries studded with sesame seeds. She bit into one and, sighing happily at the taste of spiced potatoes and lentils, she allowed her mind to wander.

'I'm telling you, something isn't right. Why would he have us go all that way and risk our lives for this? There must be something more to it, is what I'm saying.'

Yara froze, scarcely daring to breathe as she looked below. While she had been daydreaming, two men in the dark uniform of the Zehairan guards had come to a stop beneath the tree. She tucked her legs beneath her chin and made herself as small as possible – but the men were in such heated argument that they scarcely seemed to notice their surroundings. She risked a glance through the branches. One of the men was holding a small glass bottle, so smeared and dusty that it barely caught the light.

'Put it away!' the other guard hissed. 'We've no business with it.' He made a fearful sign against evil.

'Whatever's in that thing, it's powerful enough to crush us like beetles. All we need to do is hand it over and we'll be rewarded beyond our wildest dreams.'

'Rewarded with a knife in our backs more likely,' said the second man darkly. 'Whatever this thing is, whatever great power it gives him, it's not something he's going to want getting out in Zehaira. He won't even meet us inside the city walls.'

'Exactly. So we do the job, we collect our money and we don't ask stupid questions or run our mouths. If you want to double-cross the Sultan's alchemists, be my guest – but I don't fancy being in your shoes when they catch up with you.'

This seemed to silence the second man. 'Come on. Let's have something to eat – it's still a long way back.'

They sat beneath the tree, still bickering, and Yara's mind began to race. These men were working for the alchemists. She remembered Meri's words: *There are rumours that the alchemists were not satisfied with the Inquisition, that they won't rest until they wipe sorcery out for good.*

She thought of Mehnoor hidden away in the apartment, and the pain in Meri's eyes when she had talked of people being killed. If whatever was in that bottle truly would make the alchemists stronger, then she couldn't let it reach the city.

Yara began to run through her options in her head with the same careful precision she had used to come up with schemes for the library with Rehema. It seemed unlikely that the men would leave the bottle unattended. Maybe she could distract them – but how could she hold their attention for long enough to get away? She could only imagine what they would do to her if they caught her. The thought made her feel sick, the reality of the situation hitting her full force. Maybe there really was nothing she could do.

Then, to her horror, her bag began to slip from where she had left it in the fork of the branches, and she had to lurch to catch it before it fell. As she did, Mehnoor's bottle of sleeping tea rolled into the palm of her hand, as though summoned there.

Yara stared at it, the cogs in her mind turning. Mehnoor had said that this would be the best way to repay her. Was this what she had seen – that she could use it here, on these men? It seemed a fantastical thing to do – like something out of a fairy tale. But then she remembered Mehnoor's words: *You're like a character from a poem.*

The thought filled her with a strange kind of courage. She undid the stopper from the vial and leaned down from the tree, careful not to make a sound. In their bags she could see joints of meat wrapped in muslin, and with a glance over her shoulder for the men, who were still absorbed in their quarrel, she emptied the tea over the meat and made a stealthy retreat. Moments later, the first guard reached into the bag and grabbed a piece by the bone, handing it to the other.

'Eat up. We'll have to get moving soon.'

Yara watched with bated breath. After just a few minutes, in a voice already thick with drowsiness, the second man said, 'Here, why don't we have a little rest? The sun's high in the sky, and he's not expecting us back till tomorrow.'

'You heard what he said,' his companion snapped back. 'We're not to take our eyes off the bottle.' But then he gave a yawn. 'Just ... just keep your wits about you, all right? I'm going to rest my eyes for a few seconds, but don't you go falling asleep, or it's both our heads.'

Yara waited. Soon she could hear the overlapping snores of the two men beneath her, and with a silent thank-you to Mehnoor, swung herself down from the branches of the tree. Hopefully whatever was in the sleeping tea would knock them out for a while. She began to search through their bags, one eye on their slumbering forms, but there was no sign of a bottle. Her heart began to patter uneasily in her chest.

A wink of light caught her attention, and she turned round. The first guard had a bottle attached to his belt; it rose and fell with his snores. Yara stole closer, reaching out with careful fingers and loosening it from its hold.

The guard grunted suddenly, his eyelashes flickering, and Yara's heart stopped beating as she reached wildly for excuses as to how she came to be standing over him. But his eyes didn't open, and as he rolled over in his sleep Yara lifted the bottle from his belt. Thinking quickly, she fastened the emptied vial of sleeping tea to the man's side.

For a moment Yara stepped back and surveyed her work with pride. But then the guard gave another great snort and she fled, not stopping until the tree she had sheltered in was a mere speck on the horizon.

Now a safe distance away, she examined the stolen bottle. It didn't look particularly powerful – and there was nothing drinkable in it as far as she could tell. It was sealed tight, and she prised at the stopper with her nails.

The bottle began to vibrate beneath her fingertips, growing hotter and hotter until Yara dropped it in alarm. As it fell to the ground, the seal appeared to melt away, and from the neck of the bottle came thick, dark smoke that rose until it formed a cloud. But it did not fade into the air. It didn't even leave the bottle entirely; it was as though something had tethered it to the glass. Yara thought she could make out leathery wings and claws, but each time she tried to look closer they would shimmer nebulously and fade into the smoke. And then, to Yara's astonishment, the cloud began to speak. It had a smooth, low voice, like burning incense.

'What is your command, young mistress?'

For a moment Yara simply stared, too stunned even to consider the question. Her mouth opened and closed without sound, her legs wobbling beneath her.

'Who ... who are you?' she breathed.

The cloud shifted kaleidoscopically. Yara thought that if she looked at it long enough, she might see all the colours of the universe.

'I am the jinn of the bottle, bound in service to whomever comes to possess it.'

Yara's mind raced. A *jinn*. She and Rehema had frightened each other with stories of jinn preying on unsuspecting humans and luring them to their doom since they were little. Yet here was one in front of her, not solid exactly but *real*, unquestionably real, and looking at her expectantly. She racked her brains for what to say.

'Um, do you have a name?'

The jinn flared and then seemed to withdraw into itself. If Yara were more confident in her ability to interpret clouds, she might have said it was surprised.

'My name is Ajal. Ajal of the ten-flamed supernova.'

He waited. 'And you? Do you have a name?'

Yara swallowed, her mouth suddenly dry. 'Oh, I'm Yara Sulimayah.' And then, remembering Mama's insistence on manners, added, 'Pleased to meet you.'

'Well, Yara Sulimayah, allow me the privilege of carrying out your first desire.'

Yara frowned. There was more than a hint of irony in the cloud's tone, and her curiosity was rapidly overcoming her fear.

'Do you not want to?'

'It is not a matter of what I want. I am the prisoner of the bottle, to hear is to obey.'

'But that's *awful*,' said Yara. 'How did it happen?'

The cloud flared again, and this time it was definitely in surprise.

'I was trapped by a powerful sorcerer hundreds of years ago. A jinn bound in this way is an invaluable treasure – I have been passed from sorcerer to enchanter to brigand, each time causing theft and bloodshed and treachery. Eventually I will be taken from you too, but until then you may ask anything of me that you wish.'

'I . . . I can't!' said Yara, horrified.

'I assure you, you can. I am a being of great might and wisdom.'

Yara wasn't entirely sure, but she thought Ajal sounded a little insulted.

'No, I mean, um, I'm sure you are mighty and wise, very. But I couldn't possibly ask you to do things for me.' She looked down at the bottle. 'Is there any way for me to free you?'

'I ... well ...' The cloud sputtered and sparked. 'Do you have any idea what it is you're giving up?'

'Probably quite a lot.' Yara thought with a sudden pang how much easier things might be if she had an all-powerful jinn on her side. 'But it wouldn't be right. I would be ... exploiting your labour,' she finished, remembering the phrase from a book she had borrowed from the library. 'I believe in animal welfare, you see.'

'*Animal*.' There was no mistaking the revolted expression from the cloud this time. 'So that is it, you consider me to be no more than a common beast of burden to be pitied and scorned?'

'I never said anything like that,' Yara replied hotly. 'Don't you want to be free?'

Ajal took a moment before he answered her.

'I want to be free. I am a being that should run like wildfire through the wasteland, that should rise up like smoke and descend like falling ash. But with my help you could become the most powerful person in the world.'

'Oh,' said Yara uncertainly. 'Well, I still don't think it

would be right to keep you in a bottle. Can I command you to be free perhaps?'

The jinn was silent.

'Um, Ajal of the ten-flamed supernova, I command you to free yourself.'

'To hear is to obey,' came the murmur from the cloud.

There was a great shimmer, and then the cloud seemed to grow until it was larger than a house, and then grew larger still until Yara could no longer make out its perimeter. There was a rustle of flames as it rose, and instinctively she ducked, covering her head as though the fire might move forward and devour her whole. The sound crescendoed to a roar, powerful and fierce, the roar of a mighty beast that has been freed from captivity.

And then slowly, slowly, the noise died down until it was like the crackling of a log fire. Opening her eyes, Yara pulled herself to her feet, until she was face to face with the jinn.

Chapter Eight

The jinn looked much the same as he had before, save that he was no longer emanating from the bottle, which now lay discarded on the ground.

'You freed me,' said Ajal. Yara couldn't see a face, but there was a reluctant wonder in his voice, as though he were not used to being surprised by people. 'I am in your debt.'

'You're not. You should have been free; you said so yourself. It would have been wrong for me to do anything else.'

'Interesting,' the jinn murmured. 'I wondered perhaps if you freed me for my gratitude. But no, you believed I should be free more than you wanted my help.'

'Of course.'

Ajal spluttered again. '"Of course" she says. Where are you going, child?'

Yara shifted her shoulder bag, wondering how much

she should tell him. 'I'm supposed to find someone.'

'I can see that from the locating spell on your wrist. Come, you have nothing to fear from me – you freed me from your own service.'

Yara considered this. 'I'm seeking out a sorceress.'

'For a spell?'

'I don't know. My mama said I had to find her. She said that she would give me the help that she could not.'

'And what help do you suppose that to be?'

'I ... I don't know. A new home, I guess.' Realising how uncertain this sounded, Yara quickly changed the subject. 'Those soldiers you were with, they were taking you to the alchemists in Zehaira. Did you hear what they were planning?'

'They never summoned me; what I heard from inside the bottle was hazy and indistinct.' The jinn paused. 'Yet I remember they spoke of the alchemists, and a reckoning that was coming, a time when the sorcerers would be ground into the dust and the alchemists would walk like gods.' He chuckled. 'I imagine that you have put quite the dent in their little scheme.'

Yara shivered. Perhaps saving Ajal really had been enough to avert whatever the alchemists had been planning – but the memory of Omair Firaaz prowling beneath Istehar Way lingered in her mind, until she almost missed Ajal's next question.

'Do you know how much further it is you must travel?'

Yara came to her senses. 'No, all I have is the spell.'

The jinn let out a long sigh, a sound like the wind rushing through a bonfire. 'Well, it is a wonder you have not been robbed by bandits. Or eaten by wolves, or wild jinn.'

Yara bit her lip. It had been one thing sleeping in the basket last night, but the sun was already in the west, and there was a definite chill in the air.

'Could . . . could you stay with me? Just for tonight?'

'I am a great and powerful being, not a minder of children,' Ajal replied crisply.

'I'm not a *child*.' Yara seethed. 'And if you're going to be like that, then fine, go. I suppose I'd better hope that I get to Leyla Khatoun's before the wolves or the bandits or the wild jinn get me.'

And she turned on her heel and marched on. She had not gone far before she felt a strange sparking heat on the back of her neck and heard the sound of crackling. Still, she pretended she couldn't sense the jinn.

It took almost twenty minutes for her to snap. 'Why are you following me?'

'Novelty.' To Yara's deepening annoyance Ajal sounded amused. 'It is rare to meet a girl who would free a jinn. Rarer still to meet one who thinks the jinn owes her no debt of thanks after – and I do not think there has been a girl in the thousands of years since my birth who has stamped a foot before a jinn and walked a mile in the other direction.'

'I did not *stamp my foot*.' But the corners of her mouth quirked up grudgingly, and she turned round to face the jinn. 'Anyway, I would've thought the novelty had worn off by now.'

'It should have,' he admitted. 'So how does a girl like you end up wandering the mountainside with only a locating spell to guide her?'

By the time Yara had finished her story they had walked a great deal further together, the sun low and heavy in the sky. It was not yet evening but there was already a firefly glow about the jinn; hopefully, if she did end up travelling into the night, he would be a guiding light. At least the spell had brought her back on to a path, although it was rougher and narrower than before.

'That is quite a tale,' Ajal rumbled, as she drew breath. 'What was the name of the land you came from?'

'England. In the United Kingdom.'

'Intriguing. Before my captivity I circled the globe more than a hundred times; I have travelled from desert plains to the frost of the Russlands – and I know of no country named England.'

'Really? Because I saw a map of Europe on my way

here, and it *looked* the same but everything had a different name. And when I was travelling ... it was like the stars were rearranging themselves in the sky.'

Ajal pondered her words. 'There are myths among the jinn of beings who travelled between the seven spheres – the different worlds, of which even sorcerers know very little. But I have never heard of mortals doing so, and certainly not children.' Yara got the feeling of being watched intently. 'You are sure you are a twelve-year-old girl and not an eternal being under an enchantment? Or a very confused jinn perhaps?'

'Very sure,' said Yara. 'For one thing, I'm sure Mama would have told me if I were a jinn and not a girl.'

'Are you really so sure? It sounds to me as though your mother kept a great many things from you.'

They walked on in silence, and the clouds began to take on a deeper hue until it looked as though they were singed round the edges.

'Do you think I had better find somewhere to shelter for the night?' she asked anxiously. Just then, the strand round her wrist gave an insistent tug, hard enough for her to be jolted forward.

'It seems your spell has other ideas. I would press on, if I were you.'

Ajal was right. Within the hour she was dragged down a slope and into another valley, hills rising either side and dense forest just beyond. Somewhere she could hear the gentle rush of a stream, almost masking the sleepy cricket chatter. The sun was almost fully set now, and everything around her was bathed in pink – Yara held out her own hand and saw rosy shades dance across her skin as the clouds moved above. She had no time to stop and wonder at it, however. She was struggling not to be lifted off her feet and propelled forward, so impatient was the spell on her wrist.

'But there's nothing here,' she said as if in reply. 'Is there?'

'Nothing that can be seen,' said Ajal. 'It may be that there is something magically concealed.'

'Well, if it's hidden, then how am I supposed to find it?'

He regarded her intently. 'Concentrate on what it is you want to see.'

Yara squeezed her eyes shut, feeling foolish as her thoughts flitted around things with irritating indecisiveness. What was it she wanted to see? She tried to think about Leyla Khatoun but her shape was shadowy and uncertain. Was she looking for a house, a group of tents, a city like the one she had left behind? She opened her eyes and growled in frustration.

'It's not *working*.'

The jinn shimmered in thought. 'You might try

focusing on the locating spell itself. If it's strong enough, you might be able to slip under any magical protection.'

'Focus?'

'I don't know how else to explain it. If it is sorcery, then it is beyond my understanding.'

'Helpful,' Yara grumbled. She shut her eyes again, covering her wrist with her hand and taking long deep breaths.

She thought of Meri's magic, warm and honey-scented. She imagined it flowing up her wrist and through her like a current, coming down through her legs and feet and into the ground, and she willed the spell to show her where it had promised to lead her. But thinking of Leyla Khatoun again she faltered and felt the spell break. Still, she had been close that time; she knew it.

She began again, flexing her wrist as she felt the magic travel up her arm until it glistened beneath her skin. *I want answers to my questions, and Leyla Khatoun has them. She'll tell me about Mama. Take me to Leyla Khatoun.*

She breathed in and then out, and opened her eyes.

The valley was still there, the stream still rushing – but now she could see where it was rushing to. Below her was a huddled collection of houses surrounded by fruit trees and rice fields. Even from this distance she could hear sounds of walking and murmuring and children playing.

Yara let out a small choked sound. Leyla Khatoun was somewhere in this valley.

'Can you see that?'

'I can,' Ajal said slowly. 'I shouldn't be able to, though. You must have invited me in.'

The jinn said nothing more, but Yara had the impression that he was thinking deeply.

'Well,' she said awkwardly, 'thank you very much for bringing me here.'

Ajal bristled. 'Do you expect me to abandon you now? To people who feel the need to conceal themselves with magic?'

'Well, yeah, that was the plan. I thought you would have had enough of sorcerers by now. Anyway, you must have friends, family – don't you want to see them?'

'What family I had I left behind when I chose to wander the earth; what friends I had will be long gone after centuries spent in a bottle.' He paused. 'Still, perhaps it would be ... prudent to conceal my true nature.'

The jinn gave a great shudder and began to swirl darkly, his cloud-like form contracting and solidifying until, with a sudden pungent smell of burnt hair, there was no longer a cloud floating next to Yara. Instead, several metres below, there was now a large black goat, with dark eyes and pointed horns.

'Ajal?'

'Indeed,' the jinn said, his voice still flickering but with a roughness to it that had not been there before. 'I should be perfectly safe accompanying you in this way.'

'Are you sure you want to be a goat, though?' Yara asked, disappointed. 'I mean, wouldn't you rather be a wolf – or a leopard . . . ?'

'Yes, very inconspicuous, wandering into a vale of sorcerers with a leopard.' Now Ajal was a goat, Yara could see him rolling his eyes quite clearly. 'I will play the part of the dumb beast until you are settled. No longer, mind.'

'Really?' Yara asked, trying and failing to hide her grin. 'I thought I must be boring you.'

'Don't be snide; it doesn't suit you. And you have not yet found this Leyla Khatoun you are seeking.'

Yara was well aware of this; the bracelet was now wrenching at her wrist. She moved forward and the goat that was Ajal trotted next to her, letting out the occasional bleat.

As she drew closer, she passed people working on the outer edges of the fields plucking apples and persimmons, and laying them out on their shawls. Absorbed in their work, they barely noticed her, but their children stopped their game in their tracks, looking at her in astonishment.

She drew closer to the houses, treading makeshift

streets paved with straw, the smell of slowly cooking dinners wafting in the breeze. By now she had begun to attract attention, conversations halting as she passed.

'Little girl with the goat,' one man holding a tray of halva called out, 'are you lost?'

Yara turned round, heart thumping. 'I'm looking for Leyla Khatoun.'

'Ah.' His expression softened. 'That house there, just at the edge. You can't miss it.'

Yara gulped, feeling sick with anticipation as the spell pulled her along faster.

'You're shaking.' Ajal remarked helpfully.

'I'm cold.' Yara's voice rang hollow even to her own ears. Before Ajal could comment further, she was brought to a sharp stop before the door of a small house set slightly apart from the others.

'This is the one.' Her voice was barely audible – she could feel her heart beating in her throat.

'Well, then.' Ajal nudged her with a horn. 'We should enter.' Yara didn't answer. 'Should we not?'

'I should knock,' Yara murmured to herself, as if he had not spoken.

'To warn her of your arrival? An understandable custom.'

Before Yara could stop him, Ajal walked forward and rapped his horns on the wood.

'Ajal!' Yara hissed, panic rising in her until she thought the best course of action might be to turn on her heel and run away. The latch lifted and she held her breath.

'Can I help you?'

The boy who answered the door was far taller than Yara, although he couldn't have been more than a couple of years older. There was a patch of soot below his right eye that had clustered like a birthmark, while his weighty brow and long jaw gave him the look of someone in a perpetual bad mood.

Yara lifted her chin in the air. 'I'm here to see Leyla Khatoun.'

The boy raised an eyebrow back at her in haughty disbelief, looking her up and down. Yara shifted uncomfortably, the locating spell still tugging at her wrist.

'Madam Khatoun is not seeing any more *ordinary* people today,' he said, looking down his nose at her. 'What do you want?'

Yara glared at him. She had half a decade of thrusting petitions under the noses of unfriendly householders under her belt, and she wasn't about to let some soot-stained boy turn her away now.

'I want to see her. My name's Yara Sulimayah; my mum sent me.'

'Doesn't matter. Go back to your village – you shouldn't have been allowed past the protection spell without Madam Khatoun's permission anyway.'

He made to shut the door, but Ajal leaned forward and blocked it with one of his horns.

The boy looked at him with disdain. 'Remove your goat.'

'No,' said Yara, her eyebrows lowering threateningly over her eyes. 'I'm here to see Leyla Khatoun, and I'm not going to take no for an answer. Tell her I'm here.'

Just as the boy looked as though he were about to physically eject her from the doorway, a woman's voice sounded from inside.

'Rafi? Is everything all right?'

The boy turned his head. 'Fine,' he said quickly, glaring at Yara. 'Just someone who wants to see you, but I told them to come back tomorrow.'

'A villager?'

The voice was raised in surprise, but Yara didn't have time to reflect as she realised who must be speaking. She heard footsteps approaching and the door opened wider.

At that very moment the locating spell gave one last jerk at her wrist, and Yara was propelled violently past the boy at the door, crashing head first into the woman standing behind.

Yara looked up into the eyes of Leyla Khatoun.

Chapter Nine

'**S**orry.' Yara sprang back, her face growing hot. 'I didn't mean— It's the ... sorry.'

'No harm done,' the woman – Leyla, this must be Leyla – said.

It was a strange thing, seeing a person she had clung to as an idea in her head; Yara half expected her to vanish in a puff of smoke. Yet here she was, a solid living person. She was tall, her body arranged in angles beneath her practical abaya, her hair wound in a turban and pulled so tightly back beneath it that it seemed to draw her face to sharp attention. There were faint lines on her forehead and at her mouth – it was a face, Yara thought, that worried too much and took things too seriously.

Right now, however, it was creased in confusion, and Yara realised she had been staring.

'Sorry,' she said again. 'It's just ...' She took a deep

breath. 'My name is Yara Sulimayah. My mother is – was – Nahzin Sulimayah, she sent me here to find you.'

Leyla's look of bemusement only deepened.

'Sulimayah? I can't say I recognise the name. You said she sent you – where from?'

Yara frowned. Panic was rising within her. 'You must have heard that name before,' she said desperately. 'You're Leyla Khatoun – my mama promised that you would help me. Please, I've come so far.'

Leyla's eyebrows came together in a frown that pinched at the bridge of her nose.

'Very well. Come through. You can sit down and explain.'

'Leyla?' the boy said uncertainly. Until then he had been pretending not to listen.

'You can go home, Rafi. We'll continue our lesson tomorrow.'

'But I thought . . .'

'It's fine. I'll clean it up.'

Yara looked between them. By the way Rafi's ears reddened she got the impression that whatever it was that needed to be cleaned up was his fault.

Yara followed Leyla into the house, looking around her in wide-eyed curiosity. There was only one room, and it was far more spartan than Meri's apartment. Leyla didn't seem to possess much furniture – there were only a few cushions by the fire and a long wooden worktable that looked roughly hewn. Instead of bookshelves, thick tomes were stacked upon each other until they formed small columns.

But there was no doubt about it: this was a magical house. Where else would there be a simmering cauldron over the hearth emitting a potent purple smoke and sputtering on to the rug? (Yara guessed this was the mistake Rafi had made.) Or all manner of herbs and chillies suspended from the ceiling in bunches, only a few of which she could have named? Or neatly labelled jars on the windowsills and counters – the same kind Yara's mum had used for her spices – only with FROGSPAWN and NIGHTINGALE FEATHERS written on them? Even the air around them was thrumming with something Yara couldn't name but which filled her with the same warm feeling as the whispering of the eucalyptus in Zehaira.

'Tea?'

Leyla was poised by the hearth, looking at her expectantly.

'Yes, please.'

'Right. Have a seat.' As she spoke Leyla waved a hand over the cauldron, which shimmered and vanished before Yara's eyes. With a snap of her fingers, a smaller pot materialised in her hands and she set it above the fire, beckoning the flames until they rose high enough to set the pot steaming.

Yara's mouth fell open. It had been one thing seeing Meri perform the locating spell, but it was quite another to see Leyla Khatoun use magic. Each spell seemed as easy and as natural to her as breathing.

Leyla caught her staring. 'Surely you've seen a heating spell before?'

'No, never.'

'Is your mother not a practising sorceress, then?'

'I don't think she was any kind of sorceress.' Yara stopped, correcting herself. 'At least if she was, she never told me.'

'I see. And your mother . . . ?'

'She's gone,' Yara said dully.

Leyla nodded, kneeling by the fire with her back to Yara. 'Have a seat,' she said again, her voice softening by a fraction.

Yara did as she was told, arranging herself on a cushion and stretching out her hands towards the flames to warm them. Ajal came with her, sitting on his hind legs like a dog.

'You are welcome to put your goat out to pasture,' Leyla said, watching from the corner of her eye.

Yara shook her head, well able to imagine how Ajal would feel about being sent outside, especially as she heard the first patter of rain on the roof.

'No, thanks. I'd rather he stayed with me.'

'Hmm.' Leyla summoned two cups, dipping each into the pot and filling them to the brim. 'We've had quite a few unaccompanied children come to our settlement, but you're the first to be accompanied solely by a goat.'

'Unaccompanied?' Yara asked uncertainly, as she took her cup.

'Most of them orphans, like yourself. At least, I assume that is your situation.'

Yara bit her lip. She had never had it put to her so bluntly before – Stephanie had used words like 'bereaved' and 'parentless' but never 'orphan'. Her stomach clenched and she looked down at her tea, blinking furiously.

'Well, we've had fewer in recent times. After all, why teach magic to a child when it will only put them in danger? Why continue a practice at all, when all the knowledge and teaching built up around it went up in smoke? Beyond our boundary you would sooner teach a child to steal a loaf of bread.'

Yara raised her cup to her lips and thought of Meri, closing all the windows before labouring over the locating spell. 'What about the alchemists and the Sultan's guards?' she asked. 'What if they find you?'

'They couldn't.' Leyla's tone was dismissive. 'We are

concealed by the mountains and our own protective enchantments – no one can cross our boundary uninvited unless they have magic or magical assistance. There could be a hundred soldiers surrounding the Settlement as we speak, and they would see nothing more than a deserted valley and experience a strong desire not to go any further.'

'But the alchemists are plotting something new – in the city people are saying they want to wipe out sorcery for good. What if—'

'Whatever the alchemists wish to accomplish in Zehaira, it is of no concern to us here,' Leyla interrupted in a tone that brooked no argument. 'We have quite enough to worry about without speculating about the plans of those second-rate scientists and the Sultan's pack of thugs.' She levelled her gaze at Yara. 'Still, you seem remarkably well informed. How did you find us? What magic led you here?'

Yara flushed uneasily. 'A ... a friend gave me a spell. I only found out magic existed a few days ago.'

Leyla looked up, her surprise showing on her face. 'Excuse me?'

'Where I'm from ... I mean, where I grew up, no one thinks magic is real.'

'Yet your mother told you to leave your home and find me?'

'She said I had to ... She said it was important.'

Leyla frowned, her fingers drumming against her cup. 'I really can't think who your mother could be. Perhaps if you start from the beginning?'

Yara nodded, taking a deep breath.

'I found this from my mum.' She fished the letter out of her bag. 'It said that I had to return to Zehaira and find the sorceress Leyla Khatoun. That you would give me the help that she could not.'

'The help that she could not,' Leyla repeated. 'I see. So where were you when you received this letter?' Yara shifted in her seat, tracing her finger round the rim of her cup.

'I ... I think I was in a different world.'

'Oh?'

Yara reddened before Leyla's scepticism, looking at her trainers. 'Well, I must have been; it's the only explanation I can think of. Mama left me something she called a safe passage spell, and it felt—'

'A safe passage spell?' Leyla interrupted again.

'Yes, I ...' Yara looked up, and then broke off, her pulse quickening. The sorceress's face was ashen; she looked as though she was seeing a ghost not a girl. 'That meant something to you, didn't it? I had to read out this long spell, and there was a Ferryman who brought me across the sea.'

Yara hadn't thought it was possible for Leyla to turn any paler but she did, her cup trembling in her hands.

'How old are you? Nine, ten?'

'I'm twelve,' Yara replied, insulted. But her answer seemed to have confirmed whatever it was that Leyla feared; the sorceress got to her feet, crossing the room until Yara could no longer see her face. 'You knew my mama?'

'I did not know your mother. I met her once, twelve years ago.' She turned on her heel, her eyes piercing. 'She didn't say anything else in her letter?'

'Just that she knew that you would help me.'

'I'm sure,' Leyla murmured bitterly. 'I'm sure she had no qualms deciding that I would be responsible for you.'

'How do you know Mama? Was she a sorceress too?' Leyla let out a derisory snort, which Yara took to be a 'no'. 'Then how?'

'Enough.' Leyla raised her voice. 'I'm sorry, but your mother was wrong. You can't possibly stay here, not now.'

Yara felt her stomach plummet, as though she had been clinging to a thin ledge and someone had given her a sudden, sharp push off. She had thought of the possibility that she might not be able to find Leyla, or that she might not like her; but she had never truly doubted that Mama was right, and that Leyla would help.

'Why?' Her voice cracked around the word, and she cleared her throat before trying again. 'I thought you said you've had orphans here before?'

'Orphans with magic, who had nowhere else to turn and for whom I did my best to find foster parents. But I am not a foster parent, and you do not know magic. We are both entirely unsuited to ... whatever it was that your mother had in mind.'

The rain outside grew louder and more insistent, and Yara raised her voice above it. 'I'm not a child. You don't have to look after me.'

'Oh? So why are you here?'

Yara struggled for an answer. Her pride wouldn't allow her to admit the truth: that deep down she had hoped that if she followed her mother's advice, she would find someone who wanted to take her in – not because the social worker asked them to or because they wanted to hire her as an assistant, but because they cared about her. Because she belonged to them.

Instead, she glared at the sorceress, heat rising in her face.

'I want answers. Why did Mama leave Zehaira? Why did she tell me to find you?'

Leyla turned her head, not meeting Yara's eye.

'I have no idea why your mother left. As for why she told you to find me ... I gave her some help before she left Zehaira. Evidently she thought I would be able to help you too.'

'And she was wrong,' Yara finished for her.

Leyla crossed her arms, her lips pressed together.

Yara felt her clammy palms clench into fists and, beside her, Ajal gave a sharp supportive bleat. 'Well, good. I don't want charity anyway. I'll be off now. Sorry to have bothered you.'

No sooner had the words left her mouth than the dusk was split by a bolt of lightning. In the corner of the room water began to drip from the ceiling, and Leyla let out a strangled sound of exasperation.

'Oh, for the heavens' *sake*. Obviously I cannot let you go out in this weather. Sleep here for the night, and we can discuss what to do with you in the morning.'

'What do you care? You've made it clear I'm nothing to do with you.'

Leyla arched an eyebrow. 'Do you want to go out into the rain?' Yara stared moodily into her cup. 'There's a ladder up to the hayloft; I'll send up blankets.'

She crossed the room to the hearth, retrieving a lantern from the worktable. To Yara's amazement she then reached into the fire and scooped up a handful, opening the orb of the lantern and releasing the flames carefully within. 'This should last you until morning.'

'Thanks.' Yara said grudgingly. She was too proud to ask Leyla for something to eat, no matter how far away lunch felt. But her stomach betrayed her, gurgling noisily.

Leyla sighed. 'I'll send up some food too.'

Yara didn't have high hopes for the hayloft – but given that what little sleep she'd had over the past few days had been either on a rolling boat or a juddering cart, she supposed it could only be an improvement. In fact, when she climbed the ladder and pulled herself up through the trapdoor, she found a room that was small and windowless, but which had stacked bales of hay and blankets, and a floor padded with thick sweet-smelling straw.

Yara threw her bag to the ground, the rage that had been simmering downstairs reaching full boil. So this was what she had left her home, her friend, her *life* for. A selfish narrow-minded woman who was going to turn her out at the first opportunity. How could she have been so stupid as to think that Mama was trying to give her answers?

More to the point, said a small voice in her head, *how could Mama have led you here? How could she have ripped you away from home and left you with no one to turn to? How could she have been so wrong?*

Yara shook her head vehemently, banishing those thoughts to some deep, dark part of her mind. Her mum had a good reason for writing that letter. She must have done. Still, her disappointment wouldn't go away; it entwined itself with her fury until it was as though she had a heavy knot lodged below her ribs.

At that moment a wooden bowl materialised next to her. It looked like porridge. Yara was tempted to hurl it at the wall, but hunger got the better of her. She took a spoonful, swallowed and wrinkled her nose. At least it was hot.

She was scraping the bowl when Ajal who, despite his protests, had been shepherded to a paddock for the night, drifted through the wall in cloud form before transforming himself back into a goat.

'So,' he said, cocking his head to one side, 'what do you think?'

'What is there to think? She doesn't want me.'

'Of course she doesn't want you,' said Ajal impatiently. 'That much is obvious. But why was she so upset?'

'How should I know? She just seemed angry at Mama.' She set the bowl down with a clatter. 'She's *awful*. She didn't care where I went; she just wanted me gone.'

'Yes. It is interesting. She did not seem a particularly heartless person, by human standards, and yet her behaviour towards you was rather unkind. Why would she react in such a manner? It seemed as though she was . . .' Ajal searched for the word, then stopped himself.

'What? What aren't you saying?'

'Nothing,' said Ajal carefully. 'Only that the sorceress was hiding something from you. She knows about your past here – or, at least, she knows more than she's letting on. If you leave, you leave all that knowledge behind with her.'

Yara pressed her lips together. Despite herself she felt a need for answers that *burned*, that longed to shed light on the parts of her life that had been cast in shadow for as long as she could remember.

'Fine,' she said, as she felt drowsiness begin to overcome her. 'But what can I do? She's kicking me out in the morning.'

She was almost asleep when she heard Ajal's answer.

'You must give her a reason to keep you.'

Chapter Ten

When Yara emerged downstairs the next morning, the sorceress was nowhere to be seen. There was a staircase leading up to where Leyla probably slept, but Yara had enough good sense not to try to find her there.

Just as she was considering calling out for the sorceress, a raven flew into the room and landed on the table, tilting its head and regarding Yara beadily. It was a beautiful creature, its feathers jet black and smooth as silk.

'Good morning,' said the raven, inclining his head in greeting. 'I suppose you are Yara Sulimayah?'

'Whoa,' Yara breathed, too stunned for pleasantries. 'Are you a jinn?'

'Well, aren't you observant?'

Yara felt her cheeks colour. Were all jinn this sarcastic?

'My name is Shehzad. I am Leyla's familiar.'

'Familiar?'

'Her companion if you like. I am tethered to her by a strong magical bond.'

A horrible thought occurred to Yara. 'She's not keeping you prisoner, is she?'

'Certainly not,' said Shehzad, his feathers ruffling. 'I decided I would like to work with a human, she was in need of assistance, and we have enjoyed an entirely equal partnership ever since – we share our knowledge and our magic to both of our benefit. However, this morning I have been instructed to tell you that she is out, and that you are to wait here for her to return.'

'Oh, really?' Yara narrowed her eyes. 'I suppose she thinks she can tell me what to do?'

'Don't shoot the messenger.' Shehzad hopped closer, and Yara felt herself come under further scrutiny. 'I don't know what it is you've done, but you certainly have put her in a foul temper, so I wouldn't try her when she gets back.'

Yara scowled at that. 'Maybe I won't be here when she gets back.'

Even as she said the words, Ajal's knowing face floated before her mind. If she was going to stay and find out about her past, she would have to make herself useful – but what use could a sorceress have for a young girl?

She looked about the room, her brain whirring. 'Did she have breakfast, before she left?'

'No. Madam Khatoun doesn't really do breakfast.'

'Well, that's just ridiculous.' Trying to look more confident than she felt, she began to search around in the various sacks and jars by the hearth. 'Everyone should do breakfast. It's the most important meal of the day.'

'I'll take your word for it,' Shehzad said dubiously. 'But she won't take kindly to you upsetting her potion ingredients '

'I'm not *upsetting* them.' She uncovered a sack filled with red lentils. 'I'm making her breakfast. To say thank you. That's not against the rules, is it?'

'Well—'

'Exactly. Besides, if last night was anything to go by, she'll be grateful for some decent food.'

Yara turned away, aware of the raven's eyes on her back as she did so. Surely a well-cooked meal was the best chance she had of being allowed to stay? After all, if she left now, how would she ever find out what Leyla Khatoun was hiding from her?

Having scavenged enough ingredients to make something vaguely edible, Yara got to work. She hauled a clean cauldron up and over the hearth, pouring in a bucket of water and the lentils. This was the first meal her mum had taught her to cook, and she could almost hear her comforting tones issuing instructions in her head – a palmful of salt, a spoonful of turmeric, then a long gentle simmer before adding roasted onions and garlic and cumin. Soon the small room was flooded with aromas that filled her with an aching longing.

While she waited, Yara clambered on to the window ledge, getting a proper look at the Settlement outside for the first time.

In the morning light everything seemed soaked in gold – but what a different gold it was from the uneasy gleam of Istehar Way. Trees that were bow-backed beneath the weight of apricots and apples and cloaked in autumn colours; roofs of silver-birch bark made luminescent by the sun; amber rice fields stretching out into the mountains. Gazelle and wild goats wandered nonchalantly through the streets, seemingly unconcerned by the children running past them, and the adults stood before clay cauldrons that sent up bright steam outside their homes. Yara breathed in and was engulfed by a warmth that seemed to set her blood at a simmer.

As people greeted each other, Yara's breath caught in her throat – she could hear Mama's language on all sides – not lost, but spoken all around her.

'What is this place?' she asked Shehzad.

The raven, who had been watching her with interest,

inclined his head. 'The Settlement. These people are the survivors of the Inquisition – the ones who were unable or unwilling to pay off the guards and remain in Zehaira. They work for the people in the surrounding ordinary villages now – in the fields, or selling goods, or curing cattle. The lies told about sorcery in the city did not reach the mountain provinces.'

The raven flew to the window, pointing to the man with the tray who had called out to her before. 'His name is Rashiyd – he crafted sweets for the Grand High Sorceress's sugar feasts. And next to him is Bhushra Al-Qamar – she was the curator of the vaults of Istehar Way, the guardian of the greatest magical treasures of the kingdom. She handled rubies plucked from eagles' nests and pearls taken from the lairs of six-headed sea dragons. Now she keeps chickens.'

'Oh,' was all Yara could say. She thought of Meri and her bakery. Why had she chosen to stay?

'And as for her, well, you'll find out for yourself.'

Yara's eyes widened and she jumped down from the window as an elderly woman in an abaya of midnight blue hobbled over, rattling her mug. There was a milk-like film over her eyes and she appeared entirely sightless – but as she looked up, her eyes fixed on Yara's face with a strange intensity.

'So Madam Khatoun has taken in a stray,' she said,

rolling her tongue over the words. 'The kind that hisses and scratches, who wanders where she pleases between worlds.'

'This is Madam Dinezade,' Shehzad explained. 'She was once the official oracle of Zehaira – the highest office a soothsayer can hold. Madam Khatoun fills her mug with goat's milk each morning.'

With an *oh* of realisation Yara reached for a jug to her left and poured out its contents into the woman's mug. The soothsayer sniffed it and then immediately spattered the contents on to the ground, peering at the liquid as it formed pools.

'Bad,' she muttered. 'Bad, dark days ahead – and not a thing we can do to stop them.' She looked up then sharply. 'And as for you, Yara Sulimayah, mind your manners with Madam Khatoun. You need her more than you know.'

'W-what?' Yara stammered. 'How do you know my name?'

But the old woman had set off again, mumbling to herself about darkness and wells. Yara was tempted to follow her with more questions, but at that moment the pot began to boil over and she resolved to get answers from the soothsayer later.

For a while she was able to lose herself in cooking, and she was taking the cauldron off the heat when she heard a voice behind her.

'What are you doing?'

Yara froze, turning to face Leyla Khatoun. 'I've made breakfast. To say thank you for sheltering me last night.'

'You used my potions ingredients for—'

'For breakfast, yes.' Yara's heart was beating somewhere in her throat.

Leyla turned her gaze towards the raven, narrowing her eyes. 'And you did nothing to stop her?'

With a bristling of his wings Shehzad flew from the window to Leyla's shoulder. 'Don't be irritable.' He nipped at her ear. 'She wasn't doing any harm.'

Leyla's mouth disappeared in a thin line, but she said nothing more, removing her cloak and hanging it by the door.

Emboldened, Yara asked, 'Where have you been?'

'An ordinary village a few miles south. A tradesman from the city had some strange grey sickness – and then, to top it all off, they had me cast over their fields, merely because someone's uncle heard there was a crop blight spreading through the kingdom.'

She withdrew a small coin pouch from her cloak, loosening the strings and emptying it into a box in the corner of the room.

'I thought you were a sorceress?' said Yara, curious.

It seemed that was the wrong thing to say. Leyla stiffened, her shoulders hunching up by her ears. 'I am, by training. But now I must be herbalist and healer and animal charmer so that I might not starve, and so strange girls who come to my home at the dead of night might be fed at my table.'

Yara reddened. 'I can pay you.' She thought about the few pound coins sitting at the bottom of her bag, the last bit of money she had left in the world.

'Don't be ridiculous; I'm poor, not desperate. And I suppose if you have gone to the trouble of making something, I had better eat it.'

Yara bit back a retort, ladling the mixture into two wooden bowls she found by the hearth and bringing them over. Taking a seat, Leyla looked at the lentil porridge with distrust, as though anything this brightly coloured could not possibly be to her liking. She took a spoonful, brought it to her lips and tasted.

And then her eyes widened in surprise. She took another taste, and another.

Yara watched her in satisfaction, and then tried some herself.

After a time, Leyla put down her spoon. 'Well, I believe in giving credit where credit is due. I can't say that I have enjoyed a meal prepared in this house more.'

Yara tried not to look too smug, but before she could ask what this might mean for her living arrangements, there was a knock at the door.

'Enter.' Leyla said, snapping her fingers. Two small children poked their heads round the door: a boy and a girl, both staring at Yara in naked fascination. 'Ah, Imahd, Asma. I have your father's medicine here.' She made a grasping motion in the air and a small vial materialised in the girl's – Asma's – hand. 'Tell him to take a mouthful before each meal and he should be back on his feet in no time.'

The little girl clutched the bottle tightly in one hand and began to hunt around in her pockets with the other.

'Mama said she had some money for you—'

'Nonsense,' Leyla cut her off. 'It's in all our interests to get your father working again.'

She motioned them towards the doorway, and after one last curious glance at Yara the pair left.

'Who's their father?' Yara asked.

'Abdul Hussein, our craftsman.' Leyla's eyes were troubled. 'If he isn't better by winter, we'll be in a bad way if anything needs serious repairs.'

'So he's a craftsman, but he's a sorcerer too? What does it mean being a sorcerer? Is it just that you all use magic?'

Leyla surveyed Yara over the top of her bowl. A hot prickly feeling crept over the back of Yara's neck, and she knew that she had said something incredibly ignorant.

'It is not something I would expect you to understand,'

Leyla said levelly. 'Magic is a part of us. We study and practise and commune with the world around us until magic runs through our bodies like blood and we breathe it like air. Sorcery is a shared culture, a shared knowledge, a shared understanding of the universe. Or at least, it was. It's all but gone since the Inquisition.'

She returned to her bowl. 'So when do you plan on leaving?'

Yara's mind whirred. If Leyla still wasn't inclined to let her stay, then perhaps she could at least buy herself some time to investigate.

'I'll try not to trouble you for long. I . . . I might have a job I could go to actually. Before I came here, I met a baker in the city, and she said I might work as an assistant for her.'

It was almost the truth, even if Yara suspected that Meri's job offer had been more of a kind gesture than a proposal. 'It's just . . . there was some trouble before I left, and I can't go back quite yet.'

'Trouble?'

'With the Sultan's guards – I was looking for you on Istehar Way.'

Leyla gave a sharp intake of breath, colour rising to her cheeks. Yara pressed her advantage. 'So could I stay here . . . just for a few weeks? I'll make myself useful, I promise.'

Leyla said nothing, her brow furrowed in thought. Just as she seemed poised to give her answer, Rafi came through the open door, wiping his feet outside.

'Good morning, Madam Khatoun. I delivered the tonics like you asked, and—' As he caught sight of Yara, his eyes narrowed. 'What's *she* still doing here?'

Leyla pinched the bridge of her nose, visibly relenting.

'Yara, this is Rafi Al-Qamar. Rafi, this is Yara Sulimayah. She is going to be staying with me until the end of the month.'

Yara's heart soared in her chest. That gave her almost three weeks to find out how Leyla had known Mama, and she was determined not to waste a single moment.

Chapter Eleven

For days Yara spent every moment she was left alone searching Leyla's house with Ajal for some sign of her mother. Helpfully the sorceress seemed to spend most of her time out in the neighbouring villages or attending meetings in the Settlement.

Yara only really saw Leyla at meals, where all her questions would be met with stony silence, or when Rafi came for his lessons. She had Ajal – and Madam Dinezade, whose mind would wander between past, present and future as though she were browsing different stalls at a market, but who seemed to appreciate Yara's company, at least.

But at nights, when the jinn would transform and set out into the darkness, she would lie awake, her insides heavy with homesickness.

There were so many things she could have missed about home – hot showers, chocolate, walking from

Bournemouth town centre to the beach – and yet it all seemed to pale next to her longing for Mama: for the comforting shape of her hugs and warm notes of her voice as she asked Yara about her day. Sometimes the force of it would well so strongly inside her that she wanted to scream: *Why did you make me come here? Why did you send me to her?* And on the worst days: *Why did you leave me? Why won't you come back?*

A week passed and she had found nothing with so much as a mention of Nahzin Sulimayah. One afternoon Yara, scrubbing out one of Leyla's cauldrons, felt her frustration rise to a boil.

'This is ridiculous,' she grumbled to Ajal. 'How am I supposed to find out anything if she won't talk to me?'

'Perhaps you should give the matter a rest for now.' He looked at her closely. 'You haven't been yourself recently, I don't think.'

Yara huffed. The truth was, the warmth of the Settlement that had felt so comforting her first day was fast becoming overwhelming; she felt hot and restless – and prowling around Leyla's house only made her more so.

'But what else can I do?'

It was as much a question to herself as Ajal. Suppose she had to leave at the end of the month. Would she travel back to Zehaira and spend her teenage years hidden away in a bakery? Or even if she did somehow manage to return to the UK, would anyone there remember her? Allowing her thoughts to drift in either direction filled her with frantic panic, and she redirected her focus quickly. She couldn't leave without answers. There was something that would link her to Leyla Khatoun, there *was*; she just had to find it.

Yara heard voices muttering anxiously outside and sighed. Leyla must be back already – in addition to supplying the Settlement with potions and spells too complex for the others to craft, she was something of a leader of the small community, and people often brought their problems and disputes to her for resolution.

'Madam Khatoun, you must listen.' Yara could make out the sombre tones of Madam Zahrawi, the seamstress, and frowned, moving closer to the door. 'The alchemists are riding out from the city. We cannot ignore what that means.'

'Our protection spell is strong.' Leyla's voice was defensive. 'They have come to the mountains before; they have mines here, and workers to oversee. They will be gone by winter's end, I'm sure of it.'

'But the timing cannot be a coincidence.' This was from Abdul Hussein, still on his crutches. 'All our sources say there have been arrests made in the city, perhaps more killings – we have to assume they are planning something.'

Yara felt her blood run cold. Arrests? What about Meri and Mehnoor – had they been discovered after helping her?

'Darkness,' Madam Dinezade whispered, 'darkness rising up, flooding the land – every tree, every root, every flower . . .'

'I assure you, there is nothing that should concern us here.' Leyla raised her voice above the undercurrent of worry. 'We are a small community in the mountains; the alchemists have nothing to gain from pursuing us. I strongly suggest that you all return to your work.'

There was a note of command in Leyla's tone and the others dispersed, still grumbling. The door opened before Yara could jump back, and she decided it wasn't worth feigning ignorance.

'Leyla, they're right. When I was in the city, I heard the Chief Alchemist himself say he would send men out to the countryside – I don't know what they're planning, but you could all be in danger.'

'Enough.' Leyla pinched the bridge of her nose as though she had a bad headache. 'I will not argue the point with you too. I suggest you put all thoughts of the alchemists aside, particularly as you will be leaving our settlement at the end of the month.'

And sweeping past Yara, the sorceress disappeared upstairs.

Yara dug her nails into the palms of her hands, her blood running hot. Of course Leyla wouldn't listen to her – of course she would bury her head in the sand. Clearly the only way to get through to the sorceress was to confront her with something she couldn't ignore.

'What are you thinking?' asked Ajal.

'I'm thinking that there's one place we haven't searched yet. Leyla's bedroom.'

That night, when Leyla was called out to tend to some sick goats, Yara seized her chance and crept up the stairs.

Having expected the bedroom of Leyla Khatoun to be as spartan as a prison cell and as severe as the woman herself, Yara was surprised to find herself in a cosy space – a touch finer than the room downstairs, with a patterned rug on the floor. The books here seemed grander too; their binding was still intact, gold lettering winking in the lamplight.

'This is a bad idea.' Ajal was peering at her from the doorway. 'What good will it do, making Madam Khatoun angry?'

Yara, flustered and feeling cross with it, tossed her head. 'I'm not scared of her.'

Anxious to get her search over with, she began to

open drawers, feeling like a thief as she did so.

The jinn followed her into the room. 'What exactly are you hoping to find? Don't you think it might be time to seek elsewhere for answers?'

Yara rounded on him. 'Why? Because you want to leave? You're finally bored of staying here with me, is that it?'

She regretted the words as soon as she said them.

Ajal bristled next to her. 'I don't believe I said anything of the kind,' he replied coldly. 'But I see you are in a particularly childish mood, so there is no point reasoning with you.'

Before Yara could answer back, he gave a great shimmer and was a cloud once again, floating away into the breeze.

Sadness and shame twisted nastily in Yara's stomach until tears rose in her eyes – but she pushed all thoughts of Ajal away, even more determined to find something that would prove him wrong. Her hand skimmed the back of a drawer – and closed over a small round object, hard and warm to the touch.

Frowning, Yara drew it out. It was a gemstone, dark red with sunken, glimmering depths. It seemed to vibrate beneath her fingertips, and Yara had the strangest feeling that it was trying to communicate with her, its low hum a language she couldn't quite decipher. She felt her face get hotter, her skin prickling and her ears ringing until she almost missed the sound of footsteps downstairs.

Footsteps.

Yara froze. Leyla had returned early. She would catch Yara sneaking around in her bedroom and she would be kicked out before the morning. Setting the gemstone back down, Yara waited for the sound of feet treading the stairs with bated breath.

It didn't come. Perhaps if she went now, she might slip past the sorceress and make it to the hayloft.

As she edged down the stairs, her breath came out in a rush. Leyla was hunched over her largest cauldron, utterly oblivious to her surroundings. Wisps of her hair were escaping her turban and getting frazzled in the heat of the fire. In spite of herself Yara drew closer.

'What are you doing?'

Leyla jumped a metre in the air, turning to glare at her.

'*Never* interrupt a sorceress at work,' she said angrily. 'I might have slipped and blown us all to pieces.'

Yara bit her lip. 'Oh, sorry.'

Leyla huffed but relented. 'I'm making a potion,' she said, as if that put an end to matters.

'Right.' Curiosity got the better of Yara. 'But what is a potion? I mean, how do they work exactly?'

She expected to be immediately dismissed, and could

barely mask her surprise when Leyla replied.

'Think of it like this: ordinary energy comes from the sun and is absorbed by plants and animals – you know that I presume?'

'Of course. In my home country we called it *photosynthesis*,' she said, wrapping her mouth around the English syllables.

'Well, here there is a different kind of energy at work too. We think – at least, the scholars I agree with think – that magic comes from the stars, and is absorbed by every animal, tree and flower in much the same way. The difference being that we can communicate with it; it responds to our command, and it responds particularly to poetry.'

'To poetry?' Yara said disbelievingly.

'You sound surprised.' Leyla stirred the mixture in her cauldron. 'Have you never been moved by the rhyme and rhythm of a verse? Have you never had something read aloud so vividly that you believed it had been brought alive before your eyes?

'A powerful spell needs powerful language, language that can bring things that are strange and marvellous to life. The combination of a well-made potion and a verse spell – it is there that wonders have been achieved. Sorcerers have flown like eagles and held masquerades in the clouds, have swum like dolphins and brought back treasures from the mermaids. I once saw the Grand High Sorceress grow a pleasure garden in mere minutes and teach the birds there to sing love songs.'

The wistfulness in her voice moved something in Yara. 'Could I help? I could chop ingredients for you.'

'Well,' Leyla said slowly, 'I suppose you couldn't conceivably do any harm chopping persimmons for me.'

She indicated where she had arranged her ingredients in neat piles, and Yara came to sit by the hearth, all thoughts of the gem gone from her mind. 'Small pieces, please.'

Yara nodded and got to work. She chopped persimmons, and then deseeded strange-looking purple chillies and removed the wings from hornets. As she did so, her blood seemed to cool, the frenzy with which she had searched Leyla's bedroom becoming more distant.

'It's sort of like cooking,' she said, looking at the steaming contents of the cauldron.

'I wouldn't know. My parents were archivists in the Great Library – I never learned to cook. We used to eat in the hall.'

'Hall?' Yara asked, confused, imagining the canteen at her secondary school. But Leyla's gaze had softened, and, as she stirred methodically clockwise, it was as though she had gone somewhere far away.

'We used to walk through underground passages

to get there from the library – I remember when I was small it felt as though I were travelling through a labyrinth – but the hall itself had a glass dome, and there were carpets and cushions spread across the floor with designs that mapped the heavens. People would meet there to debate, and the cooks would bring up food from all over the world—'

Leyla broke off, looking embarrassed – but there was a bright animated look about her, as though it had done her good to remember. Then Yara had a sudden thought.

'Madam Khatoun, what if that's why my mum sent me to you? Because she wanted you to teach me magic?'

The sorceress went rigid. 'Impossible. Your mother knew nothing of sorcery.'

'But maybe she wanted me to. Why else would she want you to take me in?'

Leyla opened her mouth, and for a moment Yara thought she saw her resolve wavering. But then she closed it again, and her shoulders straightened.

'It's late,' she said, her voice tight. 'You should go to bed.'

'But—'

'Go, now.'

She turned back towards her cauldron, her face hidden from view.

Yara seethed at Leyla's back, her fists clenched so

tightly it felt as though there were lights behind her eyes. She turned on her heel and stalked back up to the hayloft, her thoughts racing. Surely that was the reason Mama had been so insistent she find a sorceress – even one as cold and unfeeling as Leyla Khatoun. And if she could just show that she had talent, surely Leyla would have to start listening to her.

Yara spent a sleepless night plotting how she could prove to Leyla that she ought to be taught magic. The next morning, when Rafi came to the house, Yara concealed herself below the window, kneeling on the floor of the workroom and listening intently to his lesson, which was taking place in the garden. As usual, it wasn't going well.

'Now, Rafi, this should be easy for you,' said Leyla. handing him a glass vial. 'Rub the powder between your fingers and imagine your words heating the air until it ignites.'

'I am imagining,' Rafi replied sulkily.

'Well, then, say:
"As green bark became brand,
Let flame fly from my hand."'

Rafi repeated the words, his eyes tightly shut, as though he might put an idea into his head through sheer force of will.

'Your thoughts are quenching the flame,' Leyla told him. 'Clear your mind, and let *only* the image of the flame enter it.'

'As green bark became brand,
Let flame fly from my hand'

There was a spark, and a meagre flame appeared just above Rafi's hands, as though he had lit an invisible match.

'Well, it's a start,' Leyla said unconvincingly.

'Madam Khatoun?' Asma appeared at the doorway. 'Someone from one of the villages wants to see you – something's wrong with the soil, and a tradesman who needs more healing tonic—'

'I could help—' Rafi began, but Leyla cut him off.

'No, it's fine, this shouldn't take too long. Go for a walk and we'll try the spell again soon.'

Scowling at the ground, Rafi stalked away into the Settlement. Leyla watched him go for a while, her forehead pinched, before following Asma out of the front door.

Yara seized her chance. Emerging from her hiding place, she crept out into the garden and picked up the vial from where Rafi had left it on the table, pouring some of the powder on to her palm. It had a smoky, earthy scent, and she could feel it vibrating, a million tiny whispers against her fingers: *Ignite me. Show them you're special. No one can deny it once they see me burn* ...

Yara stared at the powder, transfixed. Her pulse was pounding in her head, the sparking feeling behind her eyes and at her fingertips almost unbearable. She could do it; she knew she could.

'What are you doing?'

Yara spun round. Rafi was standing behind her, evidently still smarting. Their relationship had not improved since their first meeting.

'I, um.' Yara floundered. 'You spilled this.'

'No, I didn't.' Rafi narrowed his eyes. 'You were trying to do magic, weren't you?'

Yara attempted to smooth out her face but knew how guilty she must look.

'So what if I was?' She levelled her eyebrows as fiercely as she could muster. 'I don't see how I could have done a worse job than you.'

Rafi's face went pink. 'What are you doing here?' he hissed. 'No one wants you. Why don't you just leave?'

Afterwards, Yara could not say why it was that remark out of all of them that broke the dam of her self-control. She only knew that one moment she had been standing in front of Rafi, her fists clenched and her heart pounding, and the next she had thrown herself on him like a wild animal, pinning him to the ground.

Yara would have liked to land a great many more punches before stopping, but she felt herself being pulled away by an invisible force, and could make out the furious figure of Leyla, her hands outstretched.

'That is quite enough!' The sorceress was spitting with rage. 'Rafi, go home. We are done for the day.'

With a final glare for Yara, Rafi stormed off. Meanwhile, Leyla was taking in the scene.

'Were you attempting a spell?' Her voice was so cold that the temperature of the air around them seemed to drop several degrees. Lying seemed pointless now.

'I just wanted to try it, that's all.'

'You had no right.' Leyla's voice was still calm, but her fingers were twitching, her eyes blown wide. 'Magic is not a *game*; it is not something you can conceal from me – and the very fact you seem to think so is exactly why I was right not to let you anywhere near it.'

'That's not the reason.' Yara was shaking with fury now. 'You're just so scared of me wanting to stay that you won't do anything to make me feel like I could belong.' Leyla was silent, two red spots high on her cheeks. Yara carried on, her voice high-pitched and cracking as she forced it above her tears. 'I wish Mama had never sent me here. I wish she had never told me to find you – I wish I had just stayed in Bournemouth. She said you would help me.'

'I never—'

'But you wouldn't help me if I were the last person on earth. You hate me – well, I hate you! I hate you!'

'That's enough.' Leyla's voice was trembling now too; her face even paler than it had been before, her expression unreadable. 'You can pack up and leave first thing tomorrow morning. Since you clearly dislike it here so much, that should be no great hardship.' She turned on her heel, her abaya sweeping behind her in the wind.

As she watched the sorceress leave, Yara thought she had never felt so much loathing for anyone in her life. Turning quickly, she snatched at the powder and threw it after Leyla, shouting herself hoarse.

'As green bark became brand, Let flame fly from my hand!!'

The powder hit the ground, and huge columns of emerald flame roared to life, encircling Yara with the hungry advance of a beast that has trapped its prey.

Chapter Twelve

Yara stood frozen with terror as the air grew thick and heavy with smoke. She could hear whimpering – her own high-pitched voice – but even that became inaudible beneath the green flames, which seemed to leap out and snarl at her like a wild animal. And then she began to scream.

Dimly she could hear shouting, but the fire only roared louder, and Yara's panic rose until her ears rang with the thump of her own heart.

'Leyla! Leyla, help!'

Yara!

Leyla wasn't shouting any more – it was as though she was somehow speaking directly into Yara's mind, her voice amplified above Yara's thoughts. *Yara, stop – you have to calm down.*

Yara couldn't concentrate on her words. She was too busy watching the flames creep and twist above her until they seemed to be reaching out for her in tendrils. *Yara. Yara! Yara Sulimayah, will you pay attention?!*

Leyla's voice sounded sharply in her head, and it cut through the panic.

Yara took a few rapid breaths. *What do I do?* she thought.

Say very clearly and very calmly, "As night follows day, let my fire melt away." Do you understand?

I ... I don't know how ...

Yara, listen to me. If you don't put this fire out while you still have some control over it, it won't stop burning until it has destroyed everything in its path, including you. Now picture the fire going out and say, "As night follows day, let my fire melt away."

Yara nodded, squeezing her eyes shut and trying to block out the encroaching smoke.

'As night follows day,

Let my fire melt away.'

For a moment it seemed as though the flames were dying down, but then they gathered strength once more, until she could feel the smart of their heat on her skin.

'I can't!' she cried out desperately. 'I can't do it; Leyla, I'm trapped.'

Just as she was about to sink into despair, there was a

break in the flames, and Yara could make out the shape of a goat emerging from the fire.

'Ajal,' she said on a sob. 'Ajal, help me, I don't know what to do.'

'Yes, you do.' He butted her with his horns. 'Madam Khatoun has told you what to do. You just have to stop being so scared.'

'Easy for you to say. I wouldn't be able to walk through the fire so easily.'

'No. But it belongs to you, this thing. You must command it.'

At his words Yara remembered her mother's letter: *Make them know that you will not take no for an answer*. She thought about how Mama might address an unruly fire: with lowered eyebrows and a stubborn set to her mouth.

Feeling for where Mama's headscarf was wrapped round her neck, she opened her eyes, held up her hands and glared at the flames. In a voice that seemed bigger than herself she said:

'As night follows day,
Let my fire melt away,'

To her astonishment the flames seemed to curl in on themselves, as though ashamed at having got so out of control. Within seconds they were the height of Yara's head, and not long after that they burned dark and low by her feet until they were nothing more than a pile of emerald ashes and cinders. The smoke began to clear with the breeze, and Leyla came into view – along with half the Settlement, who seemed to have dropped their work in the fields to run to her aid.

The sorceress ran forward, gripping her arms. 'Are you all right?' Leyla asked urgently, tilting Yara's chin and looking intently into her eyes.

'I'm fine,' Yara reassured her. Her knees felt as though they had turned to cotton wool, her stomach still clenched in fear. She looked at the floor, waiting for Leyla to tell her how stupid and reckless she had been, to say that Yara could pack her things and leave that very night. But Leyla only nodded and released her, her mind clearly elsewhere.

'Inside. Come on, I'll make us some tea.'

Yara made to follow but her legs refused to obey, buckling beneath her. Before she could do anything so embarrassing as fall over, strong arms hauled her back to her feet.

'I'm fine,' Yara said again, feeling silly but also as though she might cry.

'Come on.' The sorceress's voice was almost gentle, and she guided Yara past the anxious villagers and into the house. Ajal followed them at a trot, coming forward so that Yara could feel him on her other side, guarding her.

Leyla's house felt so ordinary now that Yara could have sobbed in relief. She moved to the cushions by the hearth and thanked her stars that the fire burning merrily within showed no signs of getting any taller. Ajal flopped down next to her, and she stroked the velvety patch of hair between his ears.

To Yara's surprise Leyla joined them, kneeling wordlessly before the fire and setting the tea cauldron above it. She had still not quite returned to her usual colour, and her hand shook slightly as she stirred at its contents.

'Did I give you a fright?' Yara asked.

Leyla let out a short huff of a laugh. 'Not at all. It's not frightening in the least to see a child in your care go up in an emerald blaze.'

'I'm not a child.'

Leyla looked as though she would rather like to contradict her, but she kept quiet.

Yara felt compelled to speak, even as her voice rose with panic. 'I didn't mean to make all that fire, I promise. Why was there so much of it?'

Leyla did not answer at first. She decanted the tea and

handed Yara a cup, settling herself back on the cushions before answering.

'A number of reasons. First of all, your anger. You weren't in control.'

'Oh,' Yara said, her voice small. 'I'm sorry. I only—'

Leyla cut her off, her long fingernails drumming on the side of her cup. 'It's all right. That is, I – both of us, I think it's fair to say – said and did things that we now regret. If you are happy to leave them in the past, then I certainly am.'

Yara nodded, a wave of relief washing over her at the thought that Leyla was not about to send her packing. 'What's the second reason? You didn't say.'

'I didn't say it because I haven't finished working it out. The magic you displayed in conjuring those flames wasn't just extraordinary; it was impossible.' She leaned forward, surveying Yara until she shifted uncomfortably in her seat. 'It would take years of magical training to muster the power you have shown me today – and you told me that you had never used magic before.'

'I haven't. I swear on my mother's life, I haven't.'

'I believe you. Which makes this all the stranger.' She squinted at the goat. 'It wasn't your jinn, was it?'

'Ajal? No, he—' Immediately Yara knew she was caught, and she blushed. 'Sorry.'

'No harm done,' Leyla said crisply. 'Still, you will

know better next time than to conceal a jinn from a sorceress of my power.' She looked directly at Ajal this time. 'You are her familiar, I assume. Have you seen anything like this before?'

'Upon my immortality, no.' There was no trace of sarcasm in Ajal's voice. 'I am no familiar and thought that she was no sorceress.' He gave an exasperated bleat. 'Is this what it is like accompanying human children? Am I to fear that she will blow herself up until the day she stops growing?'

Even Leyla managed a terse flicker of a smile at that. 'I suspect that may be the way with this one.'

They might have spoken for longer, but Yara was overcome by a sudden, consuming wave of tiredness, her eyelids drooping and her head nodding into her chest. Leyla, noticing, sent her swiftly upstairs.

As Yara climbed the ladder to the hayloft, each step felt more difficult than the last, and by the time she reached the top it was all she could do to stumble over to her bed before she flopped down on her blankets fully clothed.

Bright light that was growing, growing until it was blinding, until it filled the room and flooded her bones. There was someone above her, whispering words of such aching sadness.

'You must come back. Whatever happens, you must come back . . .'

Yara woke with a start, her breathing heavy and her eyes still full of light. She turned over and was greeted by a strong smell of goat's milk and burning sulphur, followed by Ajal, who was sitting so close that his nose was almost touching her own.

'Argh!'

'Ah, good, you're awake.' The jinn prodded her with one of his hooves. 'I was beginning to think you would sleep for evermore.'

'How late is it?'

'Almost midday. Madam Khatoun came to check on you twice, but she said it was better to let you sleep.'

'She came up here?' Yara sat up, mortified. She hadn't fallen asleep in her clothes since she was a very little girl. She hurtled down the ladder – but the cottage was empty, and Shehzad was waiting for her on the table.

'She's gone out,' the raven informed Yara, anticipating her question. 'A matter needing her attention in the southern villages – she'll be back soon.'

'Oh. Did she—'

'There's porridge in the cauldron. She thought you would want breakfast.'

Leyla had thought correctly. After spooning on large

amounts of honey, Yara got through three bowlfuls before the sorceress returned.

'Good afternoon.' Leyla's eyes travelled to the bowl in Yara's hands. 'I'm glad to see that yesterday's events did nothing to suppress your appetite.'

Yara shrugged, swallowing her last mouthful with difficulty.

'Do you want some?'

Leyla exhaled audibly, hanging up her outer coat by the door and sitting down by the fire.

'Thank you, Yara. That would be nice.'

Yara ladled the remaining porridge into a bowl and handed it to Leyla, hoping she wouldn't notice quite how much honey she'd added. 'Was there a lot of work in the village?' she asked. 'You look like you haven't slept in a month.'

'Thank you,' Leyla said drily, massaging her temples with her fingertips. 'The blight in the villages is in fact more serious than I thought – half the crop has died of it already. And to be quite honest I had already spent a sleepless night trying to work out what to do with you.'

'What to do with me?' Yara bit her lip. Perhaps Leyla had decided she was no longer welcome here after all.

'Mmm.' Leyla took a spoonful of porridge, her eyebrows coming down over her eyes – whether at the sweet taste or the problem at hand, Yara could not say.

'You see, it's not so uncommon for children to have magical outbursts when they first begin practising. Sorcerers begin and sustain their practice by drawing magic from the world around them, and it requires discipline and control to commune with a force as old as the universe.

'However, what you showed me was no magical outburst. If I'm right, then for some reason you have an inordinately large store of magical energy *already inside you.*'

Yara blinked, sitting across from Leyla. 'But ... but how? Where from?'

'I don't know.' Leyla looked down at her porridge uneasily. 'It must have lain dormant while you lived in your non-magical world, shut up inside you like a jinn in a bottle – and then last night your anger let it loose.'

'I've been feeling strange for a while now.' Cogs were turning inside Yara's head. 'Like something inside me was trying to get out – it got worse every time I went out into the Settlement.'

Leyla paled. 'It's a good thing I didn't send you away that first night. If this had gone unchecked, it might have done serious damage.'

'Is that . . . Do you think that's why Mama sent me to you?'

'No, she—' But then Leyla paused and seemed to

consider the question. 'I don't know,' she admitted, and for the first time Yara could see that she was telling the truth. 'It's a possibility certainly.' She looked at Yara closely. 'Your mother never said anything to you?'

Yara racked her brains. Had Mama kept this from her too? Was that why she had sent her to Leyla, because of another secret she had deemed too dangerous, too important to trust Yara with? Somehow her own mother was becoming someone strange and mysterious to her.

She was so lost in her thoughts that she almost missed Leyla's next words: 'My hope is that with a few months of lessons—'

'Lessons?' Yara sat up. 'Leyla, you're going to give me lessons – in magic?'

'For a few months, yes. Hopefully then it will be safe enough to have you lodge with someone else in the Settlement.'

'Oh,' said Yara, deflating. 'I wouldn't stay here?'

Leyla shook her head determinedly. 'I meant what I said that first night; it would be entirely unsuitable. You are still a child, and you need someone who can look after you properly.'

Yara nodded, ducking her head. She knew it would be no use arguing with the sorceress. She wasn't even sure why she wanted to argue – Leyla was right; it wasn't much fun living somewhere where there was no one to take care of her, and she had to cook if she wanted a decent meal. Why should she prefer the gloomy abode of Leyla Khatoun over a foster family? Still, the hurt rankled in her chest.

Leyla took her silence as assent. 'Good. Well, then, I suppose it only remains to give you this.'

The sorceress waved a hand and a book materialised in Yara's arms. It was about the same size as her torso, cloth-bound and embroidered, and the writing on the cover was so faded that Yara could scarcely make it out. She opened it, her fingers tracing gossamer-thin pages.

'This is my family codex – or book of wonders, as ordinary people might know it. In it is a history, some basic spells and the law.'

'The law?'

Leyla looked solemn. 'If you are to practise magic, then there is a strict code you must follow. We may no longer have the Grand High Sorceress and her Great Council to uphold our rules, but that makes them all the more important. When you practise, you hold the laws of nature in your hand, and that comes with a duty to the world around you. I need your word that you will never forget that.'

Yara met the sorceress's eye and saw how serious she was. She tried to tamp down her excitement.

'I won't forget. Leyla, thank you. For the book and

for teaching me, and . . . I promise I won't let you down.'

Leyla flushed awkwardly, folding her arms over her chest. 'Yes, well—'

At that moment the door flew open, and Asma hurtled in.

'Madam Khatoun,' she said breathlessly, 'the hills – people – black robes.'

Leyla's face lost all its colour. She set aside her bowl and twisted her hand, vanishing into thin air.

Yara got to her feet and sprinted after Asma, following her to the Settlement boundary. By the time she got there the people working in the fields and orchards had already gathered at the edge of the protection spell. She found herself standing next to Rafi, who looked uncomfortable but nodded awkwardly in her direction.

'Sorry,' he muttered, 'about yesterday. I— I'm sorry, all right?'

'All right,' Yara whispered back. 'I'm sorry too.'

In the distance were men in the same black-and-gold robes Firaaz had worn in his laboratory in Zehaira. They had pitched a grand tent and were walking purposefully around the hills, their cloaks flying behind them in the wind until they looked like carrion crows circling wounded prey.

'This is bad.' Abdul Hussein shook his head. 'I tried to warn Leyla . . .'

A voice rose from the crowd. 'They've never been this close before – what if they see one of the children?'

Several of the younger ones began to wail, and to Yara's surprise she saw Rafi put his hands on their shoulders.

'Don't listen,' he said, awkward but undoubtedly kind. 'They can't see or hear us in here, remember, and Madam Khatoun wouldn't let anything happen to you.'

Rafi's words quieted the children, but the adults were not so easily soothed.

'They know we're here; they must do. Why else would they come so far out?'

'They could be looking for the Grand High Sorceress. I heard that five years ago she turned herself into a panther and escaped into the mountains.'

'They will burn our village to the ground; we should flee—'

'Some quiet, please.' Leyla's voice cut through the alarm. Shehzad was perched on her shoulder. 'I know this will alarm some of you, but from what my familiar has overheard they are merely looking for a source of water.'

'If that's why they're here, then they'll be talking to the ordinary villages,' a man called out. 'How do we know we won't be betrayed?'

'Our protection and concealment spells will hold,

regardless,' Leyla said, with only a flicker of worry passing across her face. 'Any attempt to search for us will fail; we have nothing to fear. I suggest you all return to your work.'

There were grumbles but most obeyed the sorceress.

Yara ran to Leyla. 'I told you, the alchemist said he wanted whatever they were planning in the city to spread – he said he would send men to do it. What are we going to do?'

Leyla looked down at her, her face etched with concern. 'Yara, the only thing you need concern yourself with is getting your powers under control,' she said, her voice low. 'It is of the utmost importance. If the alchemists detect a magical outburst, then all is lost for this Settlement.'

Chapter Thirteen

Rafi had been less than happy to hear that Yara would be joining his lessons. As they carried Leyla's worktable out into the garden, he glared at her from the other side. Ajal, who was sticking firmly by Yara's side, did his best to match the boy's expression, tossing his horns in a barely concealed threat.

'So,' Rafi said as they set the table down, 'who are your people?'

'My people?' Yara looked at him in scornful confusion.

'Your family. I've never heard the name "Sulimayah" associated with sorcery before. Do you have practitioners on your mother's or your father's side?'

'No idea,' Yara said, unsettled by the thought. Mama had always said their other family – even her father – were long gone. 'Stop annoying me.'

'Well, you must have some sort of background in

magic. Show me your birthstone; I'll see if I can work it out from that.'

'What a nosy young man,' Ajal whispered. 'Should I turn him into a beetle?'

Yara snorted. 'I'll let you know.' She turned to Rafi. 'What's a birthstone?'

Rafi flicked back his sleeve, showing Yara a jagged piece of amethyst secured to his wrist by a band.

'They're gifted to you by the most senior member of your family, as a symbol of magical tradition,' he said, with exaggerated patience. 'The Al-Qamars were one of the most distinguished families in the city – my uncle trained Madam Khatoun herself and was so renowned that he went to the Russlands as an honoured guest of the Northern Sorcerers. I bet even the smallest family would have a stone, though.'

Yara was tempted to invent an illustrious past with sorcerers stretching back centuries on her family tree, but her democratic sympathies won out.

'That's stupid,' she told him indignantly. 'Why should it matter who my family were? It's got nothing to do with magic.'

'Maybe not. But there must be *some* reason Madam Khatoun agreed to let you stay.'

Before Yara could think of an answer to that, the sorceress herself emerged from the house.

'We'll start off simply,' she told them, setting down a jar of indigo paste on the table. 'Smear this on the stone in front of you and command it to rise ten centimetres above the table.'

'Which command are we using?' Rafi asked almost instantly. He seemed to have decided that the best way to minimise Yara's presence was to stop her from getting a word in edgeways.

'No verse command for this spell; it's simple enough that you should be able to do it using the potion and your powers of persuasion.' But she looked at Yara out of the corner of her eye as she spoke, and Yara thought the lack of a verse was probably to prevent her from causing chaos.

'Easy,' Rafi muttered.

Unfortunately for him Leyla overheard. 'Well, then, you won't mind going first.'

For a moment Rafi looked as though he regretted speaking. Then, smearing paste all over his stone, he said stiffly, 'Stone, I command you to leave the table.'

Yara watched in fascination as the stone gave a tiny flip before settling back into its former position.

'Whoa,' she breathed.

'A poor effort,' Leyla said sternly. 'You were not specific enough.'

Rafi nodded, redirecting his focus. 'Stone, I demand

that you rise ten centimetres from the table.' It wobbled a little. 'Stone, you must rise ten centimetres exactly at my command.'

Yara wasn't sure whether 'reluctant' was a fitting description for a stone, but it certainly gave several half-hearted attempts at the task before Rafi managed to convince it to hover above the table. His face was tinged pink, his muscles straining as hard as though he were lifting a boulder.

'All right, that will do,' Leyla told him. Rafi let out all his breath in one go, and the stone dropped to the table. 'Yara, if you please.'

Her palms clammy with nerves, Yara stepped up. She noticed with alarm that there were more of their neighbours around than usual, the adults pretending to get on with work, the children looking at her expectantly.

Before she started, Leyla said in an undertone, 'Just ... take it slowly.'

Yara nodded, reaching into Leyla's jar and daubing her stone with the mixture. 'What ingredients are in this? Do you make pastes in the same way you make potions or—'

'Yara.'

Yara fell quiet. Feeling as though it might help, she held out her hand.

'Stone, please rise ten centimetres.'

She only just got out of the way in time. The stone shot up into the sky like a missile, travelling so fast there was a flame-like aura around it as it hurtled upwards until it vanished into the morning mist. It did not make a reappearance.

'Let's try that again,' Leyla said after a while, her neck craned as she squinted up in the direction the stone had travelled. 'Perhaps you could ask a little less directly.'

Yara hurled stones of various sizes into the sky for a good while, as the others from the Settlement gave up pretending to work and called out advice.

'It's your stance, that's the problem.'

'No, it's her posture. Straighten your back, goat girl.'

'I think perhaps that's enough for today,' Leyla said, raising her voice above the torrent of criticism, and their neighbours grumbled in disappointment.

Her voice had betrayed no emotion, but as Yara cleared away, she turned and saw the sorceress watching her with eyes that were dark and troubled.

Filled with fears of bringing the alchemists down on their settlement with an ill-timed spell, Yara redoubled her focus in lessons – but controlling her magic was far harder than she could have imagined. She felt *everything* now: the whispering of the trees in the wood and the hum of the earth and the flame-like flicker every time Ajal walked past. Her body was constantly vibrating – magic seemed to be something that prickled beneath her skin and set the blood racing around her body at an inhuman speed. It was wonderful. It was suffocating. It was as though someone had draped a jewelled cloak over her shoulders; she felt imbued with a kind of majesty, even as the weight of it crushed her.

Leyla seemed determined to work her so hard that she would not have the energy for an outburst, making her study diagrams and brew potions and memorise laws as though Yara hadn't only found out what magic *was* a month ago. She did so with all her usual briskness – but on more than one occasion Yara caught the sorceress regarding her with obvious unease. Then again, the Settlement was filled with disquiet these days. The alchemists still had them surrounded, and no one could understand why. Each day they set out to scuttle around the mountains, and each night they would return empty-handed to their tents and talk with each other late into the night.

Yara tried to think about what the alchemist Omair Firaaz had said, that he would send his men out to *make sure it spreads* – whatever 'it' was – but thinking was getting increasingly difficult. Even with Leyla's efforts, she would find herself hopping from foot to foot while cooking or twitching uncontrollably as she tried to read from the book of wonders, magic surging violently inside her. One time, coming home from her work in the neighbouring village, Leyla caught Yara rushing around the kitchen like a wild thing, their dinner long forgotten as she slipped and danced her way around the room.

'Easy does it.' She took her by the elbows, steering her to an open space of floor. 'Deep breaths in and out.'

Suddenly there were bright sparks where Leyla had been holding her, and the sorceress dropped her, as though she were hot to the touch.

'What was that?' Yara gasped, struggling to speak.

'That was your magic trying to reach out to mine.' Leyla cradled her hand to her chest. 'And that's the result of me trying to stop it.'

'Why? What's happening? Why is it so powerful suddenly? What's wrong with me?'

'I ... I don't know.' Leyla's jaw set. Even as it was becoming increasingly difficult to think, Yara got the impression that Leyla was once again not telling her something. 'What I do know is that you need to work on calming your magic.'

'How?' Yara gritted her teeth. 'I can't breathe.'

'All you need is discipline,' Leyla told her sharply. 'You are too chaotic with your practice.'

'I'm trying!'

'I can see that. But a sorceress must not content herself with trying – she must persevere until her will has been worked into the fabric and fibre of the world.' She gave a sigh, appearing to make up her mind about something. 'Summon your jinn.'

'What?'

'Just do it.'

Yara took a steadying breath. 'Ajal!' she called. After a few moments he trotted into the room.

'Have you taken on a sorcerer's magic before?' Leyla asked him.

'Never. The sorcerers who imprisoned me wished only to draw from my own power.'

'This will be very different.' Leyla spared a quick glance for Yara. 'Under normal circumstances I wouldn't ask, but she's very young and in quite a lot of discomfort.'

The jinn let out a sigh, but settled himself in front of Yara, who by now was feeling sick with effort.

'Grab on to my horns,' he told her.

Yara reached out and gripped tightly, raising herself so that she was eye to eye with the jinn.

'Good. Now breathe out.'

Yara gave a long, deep exhale, and to her surprise the tightness in her chest and the sparking feeling in her limbs receded along with her breath. Too overwhelmed to speak, she nodded, trying to convey her thanks to Ajal.

Leyla hovered over the two of them.

'What does it feel like?' Her question was directed at the jinn. If Yara didn't know better, she would think she sounded anxious.

'Strong,' replied Ajal shortly. 'It's a wonder she was still lucid. I thought you were supposed to be helping her?'

Leyla went bright red. 'I'm trying,' she said hotly. 'It's not easy when I haven't the faintest idea how she came by this amount of magic, nor any clue of how she is supposed to manage it without destroying half the Settlement practising.'

She looked half-accusingly at her then, which Yara felt was deeply unfair.

'It's not my fault!'

'Next time you feel as though you cannot control yourself, summon Ajal. He will help you manage it.'

With Ajal's help Yara's magic calmed somewhat, and her outbursts were far less frequent, but the arrangement seemed to trouble the jinn.

'Remember,' he told her almost every time. 'This cannot last for ever. I will stay with you until you have control of your powers, no longer.'

But it felt to Yara that she would never have full

control. Worse, she had dreams every night now, of blinding light and a whispering voice.

You must come back. Whatever happens, you must come back …

Each time she would start bolt upright in her makeshift bed, her magic wild and snarling inside her. Usually Ajal would curl up next to her, telling her bloodthirsty tales of the sorcerers he had accompanied and the grisly ends they had met until her breathing slowed and she grew calm enough to sleep again. But that night, when she woke gasping and trembling, he was nowhere to be found.

'Ajal!' she called out, but knew it was no good. Since they had begun sharing magic, Yara had a certain sense of his presence, and right now she felt a strange ache in her ribs that she knew meant he would be hundreds of miles away, travelling the continent as a cloud.

She sat up, looking around. Without Ajal the hayloft seemed even more sparse and lonely than before, and she wished with a sudden desperate intensity that she was back in her own bed at home, where Mama always sat up with her after she had a nightmare. Her power surged until it crushed her chest, and she reached out for her mum's headscarf, trying to ground herself back in the world.

After a few long minutes she was able to stagger to her

feet, hoping she could perhaps walk off the rest of the feeling and then go back to sleep. The house was dark and quiet, the last embers of the fire still smouldering. It must have been long past midnight ... and yet there was a light coming from upstairs. Curious, Yara crept through the cottage and up the stairs until she was hovering on the threshold of Leyla's room.

The sorceress was curled up on a scattering of large cushions by the fire, her legs tucked beneath her like a cat and a stack of parchment on her lap. She was so absorbed in its contents that she didn't seem to register Yara's presence. But what really stopped Yara in her tracks was Leyla's hair ... it fell in thick dark coils around her, silky and threaded through with burnished copper strands. If she had stood up, it would have fallen to her knees.

Yara watched her carefully. Wearing an expression of quiet enjoyment, the firelight dancing across her face and illuminating her features, Leyla looked younger and prettier than Yara had ever seen her.

She made to retreat downstairs ... but her foot caught on the edge of the carpet and she stumbled. Leyla looked up, stuffing the parchment hastily beneath her cushion.

'What are you doing up here?'

'Sorry.'

Yara's teeth were chattering, and Leyla looked at her more closely. 'Where is Ajal?'

'Out – I can't reach him.'

'Thoughtless,' Shehzad remarked.

'He's allowed his freedom,' Yara countered, but it was difficult to make a reasoned argument while hopping from foot to foot.

Leyla gave a sigh. 'Shehzad, would you mind?'

The raven clicked his beak. 'Very well; just this once.'

He spread his wings and flew across the room, settling on Yara's shoulder. She breathed out, feeling as though a crushing weight had been lifted from her.

'Thank you.' She reached out her hand, stroking Shehzad's head. He nipped at her finger affectionately before taking off again, flying out of the window and into the night.

Leyla was still looking at her closely, her expression inscrutable. 'It is rather late for you to be wandering the house.'

'I'm sorry. I'll go back to bed—'

'I didn't mean ...' Leyla twisted her mouth, as though her words weren't coming out quite as she meant them to. 'It's a cold night. You're welcome to warm yourself by the fire.'

Surprised, Yara took her up on her invitation, sitting on the cushions opposite and stretching out her fingers towards the flames.

'It is not only anger that can make magic difficult

to control,' Leyla said quietly. 'It can be particularly powerful with fear – or sorrow.'

Yara sniffed, scrubbing at her face with the palm of her hand and staring resolutely into the fire, determined not to break down in front of the sorceress.

Leyla followed her gaze. When she spoke, her voice was soft, 'After my parents died, I would spend days in the archives, trying to understand their work. The Great Library was a magnificent place, filled with its own sort of sorcery that would invite you in and lead you to the books you needed most. Sometimes a friend and I would curl up among the stacks and feel their magic radiating out – and it was as though I could feel my parents with their quiet voices and neat penmanship.

'Then the Inquisition came, and I watched the library – and all their work – burn to the ground.'

Yara's breath caught in her throat. She thought of pages curling with the heat, the ink blackening further until there was nothing left but ashes floating in the wind. A whole world gone up in flames.

'It must have been awful,' she found herself saying.

'The worst day of my life,' Leyla agreed, 'for a number of reasons. But I know even worse is to come.'

'What could be worse than the Inquisition?'

Leyla gave her a half-smile. 'There are still people today who remember the old ways, and the knowledge that was kept beneath that dome. But those men lurking outside our settlement have destroyed every bit of our history they could get their hands on, and those younger than me are already forgetting. One day sorcery will die out, and there will be no one to remember all we achieved over hundreds of years.'

'That won't happen.' Yara's voice was fierce. 'We won't let it – we'll do something, you'll see.'

Her words seemed to cheer the sorceress, who let out a low, genuine laugh.

'Perhaps you will. I certainly wouldn't like to see anyone try to stop you.' She hesitated and then reached for the parchment at her side. 'When I find myself awake at night, reflecting on all we have lost, I try to write down what I remember from the books in the Great Library. It's something of an impossible task – but it helps.'

'What were you working on tonight?'

Leyla looked embarrassed. 'A silly thing, hardly worth the parchment and ink. A collection of old folk tales my friend used to love – I had almost forgotten about them until something you said earlier reminded me.'

Yara settled herself back against the cushions. 'Could you read one to me?'

Something changed in Leyla's face. 'Very well.' She leafed through the parchment, her eyes roaming until they settled on the tale she had been looking for, and she began to read. '*Many years ago, in a time only the stars can remember ...*'

Leyla's low voice lent itself well to storytelling; it took on an added richness as she spoke. These were stories that had crossed cities and continents and worlds, stories that cast their own kind of magic over their readers. As Yara listened, lulled by the flicker of the flames, she closed her eyes and felt the murmured tale come to life.

Chapter Fourteen

'**M**any years ago, in a time only the stars remember, there were two sisters, each as wise as the moon and as beautiful as the day. The elder was Rawiya, and the younger Naazima.

'The sisters lived in the kingdom of a sultan known for his immense cruelty. When he announced that he was searching for a bride, every woman feared for her life. Many fled the kingdom, but the sisters could not leave their elderly father, who was the Sultan's Grand Vizier.

'Rawiya and Naazima had long studied the night sky and the movements of the constellations and knew of the power they held. Every evening they would drink a potion of Rawiya's own making and go out to where the stars shone brightest, seeking wisdom and understanding. And each night the stars would grant the sisters a little of their power and they would learn a little more of their magic.

'One day, when Rawiya was at her books, her sister Naazima came and kneeled beside her. "Sister," she said, "our father received word that you are to be the Sultan's new bride. He says that you must leave this house and go to him by sundown or he will kill everyone in our household."

'Naazima clasped her sister close and wept. As she did, her tears fell on her sister like falling stars and Rawiya was enveloped in pure light. And so magic was passed on from one person to another for the first time.'

Yara's eyes were flickering shut, her limbs heavy and warm. She could hear the roar of the fire in her ears, like falling rain.

'"Sister," said Naazima. There was a strange urgency filling her voice. "You must take my magic. Take it—"'

'Take her.'

The scene had bled into another without Yara realising. Leyla's storytelling voice was gone; the woman speaking was unfamiliar. Yara couldn't see anything; wherever she was it was too dark and too strange – but she could feel herself being held very tight. The woman's voice cut through again, alive with fear.

'Take her. Hide her. You must take her to the furthest corners of the earth – further even.'

Yara wanted to reach out, to speak – but she couldn't move.

She heard the woman's voice again. 'You must be so brave. And you must come back. Whatever happens, you must come back.'

Of course, Yara wanted to say, of course I'll come back for you. But she could feel herself being pulled away, and the woman was crying out in anguish – Yara had heard that cry before, but where?

It was too late; the woman's voice was growing fainter and fainter ...

Yara woke with a start, sitting up and looking around her wildly. Immediately she winced, her neck stiff from the awkward way she had curled up in her sleep.

It was just a dream, she told herself. *You fell asleep by the fire and you had another nightmare, that's all.*

Leyla was nowhere to be seen, and her bed looked unslept in – although someone had covered Yara with a blanket during the night. Picking herself up, she made her way downstairs and opened the front door, scanning the village for the sorceress. There was no sign of her – only people beginning to make their way out to the rice fields, keeping a cautious eye out for the alchemists.

Yara shivered in the cold air. It was funny – looking out from their doorstep, there was something comforting about the crags and ridges of the surrounding mountains; they seemed to wrinkle like kindly grandfathers. She wondered if Leyla ever stood here and felt the same way.

Just then, she sensed a sparking heat on the back of her neck, and Yara turned just in time to see Ajal swooping down from the skies, rematerialising in his goat form next to her.

'You're back,' Yara said in relief. Her magic was already beginning to buzz beneath her nails.

'Indeed.' He extended his head, allowing Yara to stroke behind his ears. 'I circumnavigated the kingdom countless times, and everywhere it was the same. Men in black-and-gold robes making camps by the rivers and streams.'

Yara shivered, remembering the viciousness with which Firaaz had promised to send the alchemists into the countryside. Her magic reacted uneasily to her thoughts, the hairs on the back of her neck standing on end.

Ajal sighed. 'I sense you are in need of my assistance?'

'Please,' Yara said gratefully.

She knelt beside the jinn, placing her hand on his back and letting her magic flow into him in a white-hot current. This connection, *this* was true power – with Ajal she felt like she could do anything.

It's like we're flying, she told him, her hair fanning

around her and her skin tingling. With a start she realised that she had not spoken the words aloud, but rather her thoughts had flowed into his mind along with her magic.

Ajal jerked his head, moving away from her. 'Don't,' he said, his bleat sharp.

'I ... I'm sorry,' Yara began. 'I didn't mean—'

'I am no sorcerer's familiar; our thoughts are not for sharing. I am a free jinn, free to do whatever I like – and I am not about to give that up, not even for you, Yara Sulimayah.'

Not waiting for a reply, he transformed back into his cloud form, and was carried away on the breeze.

Yara shivered again as he left, power now vibrating in her at the speed of a hummingbird's heartbeat. Her worry for the jinn was displaced by a wave of panic. How was she supposed to expend her magic without Ajal? What if she had an outburst that alerted the alchemists?

Moving towards the pine forest at the Settlement's border, she broke into a run, her sleep-stiffened limbs loosening in the frost. Pushing her way through the trees, she tried to think rationally. By now she was far away from the alchemists' camp – perhaps if she did a few small spells, she could expend the energy without alerting anyone.

Her eyes alighted on a fallen branch, and she held

out her hand. 'Soar,' she told it, and then ducked as it shot rapidly into the air, taking flight and turning cartwheels in the sky. Yara laughed in spite of herself. Already beginning to feel better, she looked around for more branches.

'Soar! Fly east! Fly west! Fly—'

But then she stopped. As the branch had sliced westward through the air, there was the sound of a human gasp and of someone diving to the ground.

She froze, heart hammering, listening intently. Yes, she hadn't been mistaken. That was a person she could hear, and what was more they appeared to have picked themselves up and were now drawing closer.

Yara pressed herself behind a tree, her heart still racing even as her magic subsided. The rustling was growing louder, the footsteps halting and unsure. They must have heard her too.

Not stopping to think, she launched herself forward, hoping to take whoever it was by surprise and sprint past them – but she collided almost immediately with the figure, who caught her by the arms.

'Yara?'

Yara found herself looking into familiar dark eyes.

'Meri!'

She flung herself at the sorceress, who staggered several steps back with the force of Yara's greeting.

'Goodness!' Meri laughed, hugging her back tightly. When Yara pulled away, she was still smiling, but there was something behind her eyes and at the corners of her mouth that hadn't been there in Zehaira. 'Who is this strong country girl greeting me? She can't be the same little thing I sheltered in my bakery all those weeks ago?'

Yara resisted the temptation to roll her eyes in a very Leyla-ish manner, but the grin remained on her face. 'You're all right – I was so worried! What are you doing here? Where's Mehnoor?'

Just then, the girl herself came bounding towards them through the trees.

'Yara!' She gave a whoop of joy, running towards Yara before pulling herself up short. 'I found you. I knew I could – it was your aura; you're impossible to miss. Oh, it's so good to see you. I want to hear *everything*—'

Meri placed a quelling hand on her niece's shoulder. 'Yara can fill you in on her adventures later, I'm sure.'

'Of course.' Mehnoor's expression became serious. 'Yara, please would you take us to Leyla Khatoun? There's something I think she should know.'

'You want to see Leyla?' Yara looked out of the corner of her eye at Meri. 'Really?'

'I had doubts about the idea myself,' said Meri. 'But if what Mehnoor says is true, then there really is no time to waste.'

Yara led the pair down the mountain and back through the Settlement. The curiosity of the villagers, which had waned after a month of 'that strange goat girl running about the place', waxed fresh at the sight of two strangers. Meri and Mehnoor looked distinctly uncomfortable beneath their stares.

'It's all right,' Yara assured them. 'She's just over here.' And Yara dropped Meri's hand, running ahead into the cottage.

'Madam Khatoun!' she shouted. 'Leyla, there's someone here to see you.'

Leyla, bent over her cauldron, gave a start, narrowly avoiding hitting her head.

'Yara, what did I say about—'

She stopped short, her eyes travelling up from Yara until she was looking squarely at Meri. Her lips parted, her hand finding the edge of the hearth and gripping until her knuckles whitened against it.

'Madam Khatoun,' Meri said. Her tone was artificially neutral, but as she brought her palm up to her chest, Yara could see her hand was trembling. 'It's good to see you.'

Leyla's mouth snapped shut. 'Indeed, Madam Shereen,' she said, not looking away. 'You're looking ...' She coughed, apparently unsure of how to finish her sentence.

'And this is my niece, Mehnoor. Mehnoor, Leyla Khatoun.'

Leyla's eyes flickered in the girl's direction. 'Welcome, both of you.' Her voice was rough and suddenly brisk. She brought her palm up briefly, then folded her arms. 'To what do I owe this ... pleasure?'

Meri narrowed her eyes. 'I'm afraid this isn't a social call. I bring disturbing news from the city—'

'So nothing that need concern us here, then,' said Leyla, not missing a beat.

Yara groaned inwardly. There would be no reasoning with Leyla when she was in a mood like this, and a glance at Meri showed her struggling to keep her temper; her eyes were bright and her mouth was pressed in a very thin line. She decided to take action.

'Meri, why don't you sit down?' she said, steering the sorceress to the workbench and clearing a place for her to sit. 'Tell us what happened from the beginning.'

Meri took a moment to collect herself before she began again.

'There has been another attack on sorcerers in the city. They're killing people – dragging them out of their beds. I imagine they are doing so as we speak.'

Leyla recovered quickly. 'Yes. They do that to sorcerers in the city. I hope you have not travelled all this way to inform me that sorcery still carries the death penalty.'

Mehnoor spoke up. 'This is different. Ever since Yara left, people have been getting ill. I could feel it – I could feel their blood and thoughts and *magic* slowing in their bodies all over the city. And it was as though the guards had been told to kill anyone who seemed affected before news could spread.'

'What on earth do you mean?'

'We think that somehow the surviving sorcerers are being poisoned,' said Meri quietly. 'And if that is true, then none of us will be safe in the Sultan's kingdom a day longer.'

There was a horrible pause after that. Leyla seemed not to know what to say; words formed on her lips only to die away on a breath.

'Poisoned,' she said finally. 'You believe they were poisoned. Do you have evidence?'

'Is my word not good enough for you any more?' said Meri in a low voice. 'There has been talk in the city for a long time now of a strange illness that turns the blood leaden grey and leaves its victims weakened beyond hope. The men and women I saw killed had those same symptoms.'

'More than that,' Mehnoor added. 'Ever since Yara left us, I've been dreaming of a darkness welling up in Zehaira, something rising from the ground and killing everything in its path. Whatever was affecting those sorcerers, it wasn't natural.'

Leyla seemed momentarily lost for words. 'I see. Well, you'll forgive me if I doubt the dreams of a teenager, but you cannot expect me to believe that the *Sultan*—'

'Not the Sultan ...' said Yara slowly. 'When I heard the alchemist on Istehar Way, he said ... he said that the ordinary citizens wouldn't be harmed by whatever he was doing. You think this is what he meant, don't you?'

'What else can it be?' Meri turned to Leyla. I told you twelve years ago that they wouldn't forget about us, that they were biding their time. Do you really think they'll stop with the city now?'

'She's right,' Yara said insistently. 'The alchemist, he said he would send men out to *make sure it spreads*. And now they're right on the Settlement boundary.'

'And what are we to do about it? I suppose everyone will be coming here –' Leyla's voice was rising in volume – 'expecting us to share what little we have, when we had the foresight to get out twelve years ago ...'

'Clearly I was wrong to expect anything of *you*,' Meri said venomously. 'I only thought you might listen to a warning.'

'A warning. You mean fearmongering and guesswork, because it gives you a chance to tell me that you told me so?'

'That's enough!' Yara got to her feet, looking between them in astonishment. 'You are sorceresses, both of you, and you're fighting like teenagers.'

'And you.' Leyla's head snapped round quickly. 'When were you planning on telling me that it was Madam Shereen who gave you my location?'

'You never asked,' Yara retorted. 'But surely . . . surely if people come from the city, we aren't going to send them away?'

Leyla hesitated, but beneath Yara's gaze said reluctantly, 'The Settlement has always been a safe haven for those who practise magic, and that won't change any time soon. But I will believe evidence of poison when I see it with my own eyes.'

'You won't be waiting long, then,' said Meri. 'People are fleeing the city as we speak.'

Afterwards the atmosphere became so oppressive that Yara brought Mehnoor straight up to the hayloft, anxious to escape the tense quiet of the sorceresses.

'I've never shared a room before,' Mehnoor said, her eyes wide and nervous. 'I've never really talked to anyone else my own age, even. Aunt Meri always said it was too dangerous – in case I let something slip to an ordinary child, and they reported it back to their parents.'

She reached for her bag, and pulled out a book Yara

recognised. *The History of the World.*

'You brought it with you?'

'Of course.' Mehnoor hugged it close to her chest. 'It's the most fascinating thing. I thought we were the only community to go through an inquisition, but this book says that in your world they happened over and over again.' She looked at Yara seriously. 'Giving me this was the nicest thing anyone has done for me.'

Yara grinned sheepishly.

'Yeah, well, if it hadn't been for you and Meri, I would never have found Leyla.' She tilted her head. 'They really don't like each other, do they?'

'Don't you think so? It seems complicated to me.'

'Complicated?'

'Well, for one thing, I've seen Aunt Meri be civil to plenty of people she dislikes. Don't get me wrong, she has a wicked temper – but she doesn't normally get angry for no good reason.'

'Oh, I think Leyla's given her plenty of good reason.'

'Not all the time,' Mehnoor argued. 'Aunt Meri was provoking her too.'

A half-buried thought dislodged itself from Yara's subconscious.

'Meri had a lock of Leyla's hair.'

'What?'

'Meri turned a braid she wore round her wrist into a

locating spell. I think it must have belonged to Leyla –
it's what brought me to her. What does that mean?'

Mehnoor looked thoughtful. 'I'm not sure. It's a big
deal giving another sorceress a lock of hair, because it
means they could have power over you if they wanted.
You would never give hair to someone you didn't trust.'

'You think Meri and Leyla used to be friends?'

'Well, don't you think it makes sense?' Mehnoor
pressed her. 'Think about it. When they fought, it wasn't
just anger; it was this sort of tangle of feelings – like
they've got so confused I can't tell where one begins
and another ends.' She looked at the floor. Through the
cracks they could hear the sorceresses resuming their
quarrel, and Mehnoor looked suddenly afraid. 'They
need to work it out soon. If I'm right about what's
coming, we can't afford to be divided.'

Chapter Fifteen

Meri was proved right. Refugees began to pour into the Settlement the very next day; first in a trickle, then rushing like great waves into the valley. Small children were carried on backs, and grandparents were carried on chairs, all of them wearing the same tired, bewildered expression. There was so much to be done – Abdul Hussein was up until the witching hours building shelters, and Meri and Leyla worked night and day preparing healing tonics and elixirs, their hands blistered from hours of grinding and scalded by spluttering potions. Even the children were hard at work, and Yara was putting her organisational skills to good use.

'A family of five?' she said, addressing the latest newcomers outside Leyla's house, consulting the scroll she had begun to use as a makeshift register. 'Anyone sick?

'Only my father-in-law,' said one of the men, and he and his children parted to reveal an elderly man lying on a cart.

Yara gave a gasp of recognition. 'Ibn Munir!' She rushed to the cartographer's side. 'Do you remember me?'

The elderly man squinted at her. He seemed to have aged twenty years since Yara had last seen him, his breathing fitful and shallow. Worse, like all the sick people she had seen, there was a greyness at the tips of his fingers and the edges of his mouth.

'I do,' he said eventually. 'Although I am surprised to find a messenger for the alchemists in a settlement for sorcerers.'

Yara bit her lip. 'I wasn't completely honest with you. I'm sorry.'

'No, no.' Munir waved her away. 'We were none of us honest in Zehaira.' He gave a mirthless chuckle. 'There is nothing left to say now but the truth, I suppose.'

Yara stepped back, unsure of how to reply – but his eyes roamed away from her, wandering as though he had gone to a faraway place.

As Yara watched the family go, there was a sudden disturbance of the air and Ajal swooped down from the skies. Relieved, Yara reached for him – and then pulled back, hesitant.

'Sorry, I— Is it all right if I . . . ?'

'By all means,' said the jinn.

Yara placed a hand on his head, her breath coming in a rush as her magic flowed into him. Since their quarrel she had been careful not to overstep the boundary between them again, but even though her outbursts had almost stopped, she couldn't imagine what she would do without Ajal to take her magic.

'The mist is coming down from the mountains,' he told her. 'Soon there will be snow – and I saw more people making their way here from the city.'

The prospect of this winter seemed very different to every winter past for Yara, who thought with a pang of advent calendars and central heating, and Mama decorating their flat with fairy lights. Here snow meant that there would be no gathering potion ingredients, no seeking work in the neighbouring villages. In the evenings Yara would see Leyla tensed over the Settlement's accounts, her face pinched with worry.

When she returned with Ajal to the house, however, neither she nor Meri were anywhere to be seen. Instead, she found Rafi pouring wellness potions into vials and Mehnoor sat on the table next to him, her hands twisting miserably in her lap.

'And it's not just the sickness,' she told the boy, her voice high with panic. 'The darkness is still coming; it's spreading through the kingdom like cobwebs, withering every tree and flower, and there's nothing we can do to stop it ...'

'Yes, there is.' Rafi spoke with surprising gentleness. 'Madam Khatoun and your aunt will make a cure; they just need time.'

'If they ever stop arguing for long enough to find one,' said Yara as she came into the room, putting a comforting arm round Mehnoor's shoulders. At her arrival Rafi straightened his back, clearing his throat awkwardly as he busied himself with the potions.

'Are those ready?' said Yara. 'They were asking for them in the encampment.'

'Almost.' Rafi held out his hand, and Yara watched him with a complicated mix of feelings in her chest. Her own magic was still too volatile to help with the potions.

'With moon-picked willow and
   dew-touched flower,
Let poison quake before my power.'

A few of the potions glowed half-heartedly – but the majority of them stayed a stubborn green. Rafi huffed in frustration. 'Useless,' he hissed.

'That's not true,' Mehnoor argued, and Yara looked at her in surprise. 'You're good at this, you know – you're good at helping people.'

Yara thought about it. Since they had had begun helping the sorceresses, Rafi had seemed far more in his element, mixing the wellness tonics with fervency and answering questions from frightened families with seemingly endless patience.

'Mehnoor's right,' she said. 'You're much better at this than magic. Why do you keep going with sorcery when you hate it so much?'

Rafi glared at her. 'I don't hate it.'

'Yes, you do. Whenever Leyla asks you to do a spell, you look as though you would rather stick your hand inside a shark tank.'

'A what?'

'You know what I mean.'

Rafi was silent for a moment, struggling with himself. 'Fine, you're both right,' he said suddenly, and then it was as though his words were tumbling out as fast as he could think them. 'I do hate it. Not magic – you can't hate magic – but the stupid, awful *poetry*.'

'The poetry? What's there to hate about poetry?'

'Everything!' Rafi exploded. 'Why can't people just say what they think? And then it's not just enough to say it, you have to *mean* it, and you have to speak properly and not too quickly, and I hate it.' He gave a sigh. 'The truth is, I like the part Leyla despises – going into the villages with tonics and making people better. But it would never occur to her that anyone would want to learn about that.'

'Why not tell her?' Mehnoor asked. 'I'm sure she'd understand.'

Rafi scowled. 'It's not that simple.'

Yara raised her eyebrows, and Rafi went on. 'They killed almost all my family in the Inquisition. My parents, my aunts, uncles, cousins … my elder brother Rizwan, everyone said he was going to be a great sorcerer. It's not right if I get the chance to do everything they were supposed to, and then throw it away.'

'You wouldn't be throwing it away,' Yara argued. 'In my world lots of people get trained in healing and medicine. It's very respected.'

'Your world?'

'Long story.' Yara looked at him ruefully. 'We haven't talked all that much, have we?'

'No. You were too busy knocking me down.'

'And you were too busy calling me names.'

Yara grinned at him, and Rafi smiled back tentatively, as if he wasn't entirely sure how to move his mouth that way.

At that moment the air began to thicken with the sound of raised voices, and Meri and Leyla materialised in the room, arguing furiously.

'You are *impossible*.' Meri was seething, her cheeks

bright red. 'Will you not even consider—'

'What is there to consider? What would you have me do?' Leyla hissed. 'Let people die while we embark on a fool's errand – to find the source of a sickness we do not yet understand? The alchemists at our border are gone; no one from the Settlement is affected. Whatever poison they used in the city cannot harm us here.'

'You weren't there after the Inquisition,' Meri shot back. 'If you are arrogant enough to believe that a few protection spells will be enough—'

'Stop it!' Yara interrupted, silencing the sorceresses. 'This isn't how you get things done. You're exhausted, both of you, and you're wasting all the energy you have left arguing with each other.'

She held her breath, expecting them to turn on her – but Leyla was looking determinedly at the floor, and Meri turned her head, burying her face in her hands.

At that moment Mehnoor emerged from the corner she had hidden herself in, removing her hands from her ears.

'Look,' she said, moving to the window. 'They're building something outside.'

Grateful for the distraction, Yara followed her gaze. Six of the villagers were building a pyre in the centre, children dancing about excitedly around them and bringing logs in from the wood and generally getting underfoot.

'What's happening?'

'They're preparing the bonfire for the Night of the Red Sun – the midwinter festival,' Leyla elaborated at Yara's questioning glance. 'It ought to be tomorrow.' She scowled, her voice rising once more. 'It is a reckless extravagance – are we to starve all through the winter for one night of *merriment*?'

Yara might have laughed at the way Leyla's mouth twisted suspiciously around the word if she had not looked quite so tired.

Meri was watching Leyla now too, and for once there was no bitterness in her gaze. 'Our people have precious little to celebrate, and will have even less as the winter goes on,' she said quietly. 'Isn't that why sorcerers observe the Red Night? One last moment of light before the darkness takes hold?'

She met Leyla's eyes, and a silent conversation took place. For the first time since Meri had arrived something about Leyla softened.

'I suppose one night will not ruin us,' she said grudgingly.

The next day, there was a growing feeling of anticipation in the Settlement, even amid all their worry. The pyre grew taller, and the air was rich with the smell of food being prepared for the festival.

Furthermore, to Yara's surprise, Leyla found her in the afternoon and presented her with a parcel.

'I had Madam Zahrawi make you up a couple of new salwar qamis,' she said, crisply. 'It's usual to wear new clothes to the festival.'

'I— Leyla,' Yara stammered, 'you can't mean to spend your money like this . . .'

'Can't I?' Leyla arched an eyebrow. 'Consider it a small payment for all your work. Now make haste – it's almost dusk, and you don't want to miss the making of the sun fire.'

Yara took the parcel up to the hayloft, retrieving the salwar and qamis from within. They were russet red and embroidered with tiny golden suns. Heedless of the clash of colours, Yara wrapped her mother's headscarf back round her neck, her scent faint and almost lost beneath remnants of sea air and smoke but still there.

She crossed the room to her wash bucket, kneeling over it and looking at herself. It couldn't have been much longer than a month since she had first made the journey to Zehaira, but her hair was longer, she looked older – she *felt* older. Suddenly she felt an intense sadness for the person she had been before, who would have been finishing up her first term of Year Seven, and who would hang around shopping centres with Rehema and play video games until her mum got home from work. The person who stared back at her from the bucket seemed far more serious and grown-up than that girl had been.

Mehnoor was watching her from the corner of the room, lying on her stomach and stroking Ajal's head.

'Come on,' Yara said, holding out her hand. 'We don't want to be late.'

'You go,' said Mehnoor. There were dark shadows under her eyes, and Yara saw that her nails were bitten to the quick. 'I don't feel like it.'

Yara's brows pulled together in concern. 'Is it the dreams?'

'It's a different dream now.' Mehnoor looked up at the ceiling, as though she could see the stars through the thatched birch bark. 'Now I'm just going down long dark corridors. I suppose it's because I'm so confused by everything, but I ... I'm finding it so difficult to be brave, I wish I could be *useful*.'

Yara hummed thoughtfully. 'Look at it this way,' she said. 'If you come tonight, Meri won't worry about you, and she and Leyla might actually enjoy themselves enough to not rip each other's heads off tomorrow. That sounds helpful to me.'

After a moment's hesitation Mehnoor took her hand.

By the time they came down, the sun was setting and the whole village was assembled in a circle round the fire. Even some of the sick had been brought out of their tents to watch. Yara looked for a familiar face and, catching Rafi's eye, led Mehnoor over to where he was standing.

She could see Leyla in the centre of the circle, dressed smartly in a wine-coloured outfit with embroidered vines and leaves, and next to her Meri looked more beautiful than ever in a long emerald tunic, her bracelets back on her wrists. For once the pair looked relatively peaceable. Yara recognised some of the other adults standing next to them – Madam Dinezade, Rashiyd the sweetmaker, Madam Zahrawi the seamstress, Abdul Hussein. They joined hands, and their concentration was so intense that it felt tangible in the air.

Then Leyla spoke. 'For remembrance. May the souls of our families rest deep in the earth, in the wind among the trees, in the fire on the mountain, in the running of the stream. May they never roam the darkness, or the wild, or the cold. May they be at peace.'

Yara felt her breath catch in her throat, and she ducked her head, her eyes brimming over as Mama's face surfaced suddenly in her mind. She thought she had moved quickly enough that Rafi wouldn't see her – but he cleared his throat and reached into his pocket, extending a scrap of cloth.

'It's the smoke getting in my eyes,' Yara hissed, wiping at her face angrily with the end of her headscarf. She looked round the circle. How many of these people would lose family before the winter was out?

Meanwhile, the feeling of concentration grew, and grew – and then Yara could see light held between Leyla's hands, as bright as starlight. It was small and seemed in danger of sputtering out, but Leyla was careful as she placed it on the pyre. As she did so it seemed to bloom and unfurl, and Yara saw flames arching towards the sky, so tall and so bright that she had to shield her eyes just to look at them. Next to her, Mehnoor's mouth had fallen open in wonder.

Moments passed, even the noisiest of the children silenced by the effect. And then Leyla cleared her throat, clapping her hands together. 'Now. Let us eat.'

The people around her began to chant, and in an instant huge clay tureens were summoned to the centre of the circle.

Yara gasped. She could see vegetables roasted in every colour of the rainbow and aubergines that had been scorched and spread with yoghurt and pomegranate seeds. There was enough rice to feed the whole of Bournemouth, let alone the village, bright orange and studded with slivered almonds. And the flatbreads! They took up most of the space, stacked on top of each other and each the size of a small child.

A bowl materialised in front of Yara and, copying the others, she passed round some dishes and helped herself to others until her plate was almost overflowing. Looking around at the food and at the people who spoke her language, who shook off their seriousness to laugh and eat with each other, Yara felt something settle soothingly in her stomach. Once she had thought she might never feel at home again.

As she did so, an old woman next to Rafi leaned over.

'So you are the little orphan Leyla Khatoun has taken such an interest in? Rafi, remind me of her name.'

'Yara Sulimayah, Auntie.' It was hard to tell in the dusk, but Rafi seemed a little pink.

'Sulimayah, eh? Well, you know my brother, Rafi's great-uncle, taught your mentor everything she knows? His great-nephew, should the stars be willing, is bound to follow in his footsteps.'

Yara looked curiously at Rafi, but he was staring determinedly at the ground. Meanwhile, his aunt continued. 'Well, did you enjoy our sun fire?'

'I thought it was magnificent.'

Bhushra snorted. 'Magnificent? That puny little light? When we used to share our magic with the Grand High Sorceress, Ismah Parveen, it would appear as though the stars themselves were settling on our pyres like snow, and the sun fire would burn all through the winter without going out. But she's gone now, along with all the power we entrusted her with.' She looked around her with contempt. 'First the Inquisition, and now poison – driving us from a city that has sorcery in its very bones. Ismah Parveen would not have stood for it, believe you me.'

Before their conversation could go further, a hush fell over the Settlement. From the crowd there came the *thump, thump, thump* of someone stamping their foot. Another joined in, then another.

Then two elderly gentlemen were jostled to the centre of the circle. One had a goatskin drum round his neck (Yara felt glad Ajal had thought better of attending) and the other what looked like a large spherical guitar. There was a murmur of anticipation as the guitar was tuned, a few errant notes plucked and then straightened with a grimace. Then the men began to play.

It was as though the music they played was the sound of the fire given note; it seemed to dance and crackle and smoulder into the night air. Yara took Rafi's and Mehnoor's hands, and they took their neighbours', and they began to weave around each other in long coils, slow at first but gradually getting faster. Then one person would let go and join up with another coil, while another person would reach out for Yara's hand, and the dance would continue even more intricately than it had done before. Yara could see dancing feet stamping in time to the flickering drumbeat, and she tried to copy them, stumbling hopelessly. Her magic was singing inside her – for once not overwhelming or oppressive, but in perfect harmony with the music.

The flames grew higher, the musicians played faster, and Yara lost Mehnoor in the crowd as the steps of their dance grew more and more complicated. She could hardly find her own heartbeat in the noise; there were only the drums and the roar of the fire, and the stamping of hundreds of feet in time, louder and louder.

Then there was a scream.

'Stop, stop!'

'There's a man down!'

The coils of people were breaking up, crowding around one point. Panting, Yara could make out a crumpled figure on the floor, Meri and Leyla already at their side.

'Who is it?' Mehnoor asked, clutching Yara's arm. 'One of the Zehairans?'

Yara opened her mouth to answer. And then she saw two children – Imahd and Asma – running to the man's side, their voices high and hysterical as they tried to shake him awake.

'No,' she said, and the realisation filled her with icy dread. 'He wasn't poisoned in the city. He's from the Settlement.'

Chapter Sixteen

Eventually Abdul Hussein was carried away from the pyre, and Yara and Mehnoor ran to the sorceresses' side.

'What's happened? Is he sick? Is it the poison?'

'Yes,' Leyla replied shortly. Her voice was calm, but the tremor in her hands gave her away. 'He has the same symptoms – the same greyness spreading across his body.'

'But ... but Abdul Hussein never went anywhere near Zehaira; he hasn't left the Settlement in twelve years.' Then Yara remembered what her friend had said yesterday. 'Mehnoor said she dreamed of darkness spreading—'

Mehnoor interrupted. 'And of rot and decay. Whatever the alchemists have created, it's all around us, isn't it? A poison that can reach us through the earth, through every tree, every flower, every crop ...'

Yara frowned. She was sure she had heard something like that before.

'It's worse than that,' Meri said flatly. 'Abdul Hussein is far more ill than any Zehairan I have seen. He may not last the night.'

Yara thought of Imahd and Asma beside their unconscious father, and her stomach lurched. She knew exactly what they would be feeling – helplessness and disbelief and terror so sharp it felt like anger.

'What can we do?' she asked Leyla, and for once the sorceress did not dismiss her.

'Help us send everyone home. We'll call a meeting in the morning.'

Around them, however, the Settlement was erupting into chaos.

'Madam Khatoun, it's my mother.' Madam Zahrawi's daughter approached them. 'She can't get up – she's not breathing right.'

'Leyla!' This time it was Rafi, his face fraught with terror. 'My great-aunt collapsed – her fingertips are turning grey.'

Leyla and Meri were sent in several directions at once, cries for help sounding against the roar of the sun fire. Yara turned to find Mehnoor, but she was lost again in the confusion. She saw Madam Dinezade and made her way towards her.

'We need to get you home!' she said, raising her voice above the noise. 'There's too many people out here.'

'Yara Sulimayah,' Madam Dinezade said faintly, leaning against a wall for support.

Yara could see grey seeping through her palm and spreading up the veins of her arm.

When Yara finally found her way home, Mehnoor was waiting for her by the hearth, her knees drawn up to her chin and her face tearstained. Together, they sat in near silence. It was well after dark when Leyla and Meri returned, Rafi trailing behind, and the sorceresses looked even more exhausted at the sight of them.

'You're still awake.' Leyla pinched the bridge of her nose. 'Go to bed; it's been a long night.'

Yara ignored this. 'What's happening? Why are so many people from the Settlement so ill?'

Meri and Leyla exchanged a defeated glance.

Wordlessly Meri moved to the fire, filling Leyla's tea cauldron. 'We don't know,' she admitted quietly. 'Six people struck down, all of them more severely affected by the poison than any I have seen before – and we just don't know why.'

Yara looked to Leyla for reassurance, but the sorceress merely closed her eyes. 'There must be something linking them,' said Leyla. 'What, I can't imagine ...'

'Yes, you can,' Rafi said suddenly. They all turned to look at him, and Meri's eyes softened.

'Rafi, sit down – you must be—'

'All six of them took part in the spell tonight.'

A hush descended on the room.

'But that's ... that's not ...' Meri said faintly. 'What could that possibly have to do with the poison?'

'*Oh.*' Yara turned to Leyla, her heart thumping. 'You told me that people practise sorcery by drawing on magic from the world around them. If it's like Mehnoor says, and the earth has been poisoned – what if the poison is attacking that magic itself?'

Yara saw something like fear cross Leyla Khatoun's face.

'Then the alchemists would have created the perfect means of destroying us,' she murmured. 'Every time we craft a potion – every time we seek a cure for the sick, we would be taking in more and more of the poison.'

'It can't be,' Meri argued. 'We took part in the spell – we have not been affected.'

'But look at the people we've been visiting.' Yara cast her mind back to her scroll. 'The elderly, the sick – it comes for them first.'

'Abdul Hussein can't have more than a decade on us—'

'Abdul Hussein was ill before,' said Leyla. 'He had only just stopped using his crutch when you arrived.

Worse, he has been crafting homes for newcomers ever since they began arriving; he's been using heavy magic night and day. If the children are right, Meriyem, then the more one practises, the greater the danger. This poison is turning our own magic against us.'

There was a long, horrified silence.

Meri sat down heavily by the fire. 'We have to call a meeting of the Settlement; make it clear that no one can use magic—'

'Worse than that,' said Leyla. 'If the poison has taken root here, then the Settlement is no longer a safe place. We must leave, and quickly.'

'Leave?'

'Yes, and seek refuge elsewhere – with the Northern Sorcerers perhaps. Professor Al-Qamar – you remember my mentor, Rafi's uncle? – he still conducts his research in the Russlands. If he would lend us his favour, we might persuade them to transport our settlement north, beyond the Sultan's domain. The alchemists will not have travelled that far; the sorcerers there will still have use of their magic – they may help us find a cure.'

'Leave the Settlement?' Yara's voice cracked with disbelief. Leave the mountains, and the forests, and the houses with their silver-birch roofs? It seemed unthinkable.

'Of course that's your solution,' Meri said bitterly. 'To turn your back, again.'

'We can't, Leyla,' Yara argued. 'This is our ... our *home*. We can't leave.'

'What choice do we have?' Leyla shot back.

'We put a stop to them; we fight back against the alchemists!' Yara folded her arms, drawing herself up to her full height.

'Who is it you wish to fight?' Leyla demanded. 'The young families? The elderly and the sick? What good is fighting back when every spell we cast weakens us further? Or have you not heard what happened to the sorcerers who attempted to fight the Inquisition?'

'Don't you dare,' said Meri softly. 'Don't you *dare* bring that up. You left – you weren't there—'

'Yes, I left. I kept these people alive for twelve years. I saw them through conflict, and famine, and drought, and I am not going to endanger them now because the two of you want us to fight.'

Meri's eyes were bright with anger, her reply so quiet Yara could barely hear it. 'If that's how you feel, then I'll take Mehnoor and go on elsewhere. But I will not flee north. If you choose the coward's route once again, then so be it.'

Leyla called a meeting, and they gathered again round the sun fire, most people still in their best clothes. Yara noticed that the newcomers were sat on one side and the older inhabitants on the other, a couple throwing suspicious glances across the circle. Clearly some of the Settlement had decided who was to blame for their own people being taken ill.

Yara sat pointedly next to Meri and Mehnoor, throwing a disapproving look across the circle as she did so.

Meri noticed and squeezed her hand.

'Don't worry,' she said. 'They've lived in isolation for over a decade; it's natural that they should be wary of us.'

'It still doesn't make it right,' Yara whispered back, and Meri hummed in sad acknowledgement.

As she did, Leyla approached the circle, stepping through the assembled crowds until she was in the centre.

'Thank you for returning tonight,' Leyla said, looking around at the huddled men and women. 'I am afraid I come bearing grave news. I do not know how but the alchemists' poison appears to have infiltrated our settlement and infected our land. Worse still, it appears to be targeting our magic itself. The heavier the use of magic, the greater the effect of the poison.'

Anxious mutterings stole round the circle, and Leyla had to raise her voice to be heard over them. 'No one is to practise magic *for any reason,* not until we divine the source of the poisoning. But the fact remains that we cannot stay here and wait for more of us to fall ill.'

'So what do you propose?' someone called. 'Are we to flee this supposed poison only to starve in the wilderness?'

There was a general murmur of consensus.

Leyla looked taken aback – she wasn't used to people here disagreeing with her. 'I have no plans to let anyone starve in the wilderness, but neither can I stand here and watch everything we have built wither and die. I intend to seek out Professor Al-Qamar in the Russlands.'

'What for?'

Leyla cleared her throat. 'I will ask him to plead on our behalf for sanctuary. The Northern Sorcerers still have use of their magic; they can continue the search for a cure. Further … it may be that with the help of the Northern Sorcerers we can move our settlement north of the kingdom, away from the Sultan and his plans.'

The mutterings rose to an outcry.

'To the Russlands? To live with those barbarians?'

'Those wandering donkeys? Who bathe once a year and know no human decency?'

'To live in a frozen wasteland with no sun and no spices?'

'The Grand High Sorceress would not stand for this.'

'Ismah Parveen is dead,' said Leyla, two red spots high on her cheeks. 'She is dead, and I may be a poor substitute, but I am trying to keep you safe.'

The clamour rose, until Yara could no longer make out individual complaints. She glanced up at Meri, and to her surprise the other sorceress looked unhappy. It was giving her no pleasure to see Leyla in such difficulty.

Yara bit her lip. However much she might dislike it, Leyla was right – these people were not ready to fight, and they could not stay, waiting until they all succumbed to the poison.

Her mind made up, Yara got to her feet.

'Stop it! Stop fighting! This is *not* how you get things done. If we don't act, the poison will overwhelm us until we are too weak to fight back against it. Do you think it will spare your children, your grandchildren? Didn't all of you lose enough in the Inquisition?'

Every single eye was trained on her, and Yara felt her face redden. But her speech had silenced the crowd.

'They're afraid,' Mehnoor whispered at her side. 'Before it was all mixed up with anger and resentment, but now it's just fear.'

Encouraged, Yara continued. 'I know you're scared; I am too. This is our home, and all of us here have had enough of leaving our homes behind. But if we go north, we at least have a chance – of growing stronger, of healing the sick. Of returning and fighting back,' she said, meeting Meri's eyes.

Meri hesitated, and then called out, 'Madam Khatoun?'

Leyla turned to look at the other sorceress, and there was apprehension in her eyes – she knew, Yara thought, that Meri could turn the Settlement against her plan with a few well-chosen words.

'Even if you manage to find your friends in the north, who is to say that they will accept us?'

Leyla looked relieved. 'Finding them should be simple enough, with the help of a cartographer. As for the second, we cannot know. And I understand that we cannot hide for ever, but we can survive the winter, and for now that is the best that I can offer.'

'Ibn Munir's a cartographer.' Yara spoke again. 'He told me he had mapped the north before. I'm sure with him you could work out how to find your professor.'

'Indeed.'

Yara could make out the cartographer's face in the assembly. He seemed even frailer than before, his cheeks gaunt and his eyes hollow – but there was a note of pride still detectable in his voice. 'The north is a vast and desert wilderness, and yet I managed it for the Grand High Sorceress, with only—'

'Excellent,' Leyla cut him off hastily, turning to the rest. 'Well? Do I have your support?' She looked round the circle, her eyes settling on Meri.

The sorceress gave a reluctant, almost imperceptible nod, and around her, people seemed to relent.

'Good.' Leyla's shoulders relaxed. 'Now go home and get some rest. I will call another meeting on my return.'

The rest of the night passed in a frantic hurry. The three children were dispatched on a hundred different errands, and by the time Yara had retrieved the maps from Ibn Munir's son-in-law, there was only an hour left before midnight.

'Leyla, how are we going to travel all that way? You heard what he said: if the north is a vast wilderness, we can't possibly walk.'

When the sorceress replied, her voice was far too casual.

'Casting one small spell to get me there will make little difference, I'm sure. At any rate, once we are safely evacuated and have the aid of the Northern Sorcerers, I will have plenty of time to recover from the poison.'

'You can't use magic!' Yara said, horrified. 'Leyla, what if—'

'I don't recall inviting challenge,' Leyla said sharply. 'What risks I choose to take for the good of this community are entirely my own business, and I do not care to hear another word on the matter.'

Yara glowered. 'Fine. But it's not just your own business, you know. I'm allowed to worry about you.'

Leyla didn't seem to know what to say to that. Her

mouth opened and closed without effect, until finally she said, 'Come on. We have no more time to waste.'

Yara had wondered what spell could take them somewhere so far – wondered how it must feel to disappear and reappear in another place hundreds of miles away. So lost in thought was she that she almost didn't notice Leyla emerge from their house with a rug rolled under her arm. Yara looked at her in confusion – and then the penny dropped.

'That's not a magic carpet?'

'A *magic carpet*,' Leyla enunciated disdainfully, spreading the rug out on the floor. 'What an inelegant turn of phrase.'

'I always wondered how you got out of the city.'

Yara turned round – Meri had appeared behind them almost without Yara noticing. It was hard to tell in the dark, but Yara thought she saw Leyla's cheeks turn pink. Before Leyla could reply, however, Rafi and Mehnoor returned.

'I got the rest of the supplies – and gloves from Madam Zahrawi, look.'

'Good,' said Leyla, recovering her composure. 'With any luck I'll be with the Northern Sorcerers by dawn.'

She cleared her throat, standing in front of the carpet and holding out her hands. Yara knew then that she was about to witness something extraordinary. Magic usually moved through Leyla like she was breathing – if she was preparing herself like this, it must be something really exciting.

In clear, ringing tones, the sorceress called out:

'Like longing on the wind.

Like an eagle in flight.

Let us rise from the ground

And soar into the night.'

The carpet seemed to prick its ears at Leyla's words, its tassels fluttering in an invisible breeze. Then, with all the elegance of the sorceress herself, it rose, hovering a metre in the air.

'Whoa,' Yara breathed.

'Leyla!' said Meri suddenly. 'Leyla, what's wrong?'

Yara looked up. Leyla's brown skin had drained of colour and her breathing was laborious.

'I'm fine,' she said. 'Nothing I didn't expect.' But even those few words tripped her up, her consonants falling into each other. She took an unsteady step. 'Let me take a moment to catch my breath.'

She had not gone far when she stumbled, and had Meri not stepped forward to catch her, she would have gone plummeting towards the ground.

'Leyla!'

The sorceress did not reply. Her eyes had become glassy and unfocused; her jaw was slack.

'Her gloves.' Rafi's voice was taut with dread. 'Peel back her gloves!'

Yara did as she was told, holding up the sorceress's hand to the lantern light. Spreading up her wrist was a terrible leaden grey.

Chapter Seventeen

By the time they got Leyla up the stairs and into her bed, the rise and fall of her chest was so faint that she might not have been breathing at all. Already the grey had spread up her arms and fanned across her jaw, as though there were cobwebs growing beneath her skin. Yara stared, held fast by a memory of two months before, when she had stood by a hospital bed and watched life go out from her mum like the tide.

Ajal, who had come up behind them so quietly that Yara had barely registered his presence, nudged her hand until it was resting on his head. Meanwhile, Meri seemed at a loss as to what to do with herself; her face was drained of all its warmth.

There was a beating of wings, and Shehzad was at the window. He looked nothing like his usual self – his feathers dull and his eyes blank. Still, he moved to Leyla's bedside, his wings brushing her cheek.

'Shehzad, it's Leyla, she won't wake up . . .'

For once, the raven had no retorts on his beak. He regarded Yara exhaustedly, before lowering his head once again.

'That's what happens when a familiar's sorcerer begins to weaken,' Mehnoor whispered. 'Their powers are so linked that the jinn fades too. They become more like their animal form.'

'If that's happening already . . .' Rafi trailed off. 'What are we going to do?'

Meri's hands fluttered helplessly by her side. 'I . . . I don't know. We can make her comfortable, but—'

'Make her comfortable?' Yara could hear her voice getting higher in desperation. 'Meri, we have to make an antidote – there must be something, some potion or remedy. Or we could send someone else north . . . ?'

'There's no one else. Leyla might have had enough influence as the Professor's student to seek aid from the Northern Sorcerers, but without her . . .' She trailed off, and came to sit by Leyla's bedside, smoothing back hair that had fallen from the sorceress's turban. 'You know, I spent over a decade telling myself I hated Leyla Khatoun, and that I never wanted to see her again. Now I find out that neither of these things were ever true, and it's too late for me tell her.' Meri managed a thin smile that wasn't really a smile at all. 'She always was contrary like that.'

'What happened between you two?' asked Yara, no longer able to help herself. 'We know it wasn't always like this – I know you wore Leyla's braid of hair on your wrist.'

'Yes. She gave that to me when we were seventeen.' Meri's eyes softened. 'Leyla was my best friend growing up – we were inseparable. We used to meet up in the passages connecting the houses of Istehar Way and sneak into the Great Library, staying up all night wrapped in its magic and talking about all the places we would visit together, and the discoveries we would make. And as we grew older, I began to wonder – well, hope really – that we might be more than friends one day.

'Then something changed. In the months before the Inquisition we started to quarrel over the smallest thing; she stopped coming to our meeting point in the passages – and then it happened, and we fought over the right thing to do. I wanted to stay and fight; she wanted to escape into the mountains. It got out of control, and we both started saying things – awful things – that neither of us meant, but which neither of us could work out how to take back.'

She looked down at Leyla, who was frowning in her sleep. 'Even after that, I really thought we would mend things – but she left. Took off in the middle of the night without so much as a goodbye, and without telling me where she was going. She broke my heart. I understand what she did, of course I do – she was free to practise magic out here. Even if that freedom was only ever fleeting.'

'Don't talk like that. We can fix this, all of it.' Yara fought to make her voice reassuring, even as she felt her magic begin to spark at her fingertips. 'We can … I don't know … we can work on a cure, we can fight off alchemists, but we can't give up on the people here.'

'Leyla was right.' It was as if Yara had not spoken. Meri looked into the fire, her face blank with misery. 'There was never any point in trying to fight. They won twelve years ago; we were only delaying the inevitable. I should have told her to run further.'

Yara got to her feet, angrier than she had ever felt before. 'No. No, you're wrong! You're wrong!'

'Yara—'

Not stopping to hear what the sorceress had to say, she ran down the stairs and out of the house, magic coursing through her like wildfire. There was no one around to stare and point; doors were shut and the houses were dark within. She ran further.

Yara came to the edge of the Settlement, and stopped, hard. She could hear mourning wails coming from the refugee encampment. With a lurch of her stomach she made out Ibn Munir's son-in-law, his arm round his wife's shoulder, his other hand resting on the head of his weeping son.

With a wordless, frustrated sob Yara lowered her hands and sent her magic thundering into the ground, shaking the earth beneath her feet. Her thoughts were tumbling amidst rage and grief, and she barely noticed when Ajal materialised next to her.

He butted her gently with his horns. 'Give your magic to me.'

Yara shook her head, her lips clamped together. She wanted to *feel it*; she wanted it to hurt.

'You are putting yourself in danger of the poison,' Ajal reminded her.

He was right. Reluctantly, Yara wrapped her arms around his neck and let her magic flow into the jinn in a rush.

'What's the point,' she said, her voice choked, 'of having all this power, if I'm too weak to use it? If I can't help and just sit by and watch as people die over and over.'

Ajal considered her words. 'Was it this great power of yours that made you voyage to Zehaira? Or free me from captivity – or seek out Madam Khatoun? It seems to me that you did these things yourself.'

Yara didn't reply, watching as Ibn Munir's family carried his shroud to the edge of the forest. As they did, she felt the first few flakes of snow fall from the sky.

'Perhaps Meri is right. Perhaps there really is no hope left here.'

Even as she spoke, every fibre of Yara's being rebelled against the idea. Leyla hadn't given up; she had fought for their people until it almost killed her. Mama wouldn't have either – she might not have had magic, but she had helped people all her life, and she had never let herself be defeated, not by anything.

Lowering her eyebrows, Yara closed her eyes, thinking of Mehnoor and Rafi. She imagined pushing her thoughts into their heads the same way she had tried with Ajal, summoning them to her side as gently and quietly as she could.

She wasn't waiting long. The snow was heavier now, but she could see the two of them approaching, their faces painted with astonishment. In spite of everything Yara felt a spark of excitement at what she had done.

'Nine stars,' Rafi grumbled, one hand still held to his ear, but looking grudgingly impressed. 'You didn't have to shout. How did you *do* that?'

'Is everything all right?' Mehnoor asked.

'No, it's not,' said Yara, 'but we're going to change that.'

'We? What are *we* going to do?'

'We're going to fly the carpet north and ask for the aid of the Northern Sorcerers ourselves.'

Mehnoor and Rafi were regarding her as though

she had sprouted a second head. Even Ajal seemed taken aback.

'You heard Auntie Meri,' said Mehnoor. 'Even she wouldn't have enough influence with the Northern Sorcerers. What hope would three children have?'

'Not just any three children.' Yara turned to Rafi. 'It's *your* great-uncle Leyla was seeking out. You could talk to him – and then the Northern Sorcerers would have to listen if he spoke on our behalf.'

Any doubt in Rafi's eyes was pushed out by pride; he drew himself to his full height, puffing out his chest. 'Of course. He's an Al-Qamar – and the finest scholar in the world.'

'Exactly. With someone like him on our side, they can't possibly say no. We can evacuate, we can have help working on a cure – we can save Leyla. Someone like him might even be able to help us fight the alchemists.'

Mehnoor chewed her lip, her forehead dented by her frown. 'You're the one who goes on adventures,' she said anxiously. 'I just read about them. There are so many ways this could go wrong ...'

'I know. And you don't have to come if you don't want to – but this is how we can be useful. We can make the Northern Sorcerers see that they have to do the right thing.'

Mehnoor swallowed audibly. 'All right. We can't tell

Aunt Meri, though; she'll be better off not knowing until we get back.'

'Good. Meet back by the house in half an hour, with warm clothes and lanterns. I'll get Leyla's map.'

The other two left. Next to her, Ajal was silent, but Yara could sense his thoughts flickering. 'What? What is it?'

'I worry,' he said slowly, 'that you have not thought this through.'

'We have a plan—'

'A plan. That you three children will talk to these strange sorcerers and persuade them to help you out of the *goodness of their hearts.*'

'Don't say it like that.' Yara's mouth felt very dry. 'Like it's silly – like it's impossible.'

'It is impossible, because people have hearts that are small and shrivelled and closed off. Yet you continue to harbour the belief that people will help you if you ask – despite all evidence you have seen to the contrary.'

'Not in spite of that. Because of everything I've seen here.' She gestured. 'Look around. Look at all the people who've taken others into their homes!'

'Yes, and listen to the muttering behind closed doors, the discontent and accusations. You cannot simply talk people into doing what you consider to be the right thing.'

Yara clenched her jaw. 'Yeah? Just you watch me.' She waited. 'Well? Are you going to come with us?'

Ajal looked at her, and his expression was inscrutable.

'The north is a dangerous place for a jinn,' he said finally. 'We are creatures of fire – we are not made for cold climates. The people there do not understand our kind.'

'But if you were with me—'

'I am a free being –' Ajal's voice flared above her own – 'not your familiar; I answer to no human's command. I have made my decision, and if you cannot respect it then we must part ways this instant.'

Yara swallowed. She could feel a familiar angry voice needling in her head: *He doesn't care about you; he just wants to leave . . .* She shook her head, pushing it back down. 'I understand. Wish me luck, then.'

Stealthy as a cat, Yara moved through the cottage and up to Leyla's room, relying on the moonlight streaming through the window to guide her path. It cast a faint glow on Leyla's face, making her look paler in the darkness. Meri appeared to have fallen asleep on the floor beside her bed, still half sat up and her hand brushing Leyla's. She looked so troubled that Yara's heart ached for her, and ached further still at the thought of leaving her behind.

'Leyla,' she whispered, 'we have to go to the Russlands. But you mustn't ... you mustn't get any worse while we're away. You still haven't told me how you knew Mama, and there's so much you have to teach me – and still a million things I haven't forgiven you for. You are absolutely not allowed to go.'

The sorceress's face was unchanged, as serene as it had been before. Quickly and quietly Yara picked up the sorceress's shawls and retrieved the maps, pausing to look at her one last time before fleeing the room, her footsteps light on the stairs.

'Auntie Meri didn't stop you?' asked Mehnoor, as Yara rejoined their group.

'No. She won't know we're gone until she wakes up.'

Yara felt a flash of guilt, imagining the sorceress searching the house for them until she realised that she was all on her own. As Mehnoor handed her a sheepskin, she saw the same thought travelling through her mind.

'Come on,' said Rafi, winding one of Leyla's black headscarves round his face until only his eyes were visible. 'The longer we take, the longer Madam Shereen will be worrying about us.'

Yara nodded and, trying to look more confident than she felt, led the other two over to where they had abandoned the carpet. It was hovering above the ground, and she could feel the low hum of its magic, shifting and reckless after years spent warming the stone floor. Leyla's spell must still be working. They arranged themselves on the carpet, watching each other nervously.

'Have either of you flown a flying carpet before?' Yara asked. Their task suddenly felt a lot more real, hovering on the cold edge of the night.

'Leyla's already done the spell. We just tell it where to go; there's no magic to it.' Rafi cleared his throat, and gave the carpet a short sharp tap. 'Take us to Professor Al-Qamar, in the Russlands.'

Yara thought she detected a sceptical air about the carpet, the same way Leyla might regard Rafi with disapproval after a particularly lacklustre command. It gave a half-hearted flutter but did not seem inclined to obey them. Rafi tried again. 'Carpet! Do as I say – take us to Professor Al-Qamar, in the Russlands.'

This time, it didn't even bother to move. Next to them, Mehnoor made a noise of realisation.

'It didn't like you speaking to it like that.' She looked over at Rafi. 'This may go against all your sensibilities, but you're going to have to be polite.'

Rafi glared at her, but cleared his throat. 'Um – most magnificent tapestry – would you mind taking us to Professor Al-Qamar? Please?'

The carpet preened beneath them. Then, as gracefully as Shehzad might take wing, they began to gain height, speeding up until they were soaring through the air, skimming the branches of the trees.

Beside Yara, Mehnoor let out a squeak, her nails digging into Yara's arm and her eyes squeezed tightly shut. Meanwhile, Rafi was studying the atlas with intense concentration.

'We have a long way to go until we reach the Russlands. You two get some sleep; we can keep watch in shifts.'

Mehnoor did not need much persuading; she rested her head on one of the bags, clearly intending to block out her surroundings until they were on solid ground once more – but Yara didn't want to close her eyes for so much as a second. She could see forests running beneath them like dark rivers, the light of the moon on the mountains. The stars had never been so close and so bright before, and she moved to lie on her back so that she could see them laid out before her.

There's the constellation of the running women, she thought, her heart aching at the recollection of Leyla standing over her while she had memorised diagrams of the stars. What if she didn't get better? What if they got back from the Russlands and she had ...?

Yara shook herself, wiping furiously at her eyes. *There are the two jinn brothers. And that one is the*

Plough – that's the same in my world. In spite of herself she felt her eyes closing. *And there are the nine stars – the nine sisters . . .*

And then all she could see was bright light, like sunbeams, filling her eyes and throat and radiating right to the tips of her toes. Then a voice: 'You must be so brave. And you must come back. Whatever happens, you must come back.'

Chapter Eighteen

Yara opened her eyes to find her head resting on the extra sheepskins and the carpet hovering in the air almost twitchily, desperate to set off. But Rafi seemed in no hurry.

'What's going on?' Yara rubbed her eyes. 'Are we there?' She felt her magic stir uneasily, and wished more than ever that Ajal was with them.

'No. But I flew by some traders, who said that there were two men from our part of the world living on the edge of the Moscwitch Forest. We can't be far now.'

'So why have we ...?'

Yara trailed off. The night was still dark and starlit, but a glowing light was illuminating the carpet. She looked around. The sky was shifting with fiery colours, burnished and glowing, casting sunset shadows across Rafi's face. As she looked closer, she could make out ethereal swords and shields clashing, and heard horns being sounded in a battle cry.

'The war of the heavens, fought by the two jinn armies of the winter skies,' Mehnoor said in hushed tones, sitting up and rubbing her eyes, her fear forgotten. 'I read about it in a scroll, but never imagined it to be so—'

'So beautiful,' Yara finished, watching as the cloud-like creatures flung themselves at each other over and over again. 'Why are they fighting?'

'No one knows,' said Rafi. 'Leyla said the reason was either lost in time or far beyond human understanding. But every year, close to the northern summit of the earth, we get a glimpse into their world, a world of eternal conflict.' Rafi paused. 'She always said that she dreamed of coming here when she was a student.'

Yara sniffed, tilting her head towards the sky and blinking hard. Mehnoor found her hand, and they watched together in silence, until clouds crossed the sky and the battle faded into the night.

'Wow,' she breathed softly. Rafi seemed to agree, not moving the carpet on until the last trace of weaponry had melted away into the clouds. 'Is it morning?'

'There is no morning here, I don't think. But Leyla packed some flatbread and tea if you want some – they're in her bag.'

'You should have woken us – you said we would sleep in shifts.'

'I didn't mind.' Rafi ducked his head, and Yara caught something that sounded suspiciously like: *It was nice to get a bit of peace and quiet.* 'Anyway, I think we're almost there – look, there's the forest.'

He lowered the carpet until they were skimming the tops of the trees, his eyes scanning the ground.

'The traders said they could be found right at the edge of the forest, close to a village. The main thing is that we mustn't land the carpet before we've found them, because I'm not entirely sure it would get back up again.'

Mehnoor closed her eyes, her face smoothing over as she breathed deeply. Then she said, 'Bear east. There's something there – it feels like a sorcerer.'

Rafi obeyed her. For a while it seemed as though the rows of trees would never break – but then they came to a clearing where there was an old man sat at a telescope, clad in robes of midnight blue, his beard so long and white that it appeared to disappear into the snow.

'I don't believe it.' Rafi lowered the carpet until they were hovering just above the forest floor. 'Professor Al-Qamar?'

The man started, shielding his eyes from the falling snow. 'Yes?' he said warily.

Rafi let out a sigh of relief, and the carpet descended with an inelegant *thump*.

'You might not remember me, but—'

'Goodness gracious,' said the Professor. 'That cannot be my great-nephew? Rizwan, what on earth are you doing here?'

'Rafi.' Yara saw brief hurt flash across the boy's eyes. 'I'm Rafi, Uncle.'

'Rafi? But Rafi was a little boy – I left him with my sister.'

'Yes. Twelve years ago.'

'Twelve years ago? Was it really as long as that?' His eyes misted over. 'My, how time flies. And who are your little friends?'

Yara frowned. The Professor was talking to Rafi as though he had merely misplaced him at a function, rather than neglected him for twelve years. But Rafi didn't seem to notice.

'This is Mehnoor Shereen, and Yara Sulimayah – Yara is another student of Leyla's.'

'Ah, Leyla Khatoun.' The Professor rolled the name on his tongue, barely sparing a glance for Yara. 'Such a disappointment – she was by far the brightest student I ever taught, you know, and I taught all the great sorcerers and sorceresses of Zehaira. I was sure she would outstrip the rest. Yet in her last letter my sister informed me she was wasting her time with herbal remedies and village nonsense.' He fixed Rafi with a stern look. 'I hope she is nevertheless giving you a traditional education – in fact, where is she?' He peered past them, as though expecting to see her emerge from behind a tree.'

'She ... she isn't well,' Rafi said, swallowing. 'Something terrible has happened, Uncle. We've come because we need your help.'

'My help?' Professor Al-Qamar looked at them quizzically. 'Well, I don't know what help you hope to find from two elderly gentlemen living on the edge of the Moscwitch Forest. Still, my companion will be delighted to make your acquaintance.' He turned to his right, raising his voice. 'Amr Haroun! We have visitors.'

A man emerged from the trees, telescope in hand. He was as different from the Professor as it was possible to be, stocky and clean-shaven, his brow hawklike over his eyes. His eyes widened in astonishment. 'Visitors?'

He hurried forward, looking between the three of them. 'Nine stars. Children? Where in the seven spheres did you find them?'

'They found me,' said the Professor cheerfully. 'Three students of Leyla Khatoun – and one of them my own great-nephew, Rafi Al-Qamar! And his esteemed companions, Mehnoor Shereen and ...'

Yara fought the urge to roll her eyes as the Professor searched for her name.

'Students of Leyla's? She is alive?' Haroun's eyes filled with tears. 'Thank the stars. We heard of the Inquisition from the Northern Sorcerers – we owe a thousand apologies for not returning.'

'The Inquisition isn't over,' said Yara. 'This is what we came to tell you – Leyla's ill – and so are other sorcerers in the Settlement. We think they've been poisoned, and we think the Sultan and his alchemists are behind it.'

The two men looked flabbergasted.

'Poisoned?' said Professor Haroun after a while. 'Good grief. You're certain?'

'Yes, and practising magic only makes the effect of the poison worse.'

'Poison, a conspiracy – I must say this all sounds highly unlikely, children,' said Professor Al-Qamar, recovering. 'Madam Khatoun will see off this illness, I am sure. Obviously we are deeply sorry to hear of all this ... unpleasantness towards sorcerers. But then I always said the Sultan was a weak-minded fool, and his vizier not much better.'

Yara exchanged a disbelieving glance with Mehnoor, and looked over at Rafi – but he was staring fixedly at the ground.

'Believe us or don't believe us, I don't care,' Yara said through gritted teeth. 'Our entire community is in danger. We need to persuade the Northern Sorcerers to take us in as refugees.'

There was a stunned silence, and Al-Qamar's face hardened.

'Rafi, your little friend has forgotten herself,' the Professor said coldly. 'That is not the way one addresses a sorcerer many years one's senior. But perhaps such manners are to be expected from a student sorceress with no family name of note.'

Yara ducked her head, biting her lip to stop herself from saying something she would regret.

'The Northern Sorcerers are not welcoming of outsiders,' said Haroun. 'Particularly those of our ... background.'

'Yes, but Leyla thought that if you spoke up on our behalf—'

'Us?' said Professor Al-Qamar, disbelieving. 'You mean to say you wish for *us* to advocate for hundreds of sorcerers to descend on this place?'

'Are you sure that is what Leyla meant, children?' said Haroun. 'Food is scarce, the climate is intemperate ... Your people would find it difficult to make a life out here.'

Yara spoke up again, unable to help herself. 'At least we would *have* lives out here. Surely you don't want to see magic wiped out in the kingdom entirely?'

Professor Al-Qamar scowled, speaking pointedly past

her. 'Even if I were to believe that that idiot of a sultan has somehow happened upon the means to wipe out magic, it is out of the question that I put your request to the Northern Sorcerers.'

'What?' Rafi's voice cracked in disbelief.

'These men tolerate our presence because they understand the value of my work. If I were to start making such demands of them, all their tolerance would vanish, I am certain of it.'

'Does their tolerance mean more to you than our lives?'

'Uncle,' Rafi interjected, before Professor Al-Qamar could register Yara's reply. 'Could you not ask the Council of the Northern Sorcerers for an audience? You don't have to tell them what we want, only that they might hear us as a favour to you. I'm sure a mere introduction from you would help our cause.'

Yara thought that last part was laying it on a bit thick – but the Professor looked mollified.

'Yes, well, no doubt you are right. If you insist, I will procure an audience for you. However—'

Yara cut him off. 'Good. We don't have any time to waste.'

It was a tense wait for the Professor to secure them an audience with the Council. Professor Haroun had brought them back to their stone house at the edge of the forest, but soon made his excuses.

'A meteorological phenomenon – one that will go unobserved if I am not there to report it,' he said.

'Couldn't you speak up for us too?' asked Mehnoor. 'It's not that we don't trust the Professor, but surely with another sorcerer on our side—'

'Ah –' Professor Haroun gave a bitter smile – 'but I am not a sorcerer. I am – or I was once – an alchemist. Oh, you are right to be wary,' he said as the three children recoiled. 'But alchemy was once a noble discipline. We were scientists, philosophers – committed to a deeper understanding of the workings of the universe. Until Omair Firaaz transformed lead into gold, and the minds and hearts of my colleagues were corrupted by greed.'

'Omair Firaaz,' Yara said slowly. 'He was the man I heard on Istehar Way – he was the one who crafted the poison.' She looked earnestly at Professor Haroun. 'You must know more about him and his alchemists than anyone. If you came back with us to the Settlement, we might stand a chance of fighting back.'

Professor Haroun looked at her for a long time. 'I wish I shared your faith in me,' he said softly. 'Good luck, you three.'

But as he turned to leave, he stopped and said, 'Firaaz always hated the sorcerers, but his hatred is matched by his fear. And fear can be exploited.'

With that he left them alone in the house, Rafi pacing the floor and Yara sitting with Mehnoor by the doorway, looking out for the Professor's return.

'Rafi should make the request,' said Yara, turning round to face him.

He stopped pacing, looking at her in abject terror. 'What?'

'If I go up there, I'm as good as invisible – but you're an Al-Qamar, and the Professor's great-nephew; that must mean something.'

'I don't see that it does.' Rafi resumed pacing. 'Most likely I'll make a mess of it. I manage to make a mess of most things, don't I?'

To Yara's surprise he looked genuinely unhappy.

'Do you really think that?'

'I can't cast a decent spell to save my life, or do anything an Al-Qamar is supposed to. I'm a disgrace to my family name.'

Yara sighed, getting to her feet. 'Look,' she said, as kindly as she could, 'the reason you're bad at magic has nothing to do with your family name. It's because you have no imagination.'

'Yara!' Mehnoor sounded scandalised, but she carried on.

'But that doesn't matter here, don't you see? All you

need is a bit more confidence.' Yara viewed him critically. 'You want to be firm; don't mutter, and don't gabble. Tell them in plain words why we're here, and why they should help us. Oh, and stand with your feet apart and your shoulders up – that way you won't fidget.'

Rafi obeyed, regarding her with curiosity. 'When did you learn all this?'

Yara thought about it. 'From Mama, I suppose. I was always campaigning for stuff at home, but she was the one who taught me that people won't always do the right thing by themselves, so you have to persuade them that they should. And she always said no one ever persuaded anyone by mumbling.'

'She sounds wonderful,' said Mehnoor softly.

'She was more than that.' Yara felt a familiar ache in her ribs, but it was tempered with pride for her ordinary mother, with no grand name or magical background. 'She was brilliant. The cleverest, most hard-working, most caring person in the world. It wasn't easy, where we were from – there wasn't anyone who spoke our language; there was hardly anyone who looked like us, or dressed like us, or cooked like us. But she never let me feel like I didn't belong.' Yara's throat worked silently before she spoke again. 'There was always a part of me I couldn't share with anyone else. When she died—'

At that moment the Professor materialised in front of

them, his countenance solemn.

'The Council have agreed to entertain your request,' he said stiffly. 'Allow me to transfer you to the Great Hall.'

Before Yara could register what was happening, the air seemed to shimmer and swirl around them, until they were no longer in the cottage but somewhere else entirely.

The hall was dark and filled with smoke, and Yara could feel animal skins on the floor beneath her feet and see stuffed animal heads staring down from the wall. At the end of the room were three stone chairs, austere and unadorned. She shivered, drawing closer to the other two. 'It'll be all right,' she said in a whisper. 'They're sorcerers themselves – they must want to help us.'

Just then, there came the sound of footsteps, and three men strode in, taking their seats on the three stone chairs. Professor Al-Qamar stood at the side of the room, his hands folded respectfully over his middle.

Yara stared. These men had matted red beards and wore furs that reeked of rotting fish, the smell so pungent it was making her eyes water. But there was an air about the trio that Yara recognised from home. She squared her shoulders, looking directly back at them.

'Children?' The middle one spoke, his derision unmistakable. 'Al-Qamar, have we convened to welcome these infants?'

'That welcome would be gratefully received,

Councillors.' Rafi touched the palm of his hand to his heart. 'We have heard great things of your wisdom and might, and—'

'Spare us your pleasantries,' the third one interrupted. 'We may as well entertain you, now we are here. Make your petition quickly.'

Flustered, Rafi cleared his throat. Yara nodded at him encouragingly.

'C-Council of the Northern Sorcerers, we have come here to beg for your mercy. There has been an attack on our community, and we face certain death at the hands of the Sultan and his alchemists without your help.'

He paused, and Yara tried to gauge their reactions – but the sorcerers' eyes gave nothing away. Rafi continued, stronger than before. 'Last week, sorcerers began to fall ill in the old city of Zehaira, and the guards would arrest and execute them the moment their illness became known. We believe these people were poisoned. What's more, whatever poison was used, it has reached our settlement too.'

'And what is it you request from us?' the second man asked.

Taken aback by the directness of the question, Rafi stumbled. 'I ... I mean, help. Help to leave the Sultan's kingdom and find some cure for our people, until we are strong enough to return and drive out the alchemists.

We will pay whatever tax is necessary; we will give you our labour, our skill, all the magical knowledge we have.' He collected himself, looking at them squarely as he delivered his last few words. 'If you do not give us sanctuary, then our crops will wither and our people will sicken and the last sorcerers of Zehaira will be no more.'

Rafi relaxed, looking as though he had run a marathon rather than delivered a relatively short speech. Meanwhile, the council were mulling over their words, their heads bent together.

Mehnoor leaned over to Rafi. 'That was brilliant,' she whispered. 'They can't possibly say no after that.'

Before Rafi could reply, the first man spoke again. 'You expect us to cede land to you?' His eyebrows were raised in incredulity. 'You, who are not our people, and to whom we owe no allegiance? Our countrymen would never stand for it.'

'It is monstrous to ask it of us,' the second agreed, regarding them as though they were something particularly nasty on the bottom of his shoe. 'We expect the winter to be long and hard this year. Are our own people to suffer so that we might give you charity?'

'And do we know that this sickness is, in fact, a poison and not contagious?' the third asked. He had drawn his furs tighter round his face, as though he might shield himself from whatever foreign plague he imagined they had brought. 'We would not only be robbing our people; we would also be endangering them.'

'Council of the Northern Sorcerers ...' Rafi began again. 'Please, if you turn your backs on us now, we have nowhere else—'

'Enough.' The first man held up his hand. 'We tolerate your eccentric countryman for his work and his counsel. But even he would not appear to countenance the entirety of your people setting up home here.'

He turned to Professor Al-Qamar, who remained gravely silent.

'As I suspected. I have always said with your lot that to give an inch is to lose a mile—'

'What do you mean "our lot"—' Yara began, but Rafi stood on her foot, hard.

'Then it is settled.' The second elder rose to his feet, and the others followed suit. 'Children, we are deeply sorry for your losses, but I am afraid we cannot aid your people at this time.'

With short cursory bows, the three men took their leave, scarcely acknowledging Professor Al-Qamar as they swept from the room.

Chapter Nineteen

Rafi stood where he was for a while, staring after the Northern Sorcerers as though unable to believe they had left. Eventually it was Mehnoor who stepped forward, her hand hovering above his arm.

'Come on. We should leave.'

'Maybe we could go after them. It might not be too late – we just need to persuade them to do the right thing.' He turned to Yara. 'Isn't that what you said?'

Yara opened her mouth and then closed it again. For once she had no answer.

'Yes,' said Mehnoor, and there was a grave wisdom to her words. 'But we told them people would die, and they didn't care. We've done all that we can.'

'Well, children.' Professor Al-Qamar approached them. 'I did try to warn you.'

'I'm sorry, Uncle,' Rafi muttered, hanging his head.

'Yes, well, if you are truly worried about this so-called

poison, you are more than welcome to stay here. Indeed, perhaps it would be best for me to take your schooling in hand.' He waved a hand in Yara's direction. 'Your friends may stay too if they wish.'

Yara dug her nails into the palm of her hand to stop herself from speaking.

'We can't possibly stay.' Rafi's voice was incredulous. 'Didn't you hear us? Leyla needs our help.'

'Leyla Khatoun has squandered her talents and my teaching; I am only sorry that I entrusted her with your education in the first place. Still, I suppose not every brilliant student is destined to match their promise.'

Yara's self-restraint, stretched perilously taut since they had first met the Professor, finally snapped completely.

'*How dare you?*' she said, looking at the Professor with an expression of such dislike that it was a wonder he didn't drop dead on the spot. 'How dare you say that about Leyla? She gave up everything she wanted to do so that she could help people who needed her.'

'Exactly,' Professor Al-Qamar said, an angry flush to his cheeks. 'She gave it up. She threw away all that I taught her.'

'Because it was the right thing to do!' Yara clenched her fists. 'Because ...' She remembered something she had heard what felt like a lifetime ago. 'Because the only true measure of our character is how we respond to someone who needs our help. And by that measure you're no great sorcerer. You are a selfish, arrogant old coward, who would let people die so he can carry on his *research* in peace. Well, I hope it makes you happy – because if the alchemists succeed, there will be none of us left to hear about it.'

She didn't wait for the Professor to react to her words. Turning on her heel, she stalked away towards the forest, wiping her eyes with blind fury.

It was a while before she heard two pairs of footsteps in the snow beside her.

'Don't say a word,' she snapped at Rafi. 'If I hear one more word from an Al-Qamar, I'm going to scream.'

'I wasn't going to say anything,' Rafi snapped back. 'Do you think I'm proud to be related to someone like him?' Yara could see that the pillars of his whole world had come crashing down around his ears, but she had no sympathy.

'You were proud enough before. Talking about ancestry and birthstones and family background, listening to him rubbish Leyla's work like that; honestly it makes me *sick*—'

'Stop it!' Mehnoor caught Yara's wrist. 'We can't fight – you said so yourself; there's no time. We need to work out where to go next.'

'What do you mean "go next"?' Angry tears were

smarting at the corners of her eyes, and, coupled with the falling snow, it was increasingly difficult to see. 'We've failed. There's no way out – no one who can help us. We may as well just go home.'

'You can't mean that.' Mehnoor shook her head. 'I don't believe you. You crossed the sea, you found Leyla Khatoun, you took us north. You're not going to give up, not now.'

'This was Leyla's last idea,' said Rafi.

'Yes,' Mehnoor replied patiently. 'So now I want to hear what Yara thinks.'

Yara felt as though she could cry. 'I don't have a plan; I never have. It was Leyla who told us to come here; it was Mama who sent me over the sea; if Meri hadn't found me on Istehar Way then . . .' She stopped. In spite of herself the smallest kernel of an idea was unfurling in her mind.

'There,' said Mehnoor excitedly, 'you're thinking. What are you thinking?'

'That's where it all started, when I overheard Firaaz on Istehar Way.' As Yara spoke, she could feel her thoughts forming themselves into ideas. 'He was showing off the poison to the Vizier. What if we flew the carpet to Zehaira and found his work? Maybe then we could work out a way to stop it.'

Rafi stared at her in disbelief. 'I'm sorry. Do you mean to say that you wish not only for us to stick our heads into the lion's mouth, but while we're there have a hunt around for his teeth?'

'I know it's dangerous,' Yara admitted. 'But Mehnoor's right: time is running out, and not just for Leyla. We can't sit back while magic dies out in the kingdom – we have to help. It's not a choice. It's the only way we can survive in a world that's trying to destroy us.'

'We could be captured,' said Rafi. 'Imprisoned, killed – we could find the poison itself and be none the wiser.'

'Maybe. But we would have done everything we can. You two don't have to come, though, if you don't want to.'

'Yes, we do.' To Yara's amazement this came from Mehnoor, whose face was alight with a fierce courage she had not seen before. 'We're your friends. Where you go, we go. Whatever we do, we do together.'

Yara saw a brief struggle play out across Rafi's features, and then he nodded. 'Where you go, we go,' he echoed. 'What we do, we do together.'

They hurried back to where they had left the carpet, rolled up and tied lifelessly round a pine tree. As they loosened it from the branches and laid it on the ground, Rafi was visibly steeling himself, muttering the spell under his breath.

'Let me do it.' Yara bit her lip. 'This was my idea, and you saw what happened to Leyla.'

'You might catapult us to the moon,' said Rafi not unkindly. 'Leyla took that risk. If she can do it, then so can I.'

Rafi stood on the carpet, taking a deep breath and holding his hands out in front of him.

'Like longing on the wind.

Like an eagle in flight.

Let us rise from the ground

And soar into the night.'

The carpet fluttered a little at the tassels, as though it were considering stirring itself, but flopped back on to the ground with a pointed shiver.

Meanwhile, Rafi retched, bringing up a hand to his mouth.

'Ugh, I can *taste* it. It's awful – like metal in my mouth.'

He cleared his throat, his hands shaking as he repeated the words of the spell. This time he succeeded in raising them several metres off the ground, holding his breath all the while, but upon exhaling the three of them came crashing down, collapsing in an undignified heap.

'It's no good.' Rafi puffed, glaring at the obstinate carpet. 'I can't do it.'

Yara tried not to let her disappointment show too obviously. The snow began to fall harder than before, and Leyla's shawls weren't enough to keep her from shivering.

'Maybe the Professor could do the spell for us. I'm sure if I went back and apologised—'

Mehnoor cut her off, her voice quiet and afraid. 'Yara, don't look round.'

Yara felt an icy trickle of fear run down the back of her neck. 'Why?'

'Doesn't matter. I think you'll have to do the spell.'

'Her? Are you mad?' Rafi said.

'We don't have a choice.' Mehnoor's eyes were lamp-like with fright. 'They're here. I can feel them.'

Yara let out a shaky breath. In the quiet of the forest she could hear a low rumbling snarl and the sound of paws padding the snow behind her. And then it didn't matter that she wasn't looking around, because in front of her a pair of yellow eyes were blinking malevolently into the darkness.

'Rafi,' she whispered, 'behind you.'

Rafi stilled, not moving a muscle. 'Do the spell,' he managed to say. 'Now.'

'But I—'

She was interrupted by a growl that was far too close. There were more eyes now, and Yara could smell shaggy fur and rotting meat. In the corner of her eye she made out the licking of lips.

'Now, Yara!' Mehnoor's voice rose to a shout.

Panicking, she cried out:

'Like longing on the wind.

Like an eagle in flight.

Let us rise from the ground

And soar into the night.'

Yara heard the sudden flurry of snow behind her, felt hot breath on the back of her neck – and then the carpet shot forward into the air, flinging off the encroaching wolves with its force.

Within seconds the trees were pinpricks beneath them; they travelled so fast Yara expected the wind to slice through them as easily as she chopped onions.

'Stop!' Rafi howled. 'Yara, make it stop!'

'I don't know how!' Yara roared back. She couldn't see the forest now – only the lights of the Northern Sorcerers' encampment, and even they were like twinkling stars beneath them. She held on to the carpet's tassels as tightly as she could. 'Stop!' she cried out. 'Stop, stop!'

The carpet came to an abrupt halt, almost throwing its passengers overboard in the process. Then, with a graceful motion of its tassels, the carpet began to plummet down towards the earth, picking up speed as it went.

'What do we do?' she shouted.

Rafi's eyes were blown wide with fear, but his voice was steady. 'We need to slow down!' he yelled back.

'I can't! I can't control it.'

'Then don't control it. Find another force that's just as strong.'

Another force that was just as strong? Yara couldn't think what he meant. The ground was getting closer, and fear was squeezing her ribcage in a way that made it difficult to think. And then she saw his hair whipped back in the breeze, and it came to her.

'Wind!' she yelled. 'We need wind!' She held out her hands.

'Like longing on the wind.

Like an eagle in flight.

Awake, North Wind,
And save us from the night!'

And as she finished speaking, a great gust of wind rose beneath them, and their fall slowed as they were borne away on a current of air.

'I can't keep this up for much longer.' Yara fought to make her voice heard over the tempest and saw from the fresh terror on her friends' faces that she had been successful. But what could she do? The wind renewed itself, and they were blown off course once more, Mehnoor saved from tumbling from the carpet only by Rafi's claw-like grip on her wrist.

Yara closed her eyes, trying to concentrate her desperate thoughts. *Help.* She tried to send the words out like a beacon into the night. *Please, please help us.*

At first there was nothing but the howl of the gale, twisting and thrashing, but then, faintly at first but growing stronger, she sensed a sparking heat on the back of her neck, and the sound of a roaring flame.

'Yara?' Ajal's voice sounded on the breeze, and she could have sobbed in relief as a large cloud descended, engulfing them in its glow. Their flight slowed and stilled in the air, and the three children caught their breath.

'Ajal! You came. I'm sorry; I know what you said . . .'

'Never mind that.' There was a tremor in the jinn's voice that Yara did not think she had ever heard before. 'Let me take you home.'

'Not home.' Yara looked round at Rafi and Mehnoor, and drew her eyebrows down as far as they would go. 'We're going to Zehaira.'

Chapter Twenty

It was an odd sensation, travelling with Ajal. It was as though they were not moving at all, but rather time and space were shifting around them, so that they traversed rivers and forests and villages in a single instant.

Yara stretched out her hand. She could feel Ajal's magic suspended around them, as strange and flickering as his speech, but beautiful too, spiralling like starlight. It felt ancient, unknowable – as though she might bask in it for thousands of years and still have no inkling of its true power.

The sky began to pale with the oncoming dawn, and as the city domes became visible in the distance Ajal slowed his flight. They were not alone in their journey to the city. Beneath them Yara could make out a line of people streaming forward, their number steadily increasing as men and women joined their progress from villages in the hills.

Soon enough the city gates loomed ahead, and Ajal landed them in a thicket of trees.

'This is where I have to leave you. Free jinn cannot pass through the city walls – your kind saw to that centuries ago.'

'Thank you,' Yara whispered. 'We'll be back before you know it.'

Ajal looked unconvinced. 'Be careful, Yara Sulimayah,' he said quietly. 'Do not underestimate the depths of human depravity.'

'There are people going past now,' said Mehnoor, peering out from the trees. 'We should join them.'

Yara reached up to the cloud that was Ajal, and imagined her hand was where his head would be as a goat. 'Trust me. We'll be fine.'

The three of them slipped silently among the crowd. They were coming up to the city gates now, and guards were eyeing them warily, their hands at the hilts of their scimitars. They passed them and Yara ducked her head, pulling her headscarf further over her eyes – but the guards weren't interested in the children. Their eyes were fixed on the farmers: hardy men and women with weathered faces and arms that had grown strong at their ploughs. Straining her ears, Yara could hear them muttering on either side of her.

'Our winter crop black and withered …'

'Not just the crop; the soil itself is dying …'

The tension was rising around them now, sparking in the air like electricity. The guards felt it too, and then without so much as a signal they moved as one, forming a barricade at the end of the street. The march came to a halt, their progress barred by the line of guards. One marked out by his gold brocade stepped forward.

'Step back,' he barked. 'You will go no further tonight.'

A man from the crowd stepped out. 'We mean no harm.' There was a hollowness in his cheeks and eyes that gave his words a desperate sincerity. 'We mean only to petition the Sultan. Our families will perish if he does not give us grain.'

'The Sultan is aware of your plight.' The guard's grip on his sword tightened. 'His Majesty mourns the suffering of his people, but he is not seeing petitioners today. Go home.'

'We cannot go home,' the man said patiently. 'If we go home, we will watch our children starve.'

'Go home. That is an order from your sovereign.'

The man stood, unmoving, and Yara could see the guard's sword hand shaking. Somehow, without once raising his voice, the hollow-cheeked man had got the upper hand.

Meanwhile, the crowd were growing restless, murmurings and mutterings rising like the tide until a woman stepped forward, clutching at the guard's robes and sobbing, 'Have mercy, have mercy and help us.'

The woman's words broke a dam: pleas and threats and accusations were pelted at the guards like missiles, until they raised their swords and charged. There was panic then. People began to scream and push past each other, and Yara gripped tight to Rafi and Mehnoor, terrified that they would be crushed.

'Aim for the street!' she shouted, and the three of them began to slip through the hordes, weaving round those fleeing until they were able to wriggle free and run down an alleyway, not stopping until the roar of the crowd was distant behind them.

'They weren't armed.' Mehnoor was out of breath, but Yara had never heard her so angry. 'They weren't armed, and they can't run away. They'll be slaughtered.'

'Nothing we can do,' Rafi panted, leaning against a wall. 'This is our best chance at making it to Istehar Way.'

'But—'

'No time. Come on, where do we go?'

After a few reluctant looks in the direction of the crowd, Mehnoor nodded. 'This way.'

Others were pouring on to the streets now, more often than not with several guards in pursuit, and the three would have to press themselves within the shadows of the warehouses to avoid detection.

'There's a passage the flour merchants use,' Mehnoor whispered. 'No one will find us there.'

Yara and Rafi followed her down the winding path until there were no more warehouses, and they had to weave among sandstone buildings, now dull and grey. The first spattering of sleet was coming now, drops hitting the street so hard they seemed to ricochet on impact. Yara's qamis began to cling unpleasantly to her skin.

'Here.'

They came to a halt, and Yara stifled a gasp. They were in the square Ibn Munir had once directed her to, but she wouldn't have recognised it. There was the eucalyptus that had once called her name – but the bright white of its trunk was blackened, the scent of rotting leaves heavy in the air. Its branches reached out like grasping bony fingers, and Yara instinctively went to it, placing her hand carefully on its trunk.

'Yara, we need to go.'

She brushed off Rafi's impatience. 'It's dying.'

'It's the well of magic in Zehaira.' Mehnoor looked grave, coming to stand next to Yara and placing her own hand on its trunk. 'It was one of the first signs that something was wrong.'

Yara moved closer, pressing her cheek against the bark.

'Go,' she told it in a whisper. 'Go in peace.' There was another whimper, and then the tree gave a great rushing sigh like wind through its branches. Then nothing.

Yara stepped back, and it wasn't until Mehnoor put an arm round her that she realised she was trembling.

'Come on,' she said. 'We're almost there.'

In the night the street seemed even more forbidding than it had before, the gold calligraphy eerily bright in the gloom.

Rafi leaned forward to read the engraving. 'It's about how they triumphed over the sorcerers. How they showed them to be nothing but charlatans, and brought about a new age of enlightenment and reason.' He clenched his fists. 'I suppose they'll have to expand it to include their latest success.'

'This one isn't going to be a success,' Yara promised him. 'We'll see to that.'

Rafi's shoulders were hunched around his ears, his eyes fixed on the pavement. 'I didn't think it would be this different,' he muttered. 'I thought it would be like I remembered. I don't think I could even find my old house.'

'You lived here?'

'Of course. This was the Sorcerers' Quarter – we all lived here. My aunt said I used to play on this street with my cousins.'

'And me,' said Mehnoor. 'I was only a baby when

they expelled us, but my father used to bring me here to see Auntie Meri, when she was a student.' She looked over at Rafi. 'We might have known each other if things hadn't changed.'

Yara felt a twinge of jealousy at the way the two of them were looking around them. This was something that connected them, a part of their history. Yara might learn as much about magic as she wished, but she would never have that. She tried to shake off the feeling.

'Come on. The third-to-last house is just here.'

But, as she spoke, they were forced to a sudden halt. Since Yara had last been to Istehar Way, guards had been posted at the door, and as they crept round the side of the building they saw more loitering by the cellar.

'Looks like you made an impact on your last visit,' Rafi said in an undertone. 'We'll have to find another way in.'

'Where?' said Yara. 'There will be guards all the way round the house.'

'Maybe we don't need to go *directly* to the house,' said Mehnoor. 'Aunt Meri said that when she used to visit Leyla, they used the passages running under the street. Surely not all of them will have guards stationed at the threshold.'

'But these houses belong to the alchemists now,' said Rafi. 'The passages might be blocked up – or we might walk straight into their arms.'

'He's right,' said Yara. 'The alchemists stole every means of connecting that the sorcerers had. They wouldn't have left the passages.'

Mehnoor chewed her lip. 'They might have left one,' she said, and her voice trembled. 'After they burned down the library, they never built anything else. Auntie said it was to mark what they had done to the sorcerers, but I think they were too scared. An act of violence and destruction as great as that fire, with all that magical energy in the library – there are things that even the alchemists wouldn't dare approach. They might have left the passage there open.'

'Might,' said Rafi. 'That's not a lot to pin Leyla's life on.'

'Maybe not,' said Yara grimly. 'But I think it's all we've got.'

Chapter Twenty-One

Whenever Yara had pictured the Great Library, she had imagined rising smoke and falling ash, the charred remains of scrolls scattered on the ground. Of course, more than twelve years after its destruction, none of these things could be seen; yet somehow their absence made the ruined, blackened walls of the library all the bleaker. She could see the remnants of a stone staircase, and a mosaicked floor, and shelves that must have reached right up to the dome but which were now crumbling beneath the open sky.

As they stepped across the stone threshold of the library, the air grew colder, and Yara felt a powerful wave of magic wash over her. This place was as alive as the eucalyptus had once been, but with none of its warmth, or spark. Fascinated, she reached out her hand to touch a stone pillar – and was instantly drenched with an icy shock of dread and despair. Yara remembered what Leyla had said about magic that drew you in and guided you to the books you needed most. After twelve years of neglect, all she could feel was something twisted and grasping, something that wanted to lead her into the dark.

'We shouldn't linger,' said Mehnoor. From the look on her face she could feel it too. 'Whatever power this place still has, it won't tolerate us for long. Look for steps going down.'

They split up, each searching in a different direction. Yara gritted her teeth, trying to concentrate on the task at hand – but her palms were clammy, her heart beating uncertainly in her chest. The dread she had felt coming in seemed more palpable now; she could hear whispers around her, a hundred phantom hands seemed to be brushing at her arms ...

She felt something grasp at her and almost cried out – but it was only Mehnoor, reaching for her arm.

'I don't like it either,' her friend said quietly. 'The sooner we find the passage, the better.'

'It's not just that. I keep thinking about it – thousands of years of learning just disappearing into smoke and ash. Leyla said we might never recover all of it. That it might just disappear and no one would ever remember the old ways.'

Mehnoor tilted her head, considering this. 'In the

history book you gave me there was a picture of a library on fire. It said there were thousands and thousands of scrolls destroyed, just like that. But they started again. They built more libraries; they made more discoveries. They lost some things, but not everything.' She looked up at a pillar that must have once supported towering shelves. 'I don't think we ever lose everything. So long as there are still some of us left to find each other and rebuild.'

A few shelves along, Rafi gave a yelp of triumph. 'Here, I've found it!'

They hurried over. Debris from a wooden bookshelf had fallen over the entrance, and together they cleared it until they made a narrow gap. As they did so, the air grew colder and the feeling of dread grew stronger.

'The library,' said Mehnoor. 'It doesn't like that we're disturbing things. We need to go, quickly.'

They worked faster until the gap was widened and a staircase leading down was revealed. The whispers seemed to rise to a snarl, the stone vibrating with their force.

'Run!' shouted Yara.

Even Rafi seemed to realise something was wrong; he obeyed without question, sprinting full pelt down the steps. Yara felt something powerful grip on to her arm, something that wanted to pull her back into the ruins – but Mehnoor's hand was firm, and she hauled Yara down the stairs with her until they were swallowed up by the darkness.

With no light to guide the way they stumbled blindly along the passage, tripping on the uneven stone in their haste to get away.

Mehnoor gave a gasp, looking around her as though she could discern some invisible light. 'This is what I saw in my dreams,' she panted. 'All those dark corridors – it wasn't confusion; they were showing me the way. I think we turn right here.'

Yara couldn't see a thing, but she angled her body to the right as best she could. Soon enough, she made out the low glimmer of lit torches at the end of the tunnel.

'We're beneath Istehar Way now, I'm sure of it,' said Mehnoor. 'If we keep heading straight—'

She was about to lead them on, but Rafi's hand gripped her elbow.

'Listen!'

Standing still, Yara could hear the brush of long robes against the floor, and the tapping of pointed shoes. She drew the three of them into the shadows, holding her breath. Had they been further along they would have been caught for sure, but by a stroke of luck there was an alcove in the wall, and they ducked out of sight. Yara could hear a familiar voice raised in agitation.

'I'm telling you this has gone too far. People will die.'

'Enough will live. We discussed this, Abdul Malik, wisest of counsel.'

Yara shuddered. She recognised the voice all too well – there was something about Firaaz's smooth tones that made it feel as though he were pouring oil in her ear.

'Abdul Malik is the Sultan's most powerful vizier,' Mehnoor whispered. 'He used to come to the bakery.'

Abdul Malik continued. 'You said only that the crop yield would be poorer than the year before. But there are hundreds in the streets, thousands—'

'Mere troublemakers, Your Excellency.' Firaaz soothed. 'When it becomes clear that sorcery has been purged from the land, these people will take their hunger pangs in better spirit. You will be remembered as the man who brought about a new era of prosperity for the kingdom.'

'That's not what they're saying now,' said the Vizier. 'Do you know what the word on the street is? That ... that *she* cursed us.'

'Nonsense,' Firaaz replied, and he almost sounded amused. 'Goodness, how close these people stray to the truth sometimes – and yet how far they remain from it.'

'Meaning?'

'Meaning you have nothing to concern yourself with, Your Excellency. Ismah Parveen has been a captive in these cellars these past twelve years; she is, I assure you, incapable of cursing anyone.'

Next to Yara, Rafi inhaled sharply.

'But the Sultan—'

'The Sultan was only too grateful for my help, as I remember.' There was a sharp edge to Firaaz's speech now; it cut through the Vizier's bluster like a steel blade. 'My guess is that he would not care for his involvement to be brought to light. The city is a tinderbox – it would be a terrible thing if someone were to . . . strike a match.'

Silence. The only sound was the heavy breathing of the Vizier.

'You would threaten me, Firaaz? You, a . . . a—'

'A devoted servant of the Sultan and his vizier.' Firaaz's voice was smooth once again. 'You will forgive a humble man of science a little caution. The Sultan's men will have taken care of the disturbance in the square by daybreak, I am sure.'

Their footsteps started up again, the conversation between the two men growing fainter until there was silence in the corridor once more.

'That was him.' Yara was surprised to find that her voice was shaking. 'Omair Firaaz, the Chief Alchemist. The one who sent the guards after me that first day – he developed the poison, I'm sure of it.'

Mehnoor shivered. 'I've never encountered anyone as

cold as him. It was as though he was making everything around him colder too.'

'Didn't you hear what they said?' Rafi was still staring after the men. 'They said that they have Ismah Parveen captive. *The Grand High Sorceress* is somewhere in these dungeons.'

'But she's dead,' said Mehnoor. 'Auntie always said that she was the first person they killed in the Inquisition.'

'Maybe not.' Rafi's eyes were bright with excitement. 'Maybe they just wanted us to believe she was dead. The Grand High Sorceress was the most powerful sorceress in the kingdom – she could help us find an antidote to the poison.'

Yara felt a memory stir.

'When I came here first, I thought I could hear someone crying out for help.' She turned to Mehnoor, her heart beating faster. 'If they really were keeping her prisoner, could you find her?'

'I'm not sure,' said Mehnoor with a frown. She shook her head, bringing her fingers to her temples. 'In my dreams there's a particular route I take. But it doesn't feel right down here – it's all strange. Muffled, somehow.'

'Try,' Yara pleaded. 'Not just for us; if they're keeping her down here, then she needs our help.'

Mehnoor looked between the two of them. 'All right. But we need to keep moving.'

Mehnoor led them down winding corridors where the torches were far fewer, the light they cast pale and eerie. Yara kept her ears pricked for the sound of the woman – but heard only their own footsteps.

'We must be below the third-to-last house now,' Rafi whispered. 'I think this is where my great-uncle's larders used to be. Look at the state of it.'

They carried on, Mehnoor's steps slow and deliberate until she stopped in front of a wide-arching door, the wood wrought with vines and leaves.

'There's someone in here,' she said, tracing the pattern with her fingertips. 'I can feel them on the other side.' Yara came to stand beside her and saw that her eyes had filled with tears. 'There's so much pain. Worse than the magic in the library.'

'It *must* be her.' said Yara. 'We can get her out!'

'It's funny,' Rafi said slowly, 'this seems familiar too, but I can't think where from.'

'Does it matter?' Yara said impatiently. She rolled up her sleeve, holding up her hand. 'I'll use a spell to open the door.'

'Yara, don't,' Mehnoor said instantly. 'You can't use magic; it's too dangerous – you'll get sick and you'll bring the guards down on us.'

'What choice do we have?' At her friend's silence Yara began, '*Door*—'

'Wait!' Rafi knocked her hand away, his cheeks flushed with excitement. 'I know where we are! These are the vaults of Istehar Way, where the artefacts and treasures of our people were kept. The Al-Qamars have always been custodians of the vaults – the door should recognise me.'

He stepped forward and ran his finger down the door frame.

Yara held her breath. 'Please work,' she whispered, 'please, please work.'

The door gave a shudder but remained closed. Rafi's shoulders slumped in defeat.

Mehnoor stepped forward. 'Something happened, I can feel it – it's just weak. We need to push.'

The three children pressed their palms against the door, feet slipping against the flagstones as they heaved with all their might. With a horrible *creak*, the door swung open, sending them tumbling into a cavernous room with a high-arched ceiling, the walls bare stone and the floor matted with mouldy straw.

'Hello?' Yara whispered. 'Is anyone there?'

More silence. Then came the noise of a footstep, and then another, until Yara could see the figure who was stumbling out of the shadows, one hand against the wall to support herself.

She was almost impossibly thin, her face so gaunt and her arms so narrow that Yara was half afraid she would blow away in the draught they had let in. Yara rushed forward, and the woman flinched at the sudden movement, moving back into the shadows.

'She's scared,' Mehnoor whispered. She took a careful step forward, her hand outstretched. 'Sorry, she didn't mean to frighten you. We want to help – if you come with us, we can get you out of here.'

Yara waited, holding her breath. Slowly, the woman moved towards them, shielding her face from the light they had let in from the corridor. 'That's right, we're not going to hurt you. Just come a little closer.'

The woman did as Mehnoor said, lowering her hand and looking around at them with eyes that had been dulled by the dark. When her gaze settled on Yara her brow furrowed, her lips moving soundlessly. Her hand reached out, hovered and then settled on Yara's arm; her grip weak at first, and then stronger. Yara's magic pulsed uneasily beneath her skin, and the woman gave a choked gasp.

'I'm going to look further inside,' said Mehnoor. 'There might be others in here. Are you two all right with her?'

'We're fine,' said Rafi.

But Yara wasn't so sure. There was something wild

and hungry in the way this woman was looking at her, something that made her want to pull her arm back and run away.

'It'll be all right.' She attempted a smile. 'Come with us – we can get you to safety.'

The woman didn't move. Her mouth opened again; she tried twice more to speak, before giving up, frustrated.

'Do you want to tell me something?' Yara tried to conceal her nerves. The woman nodded eagerly, and then before she could reply, brought her fingertips up and pressed gently at Yara's temples.

A woman was seated on a flying carpet, her hair fluttering behind her in the wind as she soared through the air at a dizzying pace. She was laughing, her eyes bright and her cheeks rosy in the cold air . . .

Yara wrenched herself away, gasping as though she were coming up for air.

'Yara, be careful,' said Rafi. 'This is dangerous – you don't know what she wants.'

But Yara's eyes never left the woman in front of her.

'That . . . that was you?' she whispered.

The woman nodded frantically, beckoning her closer.

'I think she wants to show me something.'

Chapter Twenty-Two

The woman sailed her carpet past the market, slowing as she approached Istehar Way. At least, Yara thought it must be Istehar Way, because there was the square with the eucalyptus tree to the right – but the buildings were the same warm sandstone as the rest of Zehaira, with a large amber dome in the centre. There were people bustling to and fro, stopping to converse on the streets, all in robes of midnight blue.

The Sorcerers' Quarter.

More than that, Yara was seeing Zehaira as it once was, warm and free of fear, unstained by the bloodshed of the Inquisition. There was brightly coloured smoke coming from the chimneys, bunches of herbs hung to dry from windows – and near the dome Yara could see a garden where a crowd had gathered to take notes from a man with a grey beard down to his knees. Professor Al-Qamar. The woman, however, did not *stop, increasing her speed until the golden towers that Yara had seen on her journey to Zehaira loomed in front of her, and she rested the carpet in front of a marble palace.*

Yara had never ventured this far into the city. The palace was shimmering rosily in the setting sun, with a long line of marble steps leading up to the entrance. As they drew closer, she could see the same intricate style of gold writing that had been on the alchemists' headquarters; it was dazzling as it caught the light.

It appeared the woman was expected. A small committee had gathered to greet her, and Yara recognised the Vizier Abdul Malik at the head.

'Grand High Sorceress, Madam Ismah Parveen.' He bowed his head. 'Our thanks for your attendance – we understand we gave you short notice.'

Yara held her breath. So this was *her.*

'Not at all, Your Excellency,' the woman – Madam Parveen – said breezily. 'When one is Grand High Sorceress, one must expect urgent summons and dire warnings of new dangers to the kingdom.' She placed a hand to her middle. 'Even at the most inconvenient of times.'

'Ah, yes,' said Abdul Malik, his eyes following her hand. 'I understand congratulations are in order. When do you expect?'

'Soon. Which is why I would prefer for this meeting to be brief.'

'Indeed.'

The voice was as smooth as silk and startlingly familiar. Omair Firaaz stepped forward. 'You have spent so little time in Zehaira of late, Grand High Sorceress. My alchemists have worked wonders in your absence.'

'So I see.' Madam Parveen's voice never lost its pleasant tone. 'Well, there certainly is a great deal more gold around. I would have thought a scientist such as yourself would be bored of minting coins by now.'

'Madam Parveen,' the Grand Vizier said. 'Shall we proceed?'

'Yes.' Madam Parveen did not take her eyes off Firaaz as she spoke. 'Lead the way.'

The memory went dark. When light came again, they were standing in a great hall. It might have been a pleasant place once – the windows looked out on courtyards filled with roses, the mountains a misty blue in the distance. But inside everything in the room was inlaid with gold, from the walls and mosaics to the enormous throne in the centre.

Sitting on the throne was a man shrunken with age, his head dwarfed by his crown. He wore gold chains that seemed to weigh heavily on his shoulders; his body was slumped, and occasionally he would emit a low rumbling snore.

The Vizier kneeled before the throne, Ismah standing behind him.

'If I might be permitted to address His Majesty the Sultan?'

The old man on the chair started. 'What? Oh yes, go on, then,' he replied irritably.

'Thank you.' The Vizier bowed his head. 'Your Majesty, it has been brought to my attention that there is a blight in our kingdom growing like a cancer. Unless we act to remove it, it will contaminate your power at the root, and a great evil will rise to take your place.'

Ismah was frowning, her arms folded at her chest. Behind her several guards moved casually to the doorway, hands at the hilts of their swords.

'It is a conspiracy conducted at the highest level of the realm, implicating one of our oldest traditions.'

'Well, then,' Ismah said impatiently, 'spit it out. What is this great conspiracy you have uncovered?'

'With pleasure.' The Vizier rounded on her. 'Madam Grand High Sorceress, what exactly is it that you have been working on these past few months?'

Ismah appeared genuinely taken aback. 'Nothing terribly out of the ordinary.' She recovered herself, smoothing down her skirts. 'I see no need to bore you with the details.'

'Don't you?' asked the Vizier. 'Your Majesty, shocking evidence has come to light that the sorcerers have been plotting to seize power from the sultanate.'

Ismah's eyes widened. 'I'm sorry? Your Majesty, there has been a mistake—'

'Madam Sorceress,' the Vizier raised his voice over her protestations, 'I put it to you that under the guise of advising His Majesty the Sultan you have worked against the good of the kingdom, you have betrayed us to our enemies, you have sought power for yourself and your kind—'

'Evidence.' Ismah's voice could be heard over the intoning of the Vizier. 'What is your evidence of this?'

'We have here a signed testimony that you have been developing a new feat of magic to seize sovereign power from the Sultan ...'

'Lies! Your Majesty—'

'And upon conducting a search of her premises, your loyal servant and Chief Alchemist Omair Firaaz found the evidence himself.'

Madam Parveen fell silent as Firaaz emerged from the shadows, guards at his side. His tone was measured as he spoke, but his face was alive with malice.

'I grew suspicious of the work Madam Parveen was

conducting some time ago, and took it upon myself to search her house while she was lecturing at the university. Imagine my horror when I found details of a spell that would give her and the sorcerers supreme power over every living creature in the kingdom.'

Madam Parveen looked at him. Her outrage was fast turning to fear. 'This is not true. Your Excellency, do you not see what is happening? With the sorcerers gone there will be no one able to challenge the alchemists. The city will be entirely at their mercy.' She took a step closer. 'Believe me not for the sake of myself, nor for the sorcerers – but for the kingdom itself.'

The Sultan did not reply. His brow was furrowed so far over his eyes that they seemed to vanish beneath folds of skin. But the Vizier interjected.

'Your lies will do you no good against the word of two loyal servants to the Sultan. Grand High Sorceress Madam Ismah Parveen, by the power of His Majesty the Sultan, you are under arrest. Guards, if you please.'

The soldiers, who had been clustering like flies around a wounded animal, began to advance. Ismah looked around at them, and the pieces seemed to click in her head.

'You are making a grave mistake,' she said so softly Yara wasn't sure anyone else had heard her. 'These men will be the undoing of us all.'

And then, just as the guards were poised to grab her, there was a burst of bright white light, and row upon row of men were flung back by an unseen force.

The scene changed. Ismah was staggering in the street, her breath coming hard and fast, and the rain coming down even harder. She appeared to be limping, and Yara thought at first that she had been injured by her own spell. Then she stopped, leaning against the wall and squeezing her eyes shut, her lips clamped together. She waited, recovered and kept on forward.

They were in a part of the city Yara did not recognise – the streets were dirtier, slats missing from the shuttered windows. She walked on until she reached a doorstep swept so vigorously it made the street around it look even dirtier by comparison. Ismah knocked on the door once, twice, before she stumbled, reaching for the ground as she sat down and waited.

She wasn't waiting long.

The door opened, and there was a gasp, and a voice Yara knew almost as well as her own said, 'Mercy, are you all right, Madam?'

'Madam Sulimayah?' Ismah asked, and every word seemed to be costing her effort. 'I find myself in need of your services.'

'My services?' The woman stepped into the light.

Mama. A decade younger, with fewer lines on her face, but that was Nahzin Sulimayah, alive. Yara felt as though something heavy had slammed into her chest; she wanted to run forward and grab her mother and never let her go again.

'Madam, there are grander midwives than myself in the city. Let me help you home.'

'There's no time. Please, let me in. I need your help.'

Yara's mother helped the Grand High Sorceress to her feet.

'All right. Don't worry, my love. Of course I'll help you.'

The scene changed, and it was as though Yara was watching from the corner of the room. The Grand High Sorceress lay in her undershirt, curled in on herself on the bed.

Yara's mother was at the opposite side of the room, tending to something that was wriggling and emitting a series of sharp shrieks. With a start Yara realised it was a baby. Ismah seemed to realise at the same time, her head lifting from the pillow.

'Let me see her.'

Nahzin laid the baby, now swaddled and snuffling, on her pillow.

'She's beautiful,' the sorceress whispered. 'My own daughter.'

'You should rest.' Yara's mother was hovering anxiously. 'You're not well.'

'There's no time. They will be here soon. They will know to search the midwives, and there aren't many of you in the city.'

'They?'

Ismah finally wrenched her eyes away from the baby. 'I am sorry. I did a terrible thing to you by coming here. But please, you must help me.'

'Help you?' Yara's mother came to kneel by her other side. 'That is all I am here to do, Madam. That is my job.' Ismah's face crumpled at the kindness in her speech, and she reached out her hand.

'Take her.'

Yara's mother blinked. 'I'm sorry?'

'Take her. Hide her at the furthest corner of the earth – further, even. Go to Professor Al-Qamar at the third-to-last house on Istehar Way and ask for a safe passage spell. Don't tell him who sent you. Don't tell him anything but that you want safe passage from Zehaira.'

'Take the baby?' Yara's mother shook her head, drawing her eyebrows together. 'I am not an orphanage. If you wish to give up your baby, there are those who can assist you in doing so . . .'

She stopped at the sight of the woman on the bed, who had turned her head on the pillow and begun to weep.

Her voice softened. 'I'm happy to put you up for the night – it's a terrible storm brewing out there. We can discuss what you want to do in the morning.'

'We don't have until morning.' Ismah's voice was fainter, like a dimming candle. 'They will be here by the quarter-hour, I know it; it is a miracle they did not come before.'

'For mercy's sake, Madam, who are you talking about?'

'The guards.'

Yara's mother paled. 'The guards?'

'They want me, but if they see her, they'll kill her. Professor Al-Qamar, he knows the spell; he knows what to do. Please, I am begging you, please don't let her die.'

'I . . . you don't know what it is you are saying.' Yara's mother shook her head, getting to her feet. 'And you're not the first woman to talk nonsense after her labour. I'll make a fresh poultice, and we'll talk again.'

Once Yara's mother had left, Ismah turned to the baby, reaching out her hand once more and cradling her head in her hand.

'Oh, my darling,' she whispered. 'You must be so brave. You must come back. Whatever happens, you must come back. They will need you to come back.'

Yara thought her heart might stop beating. She had dreamed of this moment.

Ismah took a deep breath. 'I'm sorry; all I have to

give you is a terrible burden. But I love you. Oh, Mama loves you so much.'

The Grand High Sorceress drew her head nearer to her baby's, and Yara thought she meant to kiss her. But then she began to whisper, her words so quick and so quiet that Yara could not make them out. As she spoke there seemed to be a shine to her and the baby that grew until they were enveloped in a light so bright that Yara had to shield her eyes.

When the light dimmed, the woman's eyes were closed, her breathing deep and even. But the baby was still glowing, as though someone had placed a small sun within her, and its beams were radiating from her fingers and toes. And then that too faded, until it might have been an ordinary baby lying on the bed next to her mother.

There were footsteps, and then Yara's mother re-entered the room.

'There, that will be ready in ...' She trailed off. Shaking her head, she turned to the baby. 'Come on, then, we'll let your mother sleep.' She gathered the child in her arms. 'There you go. Quite the night you chose to be born, eh? What a storm—'

Then came a bang at the door, loud enough to make Yara's mother start and clutch her free hand to her heart. 'Who goes there?' she called.

'Open up in the name of the Sultan's law!'

Nahzin's mouth fell open, her arms coming tighter round the baby. The thumping at the door came again, louder this time.

'Open up, or we break the door down.'

The Grand High Sorceress's eyes flickered open. 'Take her. Please, please take her.'

The banging at the door became relentless. Nahzin looked down at the child asleep in her arms, and something shifted in her face, her eyebrows lowering over her eyes. She grabbed her headscarf – deep blue with golden embroidery, the same one Yara was wearing round her neck now – wrapping up the baby until she looked like nothing more than a bundle of old clothes. As she reached for Ismah's shawl, a small gemstone slipped into the palm of her hand.

For a moment she stared at it, transfixed. Then the sound of her door splintering seemed to break her reverie, and she ran, slipping out of the window and into the night.

'Yara? Yara what did she say? Does she know about the poisoning?'

She barely heard them. She backed away from the woman, almost tripping in her haste.

'No,' she said, trembling. 'No, you're not, you're *not*.'

'Not what?'

The white-haired woman moved forward, and Yara was drawn unwillingly to her face. It was a novel experience for her, seeing her own features reflected, but that was her mouth, and her brow, and her eyes – her own dark eyes looking back at her with such obvious love and fear that Yara's stomach swooped in realisation.

'Yara?' Rafi approached her cautiously. 'What did she say?'

Yara was shaking so badly that it was a while before she could answer. She took a step closer to the older woman, too stunned to cry. 'She's the Grand High Sorceress. And ... and she's my mother.'

'Goodness.' The voice behind them was silky, even in anger. 'Is that so?'

Before Yara could turn round, a hand covered her eyes, and the sharp point of a blade was pressed against her throat.

Chapter Twenty-Three

'Yara. Yara!'

Yara blinked, craning her neck in the direction of the sound. Blindfolded and trussed up, she had been bumped about for so long that she thought they must have tossed her down a flight of stairs and left her for dead. The voice next to her, however, was unmistakable.

'Rafi? Where's Meh—'

'*Shhh*. Anyone could be listening.'

Yara nodded. The dungeon was vast, and Mehnoor had been deep within it – hopefully she had melted into the shadows.

'Can you reach me if you stretch?'

Yara's arms were bound tightly behind her back, but she wriggled and pushed with her wrists, flexing them wildly backwards.

Then: 'Is that your hand?'

'Yes. Come closer and I can try to untie you.'

With a huff Yara wriggled again, sliding across until she could feel Rafi's fingers picking at the rope.

'How are you going to untie me if you can't see?'

'Got a better idea?'

Yara thought for a moment. Then, flexing her fingers, she said, 'Rope, please could you untie yourself?'

'What are you doing?' Rafi hissed. 'You'll cut us both into ribbons.'

Yara ignored him. 'Rope, come undone, I command it.'

'Oh, that won't work, you know.'

Yara froze, hardly daring to breathe as she heard familiar silky tones.

'Who's there?' This from Rafi behind her. 'Show yourself!'

'Now, now.' Yara could hear Firaaz biting back a laugh. 'Manners. That is no way to talk to someone after breaking into their quarters. Anyway, as I was saying, it is no good trying to untie yourselves with magic. Feel the floor beneath you.'

Yara didn't move; she could sense Rafi sitting still beside her, breathing heavily. 'Well, do or don't, it makes no difference to me. But it is rather clever – this is a particular type of marble, with stone retrieved from the molten rock of a volcano. It absorbs magical energy like light. The physics of it is ... quite extraordinary.'

Yara became conscious of the edge of his robe

brushing her bound arm. Then long fingers traced the outline of her face, before lifting her blindfold. Blinking in the bright light, Yara found herself staring into the eyes of Omair Firaaz.

The alchemist's eyes were bright and glittering, sizing her up with a cold fascination, as though she were a pinned butterfly. From what Yara could tell he was alone – there were no guards lingering at the doorway. She recognised the laboratory from that first fateful day in Zehaira.

'Extraordinary,' he murmured. 'You really are her, aren't you? The long-lost child of Ismah Parveen. I assumed you had been killed in the Inquisition.'

Yara said nothing. She didn't think she had ever felt so much loathing towards anyone in her life. She looked pointedly away, and he chuckled. 'Dear me. You have your mother's obstinacy, I see. And who do we have here?'

Firaaz moved on, and Yara felt Rafi begin to shake. 'And you are, boy?'

'Let us go,' said Rafi. 'We didn't mean any harm; the door was open—'

'Yes, yes, the door was open, and you just happened to wander into my private dungeon,' Firaaz said impatiently. 'Surely we are past these pleasantries? You meant to steal from me, just as I now intend to hurt you. I would like to learn the name of the boy I am to torture.'

Rafi said nothing.

Firaaz moved quickly, wrenching the hand Rafi had been using to try to find the knot and twisting it. 'Tell me your name.' Firaaz's voice was low and insistent, and Rafi thrashed, crying out in agony. As he moved, Yara felt something small and hard slip into her palm. Rafi's bracelet – his birthstone. It was sharp at the edges.

'Your name, now!'

'Al-Qamar,' Rafi whimpered

'An Al-Qamar; I'm honoured. And what were you two doing here, young Al-Qamar?'

'Let us go!'

'I won't stop with your arm, you know; I'll break every bone in your body if I have to. Why were you here?'

Yara looked around the room desperately for anything that could help them. And then from the shadows she heard a low hiss, a flicker of movement at the corner of her eye. A pair of yellow eyes peered at her from the darkness, and the seed of a plan began to take root in Yara's mind.

'Stop, please stop!' She tried to make her voice sound as high and childish as she could. 'We'll tell you everything, just please don't hurt him!'

Rafi went rigid with outrage behind her, but relaxed as she began to saw through the rope at his wrists.

'Good.' Firaaz was slightly out of breath. 'Sensible of you. So why were you here?'

'We were looking for my mother.' Yara lowered her head to the floor, hoping that Rafi was keeping his expression under control. 'The Al-Qamars took me in when I was a baby, but this terrible sickness ... my mother was our only hope.'

'I see. It must have been quite the disappointment, seeing the state she was in.'

Yara's eyes narrowed. She would have liked nothing better than to reach out and strangle the man, but her arms were bound – and she needed to keep Firaaz talking. Luckily he showed no signs of stopping. 'We always suspected your mother sent you to the Al-Qamars – it's why we killed so many of them at the beginning of the Inquisition.' He smiled maliciously at Rafi. 'What we left unfinished then, it would appear we have nearly completed now.'

Yara feigned confusion. 'What do you mean?'

There was another *hiss* from the corner of the room, but Firaaz did not hear it. He reached into his robes and brought out a small vial, rolling it around in his fingers.

'This is a substance that goes right to the heart of magical energy – that poisons magic at the well, so to speak.

'The sorcerers looked up at the stars, so we turned our gaze below the earth. Ores, minerals, materials that had seen neither sun nor stars for millennia, and knew nothing of their magic. We made gold, and after a decade of experimentation – with your mother as an exemplary test subject – we made this.'

Firaaz looked at the vial again, and there was something awestruck in his look, as though he could not believe his own genius. 'I sent my men around the kingdom and bade them poison every river and stream they found.'

'But everything has magical energy,' said Yara. 'Every tree, every grain – that's why the farmers' crops have died, isn't it? People will starve.'

'Precisely. There will be chaos – chaos not even the viziers can control. And through chaos comes change.'

'Change?'

'Well, why not? My alchemists gained control of the kingdom the moment we turned base metal into gold. What use have we now for foolish sultans or scheming viziers? Or portentous self-important sorcerers for that matter?' His expression soured. 'We were supposed to have the assistance of a jinn to capture the city, but I made the mistake of sending my own idiot guards to retrieve it. No matter. Soon our men will be stepping out of the shadows and into the light.'

Yara felt horror rise in her like bile. 'Why?' she asked. 'Why do you hate us so much?'

Firaaz's mouth twisted. 'Because it is people like your

mother and the Al-Qamars who have kept power for themselves for centuries. Had we allowed your mother's work to continue, then we might have lived at their mercy for evermore.'

'What do you mean?'

Firaaz stopped himself. Evidently he had not meant to go quite that far. At that moment Yara felt the rope securing Rafi's wrists give way, and she pressed the stone into Rafi's hands.

'It does not matter,' said Firaaz. 'Soon the sorcerers will be ground into the dust once and for all.'

Yara could feel the rope round her wrists loosening; it would be a matter of minutes now, she was certain.

'You won't win,' she told him, forcing herself to meet his eye. 'You might have weakened us beyond all hope, but you can never win. Sorcery is so much more than power. It's a history, and a culture, and a *community*, and that is something that you will never be able to destroy – not so long as there are stars in the sky, and people who want to understand them.'

The rope round Yara's wrists gave way. It was now or never. She turned her face away from the alchemist.

'Familiar of the House of Parveen!' she called. 'Most powerful of all jinn, I summon you to my aid. I command you to untie us both!'

Springing to her feet, Yara made a beeline for the

corner of the room, where the stray cat she had fed that first day in Zehaira was lurking, apparently investigating a mousehole. Yara scooped him up in her arms and turned round to face the alchemist.

'You have made a terrible mistake, Omair Firaaz,' she said, and to her surprise her voice did not shake. 'You have upset a great and powerful sorceress, and this cat here is my familiar. At my command he untied us, and unless you let us leave here unharmed, he will wipe you from the face of the earth.'

'Impossible,' the alchemist said immediately, but he took a step back all the same, his eyes alive with fear. 'You are lying.'

'Am I? Would you bet your life on it?' She steeled herself. 'Rafi, get out. I've got my eye on Firaaz.'

'Have you indeed?' Firaaz bit out. 'Even if that fleabag is a jinn, I do not believe for one second that you have it in you to give that command.'

Yara moved further back, trying to remain calm as Firaaz began his advance. 'Why not? Why shouldn't I kill you?'

She was backed against his workbench now.

'You're brave; I'll give you that. But I would like to see the little girl who could give an order to kill a man.'

Yara had to admit that he was right. But behind her she could hear the sound of solutions bubbling, and it gave her an idea. Looking at him directly, she said, 'I am *not* a little girl.'

She swept an arm over the workbench, not stopping to listen to the smash of glass and spatter of solutions as thick smoke filled the laboratory. Holding on tight to the cat, she ran from the room, slamming the door shut behind her and lowering the bolt. Rafi was waiting for her outside.

'Is that a cat?'

'Come *on.*'

They sprinted down the corridor, running so hard that they could barely get words out.

'We didn't find a formula or ingredients – or anything that could help Leyla,' said Yara. 'There's nothing we can do.'

'What did the Grand High Sorceress show you?'

'I saw them charging her with treason, and her fleeing into the city. And there was this moment she showed me, just after I was born. She whispered something in my ear, and there was all this gold light around me and stuff.'

Rafi came to a sudden halt.

'Rafi, we have to keep moving.'

'Golden light? And a lot of words, not just a spell?'

'Yeah, why?'

'Yara, that sounds like a passing on. It's supposed to be an important magical ceremony – it's how the Grand

High Sorceress transfers her magic to her successor.' His eyes widened. 'That has to be why you have all that energy: it's the power of all the Grand High Sorceresses who came before, of all the people who entrusted their magic to the Grand High Sorceress. That's the lost magic of our community, right there inside you.'

Yara's head reeled, and she clutched the cat closer to her chest, ignoring his sounds of protest.

'We don't have time for this – we need to keep going.'

The two broke into a run again, but Rafi hadn't finished.

'You still don't get it,' he panted, as they rounded a corner. 'If Firaaz's alchemists really have poisoned the water, then the rest of us make could only make things worse, because our magic comes from communing with the world around us. But you ... the magic you have inside you is from your mother. I'll bet anything the alchemists' poison couldn't so much as scratch that.'

'What do you mean?'

They reached the great arching door of the dungeon, the sound of the guards in the distance.

Rafi turned to her. 'With all the magic you have, you could heal Leyla with the simplest of spells. Don't you see? You could save her.'

Chapter Twenty-Four

Mehnoor sprang up the moment they opened the dungeon door, her cheeks wet with tears.

'Oh, you're all right, you're all right! I thought you'd been killed.'

'We're fine.' Yara was rather glad that the cat prevented Mehnoor from hugging her; she wasn't sure that she could keep it together if she did. Her eyes travelled to where the Grand High Sorceress was standing behind her, and feelings that had been tamped down by fear and adrenaline rose to the surface once more.

Mama had lied to her – had kept the biggest part of her life a secret for twelve years. She hadn't even chosen to have her. Yara had been thrust on her in the dead of night. Perhaps she had never been a daughter to Nahzin Sulimayah. Perhaps she had always been a duty to be borne.

'Yara?' Mehnoor and Rafi were looking at her in concern, and she shook herself.

'We need to leave. We won't have held them up for long.' She held out a hand. 'Come with us. We can take you to people who will help.'

The Grand High Sorceress took Yara's hand, but her grip was weak, and as she moved towards them, she stumbled on the stone floor.

'Yara, she can barely stand,' Rafi said in an undertone. 'She won't make it to the city gates – and Firaaz said we can't cast spells down here.'

'I'm not just going to leave her here.'

'Yara—'

At that moment the cat broke free, jumping down from Yara's arms and wrapping himself round Madam Parveen's legs. To her astonishment he began to grow, filling out until he was the size of a dog, then a goat, and not stopping until he resembled a large panther, his coat glossy and his teeth elongated.

Yara blinked in amazement. 'But ... he was just a stray. I met him my first day in Zehaira – I gave him my sambusak.'

'That's no cat.' Rafi stepped closer. 'He really *is* a familiar – or at least he used to be. He must have lost most of his powers when she did.'

The panther remained speechless, but his purr was now less like a motor and more like an aeroplane taking off. The Grand High Sorceress bent down to stroke him, and Yara let out an 'oh' of recognition.

'He was leading me to *her*. That first day in Zehaira; he was trying to find her. He'll help us get her out.'

Between the three of them, they were able to half carry Madam Parveen, and they hurried down the corridors to the sound of the guards behind them. But Istehar Way wasn't far off. Together, they struggled to get the Grand High Sorceress up the steps.

And then, with one foot on the top step, Yara felt a hand encircle her wrist, jerking her back.

She turned round.

Firaaz's face had lost all its humour; his teeth were bared in a snarl. 'Going somewhere?'

Yara froze, too frightened to fight his grip, her mouth opening soundlessly. Then there came a yell from behind her.

Before any of them could react, Madam Parveen had thrown herself on the Chief Alchemist, who let go of Yara's wrist in his astonishment. The two tumbled down the stairs, and the panther followed with a snarl.

'No!' Yara screamed.

Mehnoor hesitated next to her, but Rafi seized both of them, dragging them up to the street and never once looking back.

'Yara, there's nothing we can do. She knew what she was doing.'

'We can't leave her there!' She fought him, struggling against his hold. He didn't understand – he hadn't seen the bright, vibrant woman on the carpet sacrifice twelve years of her life to a dungeon, only for Yara to get her caught once again. Mehnoor took her other arm, and she fought harder.

'Yara, please.' Hearing Rafi plead with her slowed Yara's movements. 'We'll come back, I promise, but if we don't go right now then we will lose everything.'

Yara said nothing. With one final look back she allowed Rafi and Mehnoor to lead her down the street. The struggle was still going on around them, but it was fading, the farmers fleeing, and the trio weaved among them.

'You did the right thing,' Mehnoor panted at her side. 'That cat – whatever he is – he's with her now; he'll make sure she comes to no harm.'

Yara didn't reply. Risking a glance over her shoulder, she spotted the alchemists' guards picking their way through the crowds, scanning the face of each person as they passed.

They reached the city gates, breaking away from the stream of people. Yara cried out, 'Ajal! Ajal, we're here, we need you!'

The jinn was at their side in an instant. Yara heard the guards give a yell, heard the clash of metal as they began to run towards them – but it was too late. They were flying through the air, the farmers and soldiers and then even the domes of Zehaira soon pinpricks in the distance.

'Well,' said Yara dully, 'we got away.'

'I wouldn't be so certain of that,' said Ajal.

He slowed their flight, and Yara looked below. A black mass of soldiers was writhing through the mountains, some of them on horseback, some marching. At the sight of the swords slung over their backs Yara felt a new terror twist in her stomach.

'We're close to the Settlement. If Leyla's protection spells fail . . .' She trailed off. From the look on Rafi's and Mehnoor's faces she didn't need to continue. 'They're hours away at most. We're almost out of time.'

When they landed, the smoke from the chimneys was the only sign of life in the Settlement. The trees around them had blackened and withered, their broken branches skimming the snow, and the feeling of death and decay welled up around Yara until she could scarcely breathe through it.

The three children burst through Leyla's front door, Ajal following behind in his goat form. Meri started up from where she had been sat by her cauldron, and at the sight of her Yara felt a horrible flash of guilt. The sorceress's eyes were red-rimmed, and she was paler than Yara had ever seen her, with a tell-tale grey about her fingers.

'Where in the *seven spheres* have you been?' Yara had never heard Meri sound so angry. 'Not a word from any of you – I've been out of my mind—'

'Auntie, we're sorry,' said Mehnoor, 'and we'll explain everything, we promise, but there's no time right now. The Sultan's men are coming, and we know how to save Madam Khatoun.'

That stopped Meri's tirade.

'What?'

'It's Yara.' said Rafi, 'we were right; the alchemists poisoned our magic—'

'Firaaz said it was through the water – everything around us is infected.'

Meri looked at them blankly. 'Then there's nothing we can do.'

'We can't do anything, no – but Yara can,' Rafi interjected.

'Yara?'

Words were tumbling from Rafi and Mehnoor now, their voices overlapping. As they explained, Meri stared at them, first with disbelief, and then with a hope that was almost too much to bear. Finally she took a deep, steadying breath.

'All right. I am not sure that I entirely understand, and I am still *extremely angry* with all three of you – but Yara, do you think you could cast a healing spell?'

They went upstairs together. Leyla's dying magic was so strong that Yara thought even Rafi could feel it now; she saw him flinch and hang back, unwilling to get closer.

Sitting on the side of the bed, Meri took Leyla's hand in her own. Leyla's sleeve fell away to reveal a bracelet on her wrist – two locks of hair braided together that hadn't been taken off during almost twelve years of bitterness and hurt.

Yara could feel Mehnoor's fierce, believing eyes fixed on her, and she wished they would all step back; their hope was making this so much harder. She had heard Leyla, Meri and Rafi saying healing verses a hundred times over the last few weeks, she knew she could do this – and yet terror seemed to stop the words in her throat.

'I've never healed anyone before,' she whispered. 'I couldn't even enchant the potions. What if I get it wrong? What if I hurt her? What if it makes her worse? What if . . .' She lowered her head, feeling as though she might cry. Madam Parveen, Mama, Leyla, they had all given up so much to help other people – to help *her* – and she couldn't save any of them.

She felt Meri's hand cupping her cheek, wiping away a stray tear away with her thumb. 'I'm sorry,' she said quietly. 'If there were any other way ... but I believe in you. Leyla would believe in you too. I know she would.'

'I will be here,' Ajal added. 'I will help your control.'

Yara looked at the two of them on either side of her and nodded. Taking a deep breath, she closed her eyes and began:

'With moon-picked willow and dew-touched flower,
Let poison quake before my power'.

Yara felt magic swell within her, and next to her she felt Ajal tense with the struggle of keeping her magic under control. He wouldn't be able to hold it back much longer. She closed her eyes, concentrating with all her might.

There was a flash of light and Yara opened her eyes. Leyla lay as still and silent as she had ever been.

Yara's disappointment felt as though it could choke her. Then she heard Rafi and Mehnoor slump in despair behind her, heard Meri exhale as though someone had taken a sledgehammer to her ribs, and disappointment gave way to keen rage. How could Leyla Khatoun of all people be allowed to die?

'No! You can't let her die; I won't allow it.' Yara didn't know who or what she was speaking to, but she knew she was *furious* with it. 'Leyla's not supposed to die now. She should wake up and take a deep breath and know immediately how we can make things better.'

'Yara.' Meri's voice was tight in her disbelief. 'Keep going.'

'What?'

'Don't stop! Look at her; you're keeping the spell alive.'

Yara couldn't see much of a difference, but Meri's eyes were frantic, and she knew it would be a terrible thing to stop. She was reminded suddenly of the Ferryman who had brought her to Zehaira, telling her to make her case.

Instinctively she clutched her headscarf, which had once been indigo blue and belonged to the bravest woman she had ever known, and spoke:

Leyla Khatoun isn't supposed to die now.

She needs to finish writing down the folk

tales and brewing her potions, and

she has to apologise to Meri – but
especially she has to do the things
she's always wanted to do, because
she's been trapped here
since she was eighteen.

She cannot die because
I won't let her.'

Yara ran out of air. When she looked down, Leyla was so still and so silent that she felt her own heart stop.

Then, as though surfacing from underwater, the sorceress began to cough and splutter, her eyes fluttering open as she took breath after deep breath.

Chapter Twenty-Five

'I ... what am I doing here?' Leyla propped herself up on her elbow, looking around her in alarm. 'How long have I been asleep?'

'It's all right,' said Yara shakily. 'Oh, Leyla, we thought you were going to die.'

Leyla snorted, her breath still rasping. 'Nonsense. As if I would do a thing like that when there is so much to be done around the Settlement.'

She looked up at where Meri was standing, her eyes wide and her whole body trembling with relief. 'Meriyem, I – did you ... ?'

'Not me. Yara.'

'Yara?'

Leyla looked between them wildly, and Yara tried to find the words to explain.

'All that powerful magic I have – it doesn't really belong to me. It was passed on by my mother.'

'That's not possible . . .' Leyla began.

'Not . . . not Mama.' Yara took a deep breath. 'Ismah Parveen.'

That made Leyla sit up. She looked at Yara in pure undisguised amazement.

'Ismah Parveen? The last Grand High Sorceress?'

'I know, but I saw it myself. After I was born, she gave me all her magic, and told Mama to take me to Professor Al-Qamar and ask for a safe passage spell. She's been in the alchemists' dungeon ever since.'

'They went to Zehaira, Leyla.' Meri placed a hand on Yara's shoulder. 'Without my knowledge. It's a long story, and I'm not sure I understand it all myself, but – well, it appears what Yara says is true. She is Ismah Parveen's daughter.'

Leyla stared at Yara, her mouth opening and closing soundlessly. Yara expected more denials, more questions. Instead, the sorceress pulled back her blankets, getting unsteadily to her feet.

'Leyla, take it easy—'

'You only just woke up—'

But Leyla ignored Meri and Mehnoor. She managed to stumble over to her drawers, rummaging until she found the small red gemstone.

Yara gasped. 'I've seen that before.'

'The ceremonial ruby of the Grand High Sorceress,'

said Leyla, lifting it up it to the light. 'Held as a symbol of her magic, and her responsibility to her community. If I had only recognised it . . .' She looked down at Yara, and pressed the ruby into her hands. 'I am going to ask something of you that you will not find easy. Before I do, I need to know that you trust me. Do you?'

'I . . . yes, of course.'

'Good. Because I need you to do what you did for me for the entire kingdom.'

'The *entire kingdom*? I could barely heal you; I couldn't—'

'Yes, you can. That must be why the Grand High Sorceress sent you away with your mama in the first place – she knew that they could imprison her, but that her magic would be safe across the sea. She knew that one day you would come back and defeat whatever plot the alchemists had devised.'

'Be reasonable, Leyla.' Yara felt grateful for the sharpness in Meri's voice. 'A thing like that – it would take all the magical energy she has, even if she could manage the control.'

'Not all the magical energy she has,' Leyla argued. 'All the magical energy her mother gave her. As for control –' she took a deep breath – 'I can help with that. I can channel her magic.'

That stopped all of them in their tracks.

'You can what?' said Yara, bewildered.

Leyla closed her eyes briefly, and then held Yara's gaze.

'A little over twelve years ago, your mama came and asked me for a safe passage spell. The magic that spell requires is ancient, as old as Zehaira itself, and it required an exchange between us. So she promised you to me.'

'She *promised* me?'

'Yes. And when she did, you became my responsibility. But, more than that, it created a bond between us, in the same way a sorcerer might bond with a jinn when they share magic. It means that with your power and my discipline, we can bring an end to this. We can save everyone who is sick and suffering.'

Yara's head was spinning, a thousand and one questions on her lips. Perhaps sensing this, Leyla said quickly, 'We're almost out of time. You told me that you trust me. Do you?'

Yara looked up at the sorceress and made up her mind.

'All right. Just tell me what to do.'

Still unsteady on her feet, Leyla led them all out to the edge of the Settlement and kneeled on the ground, clearing the snow with her hands until she found what she was looking for.

'The ashes from the sun fire. There's powerful magic still in them – magic from our community. Now, Yara, take my hands. Say the words, and then breathe out, just as you would when you're sharing your magic with Ajal. Your magic will flood the earth, and I will channel it throughout the kingdom.'

'She can't do it,' Rafi argued, and for once there was fear, not petulance, in his voice. 'She'll be ripped to shreds.'

'I'll hold on the whole time.' Leyla didn't take her eyes off Yara. 'I promise, no matter what happens. I won't let you give more than you are able to.'

'I will be right here with you,' Ajal promised.

'And I.' Meri squeezed her shoulder. But Yara only had eyes for Leyla. Leyla wouldn't lie to her; she wouldn't give her false hope where there was none.

'I'm scared,' she whispered. 'What if it's too much for me? What if I can't do it? What if I don't have magic after this?' Thoughts began to pour from her in a rush, unguarded and selfish and terrified. 'The whole reason I'm here is because I have magic, and it's not even mine; it's my— *Hers*. What if you take it away and I don't belong here any more?' She looked down at her lap, mortified by her outburst. Then she felt hesitant fingers tilting her chin, until she was looking directly into Leyla's amber eyes.

'You will belong,' said the sorceress, her voice surprisingly gentle. 'With or without magic, I promise.'

'But you said—'

'I know what I said. I was wrong – truly wrong. You

belong here with me, and that wouldn't be any different if you had no magic to speak of or were the most powerful sorceress on earth.' She paused. 'As for what this will do to you – I don't know. But I can swear on my life that I will do everything I can to protect you from harm.'

At her words Yara felt something uncoil in her stomach that had been tightly wound for so long she had almost forgotten life before it.

'What do I say?'

Leyla shook her head. 'This has to be your own words. For a task this monumental it must come from your heart, and your heart alone.'

'I couldn't begin to think of my own verse. I don't know how; we never did it in lessons—'

'Does it have to be a verse?' asked Mehnoor. Everyone turned to look at her. 'It wasn't just Yara's healing spell that saved Madam Khatoun – we all saw what happened. Yara talked life back into her. She *argued* for her.'

'Mehnoor's right,' said Rafi. 'After all the things you've talked us into, you can't turn round now and say you're no good. You've never exactly had trouble finding the right words before.'

Yara didn't have it in her to glare at him. She looked up at Leyla, who said quickly, 'I trust you. Wholeheartedly.'

Yara thought about it. She thought about sparring with Rafi, and telling off the Professor, and silencing that woman on the bus – about persuading a mysterious man to ferry her across the sea and commanding green fire to snuff itself out. Rafi was right. She could do this.

They were at the sun fire. The blessing Leyla had spoken at the winter festival – that hadn't been poetry, but the air had been heavy with her magic that night.

Yara held on tight to the sorceress's hands and, closing her eyes, reached for the power inside her. For Ismah Parveen's power. She had called it a terrible burden, but as it began to move restlessly within her it felt more like a strength. A piece of the woman who had loved Yara for twelve years without her knowing.

Almost by instinct, she wrapped Mama's headscarf tighter round her neck and tried to imagine her mother there next to her, issuing a single instruction: *Do not take no for an answer.*

Moments passed, and Yara began.

Let my power take root. Let it spread deep in the earth, in the wind in the trees, in the fire on the mountain, in the running of the stream. Let it send the darkness back, back, until the rivers run clear and the flowers bud and bloom and our people are free!

She could feel magic rising within her, stronger than ever before. She started again, and this time her voice was joined by Leyla's.

'Let our power take root. Let it spread deep in the earth, in the wind in the trees, in the fire on the mountain, in the running of the stream. Let it send the darkness back, back, until the rivers run clear and the flowers bud and bloom and our people are free.

Let our people be free.

Let our people be free.'

Oh – it was like being split open. As though she had been ripped apart and turned inside out; like the feeling of magic out of control but a hundred times worse. Yara let out a cry, her whole body shaking with effort. One moment she felt as though she were something incredibly small with the earth looming large around her, the next she was a star looking coldly down from the heavens, the earth a pinprick below. It hurt, it hurt; it was agony. She could feel the earth crying out around her; she could feel it bleeding, grey and dying. Her voice rose again, and she barely recognised it as her own.

'Make it stop! Make it stop, please!'

'Leyla!' Meri said urgently.

But Yara felt Leyla's grip on her wrist tighten.

'It's not enough,' she replied.

'Leyla, look at her!'

'Moments more, I promise; Yara, just a few moments more.'

Moments. She could do moments. She could feel seconds like tangled threads between her fingers, could taste the salt strike of the hour on her tongue. The magic in her had waited for twelve years. Dormant, then agitated and restless like an animal who wakes caged after a long winter's sleep, and now gloriously running free. She felt herself soar above the mountains, the earth spread beneath her. Hers, if she wanted. She could let herself be carried away with her magic like a song on a breath and melt into the world like a fallen star.

She felt her eyes flutter and close, her head lolling back. Around her she heard voices with the far-away inconsequence of rain on the mountain.

'Leyla, she's not conscious.'

'It's almost there; I can feel it.'

'Madam Khatoun, please . . .'

'Now!'

She felt the earth shaking beneath her, heard Meri and Mehnoor and Rafi screaming for Leyla and Ajal bursting from his goat form – and she fell, deep into the dark, and knew nothing more.

Chapter Twenty-Six

When Yara woke, she was in a bed – a proper one; it was solid beneath her. For a moment she thought she must be back in Bournemouth, and that Zehaira and Leyla Khatoun and everything that had come after had all been an extraordinary dream.

She opened her eyes a crack, and then immediately wished that she hadn't. Her head felt as though someone had been using her skull as a drum. There was something heavy weighing down her legs at the end of the bed, and when she opened her eyes properly, she could see Ajal sat upright by her feet.

She managed a sleepy smile. 'Miss me?' she croaked.

'Never,' said the jinn, flashing his eyes. 'Never have I met a human with such propensity for finding herself in trouble – the wickedest of sorcerers could not hold a candle to you, Yara Sulimayah. Why I followed you I shall never know, but if I had a limited lifespan,

I would say you have shortened my life by several millennia . . .'

'I'll take that as a yes.' Yara sat up, bringing her knees up to her chest and looking around. 'Leyla gave me her bed?'

'Indeed. With all her restless pacing over the last few days, it wasn't as though she had need of it.'

'*Few days?*' said Yara. 'I've been asleep for days? Is everyone okay? Did the spell work? Did the soldiers—'

'The spell worked, we remain concealed. The soldiers appear to have caught a glimpse of us, however – we are currently surrounded.'

At his words Yara craned her neck to look out of the window. She could just about make out figures in black encamped at the boundary of the Settlement, prowling the border suspiciously.

Ajal continued. 'Meriyem, Mehnoor and that boy have been out every day with those still recovering from the poisoning, but the signs are promising.'

'And Leyla?'

At that same moment Yara heard footsteps at the bottom of the stairs.

'I believe that is my cue to depart,' said the jinn. 'I fear there is about to be far too much human emotion for a creature such as myself to bear.'

Yara pulled a face – and then an unhappy thought

occurred to her. A lump formed in her throat, and she had to swallow around it several times before she was able to get out what she knew she had to say:

'You know, I suppose I am settled now; my magic is under control, and I have Leyla's help. If you want to go, then don't let me—'

'Yara Sulimayah,' Ajal said wearily, 'if I have learned anything over our time together, it is that you will never be under control. Just know that as my familiar, you will be held to a certain standard of conduct in future.'

And with that Ajal transformed himself into a cloud and sailed breezily out of the window.

Yara watched him leave, smiling to herself. The footsteps came to a halt outside the room.

'You're awake?'

She turned round. Leyla was hovering just outside the room, her fingers splayed against the door frame.

Yara sat up straighter. 'I only just woke up. I was talking to Ajal, but …' She gestured towards the open window.

'May I come in?'

Once she had entered the room, Leyla seemed even less certain of what to do with herself. She walked to the foot of Yara's bed, then to the window, then back to the bed. Then she said suddenly, 'So. Between them, Rafi and Mehnoor have filled us in on your trip to Zehaira.'

Yara bristled. 'We didn't have any choice – you were unconscious and Meri thought everything was hopeless, and—'

'I thought it was very ... brave of you,' Leyla said quietly. At Yara's look of disbelief she continued. 'Foolhardy and dangerous beyond belief, of course, but brave nonetheless.'

Yara looked up at the sorceress and saw from the anxious lines of her face that Leyla had prepared explanations and apologies if she wanted them.

But Yara decided she didn't want them – at least, not yet. Right now, she was just glad that Leyla was standing in front of her, alive. She got to her feet and wrapped her arms round the sorceress, burying her face in her shoulder. After a few cautious seconds, Yara felt Leyla's arms came round her, stiff and awkward and sincere.

It wouldn't be right to say things in the Settlement returned to normal. Yara's healing spell had come too late for some, and grief had fallen and settled on the shoulders of the people like snow. New graves had been dug for Abdul Hussein; for Madam Zahrawi; for Madam Dinezade, who had been kind that first lonely week. Meanwhile, guards and alchemists alike watched the Settlement with unending intensity, stalking the boundary like wolves surrounding their prey.

Yet it was still there. Its people were weak, hungry and frightened – but they kept on. After a long talk with Leyla, Rafi was preparing wellness tonics to help people recover from the poison, while Mehnoor had joined their magic lessons and had taken to them so well that their bedroom became cluttered with her scribbled ideas for spells. Although Ismah Parveen's power had left her, Yara soon became acquainted with her own magic. It felt half formed inside her, strange and uncertain, but it was *hers*.

Leyla and Meri were still quarrelling; Yara suspected they always would, but their conversations were no longer tinged with hurt and misunderstanding. Something had shifted between them, and several times Yara came back to find them sitting close together by the fire, talking quietly and intently. Which was as it should be, she decided. They had been torn apart by the Inquisition, after all – seeing them reconcile felt like the beginning of things being put right.

Yet how could things be right when Ismah Parveen remained in the dungeons of Istehar Way?

It was that thought that consumed Yara as she walked the boundary of the Settlement, turning the ruby over and over in her hands. Ismah Parveen was her mother – did she have a father too? More family, who had survived the Inquisition?

She replayed in her head the way the Grand High Sorceress had looked at her, with all that love, and fear, and wonder, the same way she had looked at Yara as a baby. If they did rescue her, would she expect Yara to behave like her daughter?

She recoiled at the idea, and then felt ashamed for doing so – but she had been someone else's daughter for twelve years. Someone who had read her bedtime stories and taught her to make sambusak and listened to her worries. Thinking of Mama, however, only made her feel more lost.

'There she is.'

Yara looked round. Rafi and Mehnoor were running to catch up with her, and she stopped, waiting for them.

'Mehnoor could feel you moping all the way from the house,' Rafi told her, walking on her left-hand side. 'It was putting me off my spellwork.'

'It was *not*.' Mehnoor swatted at him from Yara's right. 'Is everything all right, though? You've been very quiet lately.'

'Everything's fine.' Yara looked down at her lap. 'It's just hard not to think about my— Madam Parveen.'

'You did the right thing,' said Mehnoor. 'She didn't sacrifice her freedom for twelve years for you to be captured now. You had to leave her.'

'It's not just that. When the Sultan had her arrested, Firaaz said that she had been working on something that would let her take power in the kingdom. Do you think that's true?'

'It might be,' said Rafi. His eyes lit up. 'We could find out. If she really was working on something powerful, it can only be a good thing for us. We could continue what she started, take the fight to the alchemists—'

'Is that really what's been worrying you, Yara?' Mehnoor interrupted, looking at her with concern. 'I feel like there's something you're not telling us.'

'I'm fine.' Yara fidgeted with the stone. 'I suppose I've just been feeling a bit out of place.'

'Out of place?' Rafi said, disbelieving. 'Yara, you're the daughter of the Grand High Sorceress. You saved practically every sorcerer in the kingdom from certain, painful death. How can you feel out of place?'

Yara swallowed. 'I know. And this is where I belong, I suppose, as Madam Parveen's daughter. This was what Mama wanted for me too – a new home, with people who are like me.'

'But?' Mehnoor pressed.

Yara swallowed again, this time with greater difficulty. She had a strong suspicion that if she voiced her feelings she would cry.

'But Mama brought me up, and she never told me what I was – who I was. Now I keep wondering whether she actually wanted me. Whether she ...'

Yara trailed off and sniffed, reaching into her pocket for something to wipe her eyes with. Her fingers closed round a small scrap of paper, scrunched and smelling of the sea. She drew it out, her eyes moving across the page.

I love you so, so much — more than the moon, more than the stars, more than my own heart.
    Good luck, my brave girl,
    Mama

Yara sniffed again, and almost without her noticing she had begun to cry, tears dripping down her cheeks and on to the page. Mehnoor wrapped her arms round her, and Rafi patted her awkwardly, but Yara barely noticed. Mama had loved her, deeply and truly. She might have lied, and kept secrets, and made mistakes – but Yara was hers. No matter how much magic she learned, a part of her would always belong to Mama.

Yara wiped her eyes fiercely and moved closer to the boundary. Barely metres away an oblivious soldier was cleaning his sword, polishing the blade until the metal was bright enough to split the sunlight.

'What are you thinking?' asked Mehnoor.

When Yara replied, her voice was full of steel.

'We can't hide away here any more; even Leyla knows that now. We're going to save Ismah Parveen, and after that we're going to take back Zehaira from the alchemists. No matter how long it takes.'

But later that night she lay awake, breathing in the almost-faded scent of castor oil and rose water from Mama's headscarf, her fingers tracing frayed embroidery. Nothing Mama had given her had been magical. There are things you can pass on that are more important than magic, Yara thought. Teaching your daughter that she must keep making demands of the world, no matter how often it denies her. Showing her the whole of the night sky in a shawl of faded blue.

About the Author

Zohra Nabi grew up inventing stories for her two younger sisters. She studied law at Cambridge and Oxford universities, but secretly dreamed of being an author. Now she lives in London, browsing bookshops and writing magical adventures. *The Kingdom Over the Sea* is her first book.

Acknowledgements

There are so many people to thank for *The Kingdom over the Sea*.

Thank you to Julia Churchill, my incredible agent, for giving the best advice, and for being the best advocate – and for just being the best! Thank you also to Alexandra McNicoll and the rights team at A M Heath for supporting *Kingdom* right from the start.

I'm lucky to be in such brilliant hands with my publishing teams. Thank you to my wonderful, wise editors: Ali Dougal and Sarah McCabe. I really love working with you! Thank you to Lowri Ribbons for your insightful edits, to Arub Ahmed for all your wonderful work on the book since, and to Anum Shafqat for your thoughtful comments. And thank you to my copy-editor Jennie Roman, typesetter Sorrel Packham, and proofreader Anna Bowles.

Many thanks to everyone at S&S UK – especially Rachel Denwood, Laura Hough, Olivia Horrox, David McDougall, Sophie Storr, Eve Wersocki Morris,

Danielle Wilson – and to Sean Williams for designing the cover of dreams, and Tom Clohosy-Cole for your magical illustrations. Thank you so much to Maud Sepult and the rights team at Simon & Schuster UK for taking *The Kingdom over the Sea* on new adventures overseas. Many thanks also to everyone at Simon & Schuster US – especially Bridget Madsen, Tatyana Rosalia, Lisa Quach, Lindsey Ferris and Karyn Lee.

Thank you to the authors and book bloggers who have got in touch to say lovely things about this book – you're all amazing! Thanks in particular at the time of writing to A.F. Steadman for such a gorgeous jacket quote, and to Sophie Anderson, Zillah Bethell, Abi Elphinstone, Lizzie Huxley-Jones and Jo Nadin. Thanks to my author group chats for your support, special thanks to Sarah Underwood, you're amazing.

And thank you to everyone who read this before it was a book worth reading. Thank you so much to Aisha Bushby, I feel so lucky to have had your advice and support so early on, I really wouldn't be here without you. Thank you to Penny Young for being a wonderful writing partner. Thanks also to Lee Weatherly and to my Faber Academy class, especially Emma Sterner-Radley for your critique of the first draft. Thank you to all my friends and family for being so enthusiastic – particular thanks to Izzy Aughterson for making me send you instalments during lockdown.

And Alice, Zia, Sophia and Saira, thanks for everything. I love you all so much.

The story isn't over . . .

Watch out for more magical adventures with Yara, Mehnoor and Rafi!